BELLTREES

Kate Paton Rogers

BELLTREES. Copyright @ 2000 by Kate Paton Rogers.
All rights reserved.

DEDICATION

For my children who supported me greatly, each in their own way.

HISTORICAL NOTE

As told to me by my father, John Paton, who was born in Lochwinnoc, Scotland. He said that a local historian, who was known to be very knowledgeable, told it to him.

The place-name, Belltrees, does not refer to any specific tree but to a hillside or hill-top grove of native, British trees, probably originally oak trees which played (it was thought) a large part in Celtic mythology.

The Celts did not have a written language and most of what is known of their beliefs is based on later histories written by Roman historians.

There are a number of sites in lowland Scotland called Belltrees that are thought to be connected with the worship of a Celtic fire deity – Bel. Only traces of these rites survive. One is Beltane Day, May 1st, when huge fires were lit and a special oat-cake, containing eggs (called Bannocks), was eaten. One unfortunate soul, who got a specially marked piece of the Bannock, was forced to shoulder all of the bad luck that the tribe had experienced for the past year. It is not known what his punishment was.

BELLTREES

by

KATE PATON-ROGERS

CHAPTER ONE

1924

The woman seated in the gazebo could have been sleeping, her head resting on the back of her chair. Her dark, smooth hair was touched by white at the temples. A brave sparrow landed on the railing not ten feet from the woman in the blue, voile dress. A slight breeze stirred her skirt and he flew away. Nora still sat, deep in memories of the past. Like a silent film, pictures followed one another through her mind.

1900

Nora McDonald stood at the rail of the huge steamer close to her husband, who was holding their small son. They watched the stretch of dark water slowly widen between them and their homeland. The tiny, doll-like people on the wharf faded away completely. Scotland looked infinitely precious as it receded from view.

"Would they ever see it or their family again?", Nora wondered.

Then she felt Angus' arm around her waist. He spoke in a thick Scotch burr. "C'mon, my dear, we'll be looking forward from now on. I'm thinking your son needs a change and we must get settled in."

They went below decks to the small cabin allotted to them. Nora busied herself arranging their belongings to make the most of the space. Angus took the canvas satchel he'd been carrying over his shoulder and, placing it carefully in a corner, he opened it and scrutinized the contents. This was a bit of Scotch soil he was bringing to their new life. In the soil were ten tiny trees, lovingly dug up and packed in the canvas bag. These would be their link with home and give roots to their new life in America. He went to the water pitcher on the stand and, pouring out a cupful, he sprinkled it over the soil. Then, turning to Tad, who had been watching his father closely, he took his son's hand and placed it on the soil.

"This is your legacy, Sean Edward McDonald, and the beginning of our future."

Not understanding, but pleased with his father's attention, Tad patted the soil with his small hand, then examined his dirty palm seriously. Angus laughed, his deep, booming laugh, shaking his whole body. Nora and Tad both laughed in response. Hilarity relieving the tension of parting with loved ones, they laughed until they all collapsed on the bunk. Nora wiped the tears from her eyes and sat up.

"Enough, now! My stomach is hurting!" She gasped. Angus gave her a hug and swung Tad up on his shoulders.

"C'mon lass. We'll go up on deck and enjoy this bonny day. God knows if we'll have many like it."

" I'll be up in a bit, love, our things need to be hung up if we're going to look decent. Go along with you, now." She gave him a kiss and a little push.

When the two had left, Nora sat down on the edge of the bunk. The finality of this move struck her. Pictures of her mother and father and her two sisters flashed through her mind. Nora was the youngest of the family. She and Angus had lived with her parents since their wedding four years ago. Her dear, little Mother would sorely miss her. They had been closer to each other than either Molly or Mairi, perhaps because she was the baby.

Father, stoic and quiet, would miss Angus, too, she thought. They had become good friends, working side by side on the farm. Edward Renfrew, dour Scotsman, admired his son-in-law's diligence and enjoyed his sense of humor.

It was her father's brother, Harrison Renfrew, who had written from America to tell them of the fertile land that could be theirs. He told them of a small farm, adjacent to his own, which had come up for sale. The old folks who had owned it had died and their children lived far away. The farm was in some disrepair, so the selling price was low. Uncle Harrison had offered to hold the mortgage on the property and Angus could repay him on an annual basis, when his crops came in. Nora and Angus had spent days discussing the idea.

Nora was reluctant to leave her family but she was aware of Angus' need to have a place of his own to work. His mother and father had fled Ireland's potato famine just before Angus was born. His mother had died as she gave life to her son. His father brought his son up to adulthood and then he, too, died, as though he had simply lived to fulfill his duty.

Nora felt tears starting to form and she quickly jumped up and finished fixing Tad's bed. There was an old, wavy mirror hanging above the washstand and she laughed when she caught a glimpse of her slightly distorted image. She took the pins out of her hair, brushed it back and remade it into the neat bun she wore. She had always envied the curly, red hair of her sisters, which they had inherited from their father. Nora had her mother's black, straight hair with the same light skin and gray-green eyes. She washed her face, then, taking her shawl, she left the cabin to join her husband.

Stepping into the corridor, she collided with a man who was walking swiftly by. Strong arms kept her from falling. Nora noticed concerned, blue eyes, a short, brown beard and white teeth. "Excuse me, Madam! Are you alright?" He asked. Flustered, Nora straightened her bonnet.

"I'm fine, thank you. It was my fault for rushing out so fast. Please, don't fash yourself." Her Scotch accent was intensified in her confusion.

"Again, I apologize, Madam". He tipped his hat and went on his way.

Nora went on up to the deck where she found Angus and Tad walking up and down. Tad pulled free of his father's hand and ran to her, all excited.

"Mama, Mama, we saw a big fish, and I saw another boy; he's going to be my friend."

Angus explained that they had seen a large fish jump out of the water and they had met another family who had a boy about as old as Tad. While they talked, a man came strolling down the deck, the same one that Nora had bumped into below decks. As he approached them he stopped and touched his cap. He smiled at Tad.

To Angus and Nora, he said, "How do you do? My name is Jack Bradshaw, from England." He extended his hand. Angus shook it enthusiastically.

"We are from Renfrewshire. It's happy I am to meet you. I am Angus McDonald and this is my wife and our son, Sean, or Tad, as we call him."

"I'm afraid I literally ran into your wife down below. I trust you are all right, Mrs. McDonald?"

He inclined his head in her direction. She reassured him again that no harm was done. Angus and Jack fell into a brisk conversation about the places they were both familiar with in Scotland and England. Jack, it developed, had not decided where he would settle in America, but he had friends in Boston. Though he did not brag at all, the McDonald's got the impression that his family owned a great deal of land near Oxford. Nora sat down in a nearby deck chair and watched the animated conversation between the two young men. Her heart swelled with pride in Angus. Although a few inches shorter than Mr. Bradshaw, he stood straight and proud. His sandy mustache and hair were in contrast to the dark coloring of the other man. They were talking as if they were old friends. It pleased Nora that Angus had found a male friend and she liked the forthrightness of the man. I think he'll make Angus a good friend, she mused.

Nora turned her attention to Tad, who wanted her to help him to spin the wooden top his grandfather had given him before they left. She showed him how to wind the string tightly around the top and then pull it quickly to make the top spin.

Then the family with the small boy strolled by and Tad called the other child over to see his top. The boy's mother, who was carrying a baby about nine months old, came to sit near Nora. Her husband joined the other two men.

"Hello, I'm Peggy Forbush and this is Cassie." She adjusted the baby's bonnet. "I see our lads have taken to each other."

"Yes, " replied Nora. "It'll make the time go faster for them to have a friend." She admired the baby, who was all smiles.

Peggy confided, "We were worried about bringing her on such a trip, but Daniel's brother has been sick for a long time and Daniel wanted to go over and help them. They live in New York

State. They have four children and it has been awfully hard for his wife."

As they talked, Nora felt that she, too, had made a friend. It was unlikely that, once in America, they would ever see one another again. However, they could enjoy the company on the trip and it was especially good for Tad to have Peter to play with.

On the fourth day they awoke to find the ship rolling and pitching. Rain was hitting against the porthole. Angus had trouble standing and pulled on his clothes while holding onto the bunk. Tad woke crying and Nora comforted him while Angus went out to see how bad things were. Nora got a basin for Tad. Her own stomach was feeling very strange. The floor seemed alive and moving under her feet. When Angus came back with some breakfast, neither Tad nor Nora could look at it.

The storm passed, but Nora and Tad were sick for three days. The fourth day Angus took them out on deck. He tucked a pale Nora into a deck chair. She lay back and took deep breathes of the tangy salt air. She could see the ocean sparkling in the sunshine. Angus patted her hand.

"Ah, you're looking better already, lass. You had me worried there for a while. You'll be fit as a fiddle in no time. Now, I'll fetch you and the lad some tea."

Nora was about to refuse the food when she realized she was actually hungry. When he came back with biscuits and honey and good hot tea she and Tad both ate every bite.

Several of the others had been sick, too, and everyone was glad for the calm, sunny day. Peggy's family was nearby and Tad soon was playing jacks with Peter. Nora and Peggy were comparing their first experience with seasickness.

"That was the worst illness I ever had." said Peggy. "Thanks be the baby didn't get it. I don't think she could have survived it."

"It was a terrible time, for sure." Nora sympathized. "I think I'd rather have another bairn than go through that again."

"I know! It's so nice to have my stomach stay in one spot for a while." Peggy said wryly.

"Maybe we should celebrate our recovery."

Peggy pounced on the idea with glee. "We'll have a party, that's what we can do!"

She called out to her husband, who was talking with Angus. "Oh, Dan'l, will you play for us? We are going to have a party tomorrow night to celebrate how lucky we are that we're well again."

Before Daniel could answer, the others on deck were begging him to bring out his fiddle and play. When he could be heard, he promised to play for the planned party the next night. The women were excited about the party; it would be a welcome change from the past few days. The children caught the spirit and began dancing around until one of the little ones fell down and skinned his knee.

The next night, after supper, Nora bathed and put on a pretty, soft, green dress that her mother had made her when she and Angus were married. It had a lace yoke and sleeves that were puffed at the top and tapered to a narrow cuff. Her eyes were shining at the prospect of music and a party. Tad was scrubbed and changed. Angus looked elegant in his wedding suit. He put his arm around Nora and took Tad's hand.

"The handsomest family on board." He declared.

He squeezed Nora's waist. Her cheeks were glowing with color as they went up to the large dining room. All the tables were pulled back against the walls so there would be room for dancing. Some of the others were already there. Daniel and another man were tuning up their fiddles. The children clapped their hands over their ears at the discord. All the ladies had worn their best dresses. Peggy had on a pretty wine colored taffeta gown, perfect with her blond hair.

For several hours they all danced, talked and laughed together. When the children got tired, they were tucked into deck chairs to sleep. Once, during the evening, Jack asked Angus' permission to dance with Nora. She was surprised at how comfortable she felt as he whirled her around gracefully.

It was a lovely evening, which was repeated twice more during the trip. For many of them it diverted their minds from what was ahead of them; an unknown country with new problems to be met and conquered.

The weather stayed pleasant and, in spite of cramped quarters, Nora and Angus did not mind the trip. Nora was always optimistic and Angus was determined not to worry about the future; at least for the time being. They took advantage of having few immediate demands on their time to enjoy each other. They were alone for the first time since they'd married.

They had lived with Nora's family at the urging of her father. With no sons of his own, Edward Renfrew had been delighted to get a strong, agreeable son-in-law to help him run his farm and engage in hours of man talk with him. Angus had truly enjoyed his father-in-law and learned a lot from him about running a farm. So it was with mixed feelings that he and Nora had decided to try their fortune in America.

Uncle Harrison had written that the farm was about fifty acres, fifteen or so acres of pasture land and the rest being covered in trees. It was enticing to Nora and Angus to think of establishing a home of their own. Dreams and then plans flew through their heads; hours and days had been spent in making lists of things to take, articles that had to be left, deciding what to do before leaving to make their absence less of a burden for Edward.

The only small cloud seemed to be Uncle Harrison's son, Supleen. He was about Angus' age and although they had not met since they were small, there had been reports from relatives who knew him that he'd grown into a selfish, unpleasant person. His mother, Aunt Clara, had miscarried, or lost in infancy, four other children, so all of her frustrated Mother love had been showered on Supleen. Clara was so afraid that something might happen to take away her only child that every whim of his was catered to, even when her husband protested. Clara's tears quickly silenced his admonitions. The result was that Supleen was totally self centered and showed no respect for anyone else. Angus, in the enthusiasm of the moment, ignored the warnings. He knew that Harrison was an honest, principled man and Aunt Clara, though misguided, was kind. So an agreement had been reached about the farm. Angus had sent a down payment to Uncle Harrison as good faith money to secure the property. He was to pay a portion of the balance each year, with Uncle Harrison holding the mortgage.

Now, on board ship, they were in a sort of limbo; Scotland was miles behind them and America far ahead. These days were to be enjoyed. Some of their time was spent with their new friends, but the best times were those when Nora and Angus were alone. Hours were spent in long conversations of their hopes and dreams for family and home; their concerns and anticipations for their children. They told each other secret feelings and dreams that they'd never had the privacy or luxury of time to do before. It was like a long honeymoon for them. Their first, because there had been no money for one when they were married.

During the time spent talking with their new friends, Angus and Jack grew to like and respect each other more and more. Jack had not decided on a place to settle and planned to look the country over well before he made a decision. One day, the two were talking and strolling around the decks at the same time. A slight breeze ruffled their hair and made it difficult for Jack to keep his pipe going. As they stopped a moment for him to light it again, Angus spoke.

"I've given it some thought, Jack, and I was wondering, since you've not decided where you want to settle, why not come with us to Vermont until you know where you want to go? I dare say I'll be needing some help to get things started on the farm. I've got the money to pay wages, but you'd share in the crops and have your keep as well. What do you say?"

Jack finished trying to light his pipe. "I say, that is a very generous offer, my friend. I know little yet about farming, but I have a strong back. And it would be good to be near a friend. Can I think it over for a while?"

"Aye, as long as you like." replied Angus. "Whatever you decide, you'll always be welcome at our home." Then, with a grin, "Maybe there in Vermont, you will find a comely lass. I've heard there are some beauties in America."

Jack laughed. "Thanks, old man, but it will be some time before I can marry. I'll never ask someone to share my life until I have a good home and money to make life easy. At least, that is my excuse for putting off getting involved with anyone. I had a lady in mind back home, but she turned me down for a rich nobleman, so I learned my lesson. I hadn't asked her yet, mind, but she knew what I was planning, alright."

Angus felt slightly embarrassed at this confidence. "No mind, you've plenty of time." They turned to other subjects then; what Vermont would be like, the best crops to plant, how many cows Angus should get and what breed they should be.

Nora, who was amusing Tad with some simple child's game, had something else on her mind. Since her bout with seasickness, she hadn't settled back to feeling normal again. Instead, each day her stomach felt uneasy and that morning she had a definite reaction to the sausage and egg breakfast. Now she knew for sure what she had suspected. She was in the family way again.

Her feelings mixed; joy at the idea of another new life and misgivings about the uncertainty of the future. Who knew what would have to be done at the farm, for sure a lot of work, and it would have been better to wait another six months or a year before another pregnancy. But her pleasure overcame her misgivings, for they both wanted a big family. If only she didn't feel so sick!

When Tad was fast asleep that night and she and Angus were cozy in their bunk, she told him. Angus held her tightly and kissed her face gently.

"Oh, lass, 'tis a good omen. We start a new life in our new country. You're feeling well, aren't you?" He scanned her face anxiously.

"About the same as it was with Tad. I hope this one is a lass, though; if it is I would like to name her after mama. Do you mind?"

Angus agreed. "A lovelier namesake you could never find. Let's hope she looks like you. With that combination, she'll be a rare one."

Within the warmth of her husband's arms, Nora's last misgivings disappeared.

Because of the spring work on his farm, Uncle Harrison wasn't able to meet the ship. He had written to a cousin of Clara's, Hanna Murphy, whose husband, Tom, would meet them and take them to the train station to continue their trip.

No one could feel like a stranger around Tom Murphy. He had a large, red face, reddish hair that stood up on his head in spite of apparent efforts on his part to tame it. He had a hearty, booming laugh and seemed to find a lot to amuse him. He found them with no trouble and soon made them feel as if they'd known him for years. He'd brought along two of his sons (he had seven) to help with the baggage, so they were all soon on the way. Tom insisted that they stay a couple of days with his family before starting the trip north. Nora had protested.

"But, we don't want to inconvenience your wife, sir. I'm sure she has her hands full with your big family."

Tom interrupted her. "Now, now, don't you fret, Mrs. McDonald, it's pleased as punch she is to have company. Com 'n, me lad." He clapped a huge hand on Angus' shoulder, and then gently took Nora's arm. He was like a big bear, rounding up his cubs.

Tom, Angus and the boys piled Nora and Angus' personal luggage, the canvas bag and Nora's trunk into the back of the large wagon. Nora had never seen a wagon like it before. Tom and his sons had put it together from parts of three other wagons that had been thrown away. It had a long bed in back to carry provisions in and up front two comfortable seats stretched from one side to the other. These had been padded and covered with some canvas. Then over both seats was a canvas top, pulled tight. A piece of the canvas came down like a ruffle on the two sides and back. It made comfortable seating for six. Tom and his sons sat up front. Nora and Angus, with Tad between them, on the back seat.

After what seemed to Nora an interminable time of riding over the roads that were full of bumps and holes, they were relieved to at last reach the Murphy's sprawling home. Hanna Murphy met them at the door, beaming in a replica of her husband's Irish face. She was firm spoken and motherly. She embraced Nora as though she was a sister, talking all the while.

"Come, m 'dear, you're looking a mite peaked. The first thing you're going to do is have a nice rest." Then to Angus, she said "Bring the wee one along, too, we'll give him a nice glass of milk."

She took them to a large, inviting room. There was a massive wooden, carved bed dominating the room and, to the side, a small child's trundle bed. Everything shone, from the wooden floor to the windows. There was a white, crocheted coverlet on the bed and hand woven rugs on the floor. A fireplace was opposite the bed. To Nora and Angus, after days in the small cabin, it looked like heaven. Hanna wouldn't listen to their thanks.

"O dearie, we'll take care of the wee one. You have a nice rest until supper is ready. You too, me boy." This last to Angus, who was bringing in the luggage.

Then away she went with Tad, who, surprisingly, went along without a protest. Nora sat down on the soft bed with a sigh.

"Oh, Angus! It's so good to be off that ship and these people are so kind, how can we ever repay them? And they don't even know us!"

"They're not the kind to look for payment, my love, now you do what Mrs. Murphy said and rest. I'm feeling fine and I'll go have a talk with Tom."

When he left, Nora took off her shoes and dress and lay down on the huge bed. She pulled the coverlet over her and was asleep in minutes. The trip had tired her enormously. She hadn't complained, but her pregnancy had been making her very uncomfortable. She often had back pain and her food didn't appeal to her so she had lost some weight and had circles under her eyes. Her sleep was deep; she didn't wake until Tad pulled at her.

"Mama, mama! C'mon, the lady says we're going to eat now. Papa sent me to get you." He put his face down on his mother's, standing on tiptoe to reach her.

"Oh, Tad, love." She squeezed him and planted a kiss on his nose. He wriggled free.

"Hurry, Mama, I'm hungry and I want you to see the doggie." As usual, he was talking about several things at once. "I want to get a doggie, can I, Mama? A big one like Tom's."

Nora sat up and slowly started to fix her hair and wash. Her stomach was feeling strange again. Maybe food would help. She hoped so.

"You can go down, Tad, and say I'll be right along. Go on now". She gave him a pat on the bottom and he ran off, excited about everything new.

Hanna Murphy made the best beef stew in the country, as Tom always bragged, and with her homemade biscuits it was food for the gods. The table was a long one, comfortably seating nine Murphys with plenty of room for the McDonald family. The Murphy boys looked to be from six years old to seventeen, all as friendly as their mother and father. It was a jolly meal with good conversation.

After apple pie, Nora helped Hanna clean up while the older boys, Angus and Tom, went to the barn to finish the evening chores. While washing the dishes, Hanna and Nora chatted about their children and Hanna wanted to know all about their trip. Nora suddenly felt weak and sat down in the nearest chair. Hanna, all motherly concern, brought her a glass of water.

"You alright, dearie? You're white as a ghost!" She patted Nora's shoulder sympathetically. "Going to have another wee one, are you? You poor thing, and traveling all over the place. But, don't worry. God will give you strength. You stay with us 'til you have a good rest. A few days more or less won't make a whit of difference." She kept up her chatter as she worked, but Nora's mind was on the child she was carrying.

"Thank you, Hanna, we'll stay a day or two and be grateful. I have been feeling pretty sick with this one, not at all like with Tad. Perhaps it was the trip and all."

"Don't worry, dearie. Look at the lot I've had, and each one different, they were." Hanna finished wiping off the tables. She said to Nora, "Go on now. Off with you! Get into bed and have a good rest. You'll be as good as new in a few days."

Nora took her advice, went upstairs and lay down. In spite of her nap, she was still bone weary. As soon as she put her head on the fresh smelling pillow, she fell asleep. When Angus came in with Tad later, she barely stirred.

After spending three days with the Murphy family, they were ready to continue their journey. Angus, in particular, was anxious to see his new property. The Murphy family seemed reluctant to have them leave. Hanna gave them big hugs and an enormous lunch of homemade bread filled with juicy slices of pot roast.

It would be a long trip, but knowing it was near the end made them eager to get started. They invited the Murphy's to visit them in Vermont. In return, they had to promise to come back some day to visit. The wagon was again loaded with all their belongings. Then, with Tom and his two oldest, John and Tim, they drove to the railway station. They were taking the train to Morristown where Uncle Harrison would meet them with a wagon to take them home.

On the way to the station Tom was his jolly self. When the wagon jounced over the road and Tad nearly fell off his seat, between Angus and Tom, Angus caught him by his jacket. Tom laughed.

"Pretty bumpy riding, eh, me lad? Maybe when you grow up you'll drive one of those new fangled automobiles. I heard a feller out in Michigan built one that can go twenty-miles an hour with no horse. What do you think of that?"

Angus replied in his quiet way. "Well, I'd be willing to try it if it came my way. Save a lot of horse feed."

"Me, too." echoed Tad, wanting to go along with his father.

Nora was quiet; as usual she was having trouble keeping her breakfast down, aggravated by the rough ride. With great relief, she saw the railroad station come into view.

When last goodbyes were said and all luggage put away, they sank into their seats. Although the seats were dusty, they felt a good deal better than the wagon. Nora and Angus alternately rested and discussed with quiet excitement what they could look forward to in Vermont. Tad amused himself by walking up and down the aisle, looking out of the window and playing with a wooden train that John Murphy had carved for him. When he got tired, he was tucked into a seat, his head pillowed on a valise.

With a lot of jerking and blowing of whistles, the train pulled into the small station at Morristown. The conductor had been around a while back bawling out the name so the McDonald's were ready. Angus gathered their belongings together while Nora caught Tad, who was taking off up the aisle, and tried to put his clothes in some kind of order. They were all slightly disheveled after the long train ride.

Uncle Harrison was waiting as they came down the steps of the train. As they were the only ones to disembark except for one old man in a straw hat, he recognized them at once.

CHAPTER TWO

Harrison Renfrew had once been nearly Angus' height but now was stooped slightly. His graying hair was plentiful still but the worried look etched on his face spoke of a hard life. He was genuinely happy to see them all. Nora gave him a big hug, which seemed to embarrass and please him at the same time.

To Tad, who was hanging back, he said. "Well me lad, c'mon now, you can help me drive the horses. Would you like that?" Tad was won over.

In Harrison's effusive attempt to explain why Supleen had not come to greet his cousins, Angus sensed that their cousin was less than anxious to meet them.

The Renfrew house had started out as a saltbox but had been added onto several times to accommodate different families. Aunt Clara, a small, round woman with a soft voice met them at the door and gave big hugs all around. She took them to a room where they could wash and change after their dusty trip.

"I'm afraid you'll have a heap to do in your house." She told them. "I sent some canned things over by Claude, our hired man. If you need anything you can let us know. It will be so nice to have family near by!".

Nora sank down on the big, soft bed, grateful for a chance to stretch out for a few minutes while Angus washed up and helped Tad to do the same though Tad protested that he was just fine. Angus sat on the side of the bed and smoothed Nora's hair back.

"How are you feeling lassie?".

Nora sat up. "I'm right as rain, love. I can't wait to see our very own home!".

When they came down for supper in the big country kitchen Angus saw there were two other men in the room besides his Uncle. They were introduced as Claude, a wiry, short Canadian who worked for Harrison, and the other one, a big, loutish man, as Supleen. The latter greeted Angus indifferently and complained that supper was late.

Nora helped her Aunt, who seemed to be agitated. They put the generous meal on the table, and as they were sitting down, an affectedly cheerful, southern voice from the doorway made them all look in that direction.

"Hello, everybody, sorry I'm late." In the doorway stood a woman who had obviously spent a lot of time on her toilette. She had on a navy blue, sateen, flounced dress with lots of white lace trim. Her hair was dressed very fashionably and she had several strings of beads around her neck. Harrison quickly introduced her as Zoë, Supleen's wife. She shook hands with them, smiling brightly, but her eyes remained cool and appraising. She spoke with a drawl.

"Ah do hope ya'll won't be too uncomfortable in that old house. Nobody has lived there for ages. Mother Renfrew and I went over there to freshen it up a bit for you."

She glided to her place beside Supleen, who was looking at her adoringly. Nora thought, at least he has some human feelings. She noticed, too, how Clara's lips tightened at Zoë's last remark. I can see who did the work, that one won't do a lick if she can get out of it.

The meal was pleasant enough, though Supleen didn't say much. Uncle Harrison and Angus talked at length about what he would need for the farm; Claude also had some helpful suggestions. Zoë chattered on about how dull life was in this tiny town. She explained in detail about how she had met Supleen when he went to Virginia to look at a particular bull he wanted to improve their cattle line.

"My dear, I froze to death here last winter, I just hate this weather. It makes your skin shrivel up. You just wait, you'll hate it, too."

On and on she went about her beloved South. Poor Aunt Clara, thought Nora, when her son married she only got another person to wait on.

After the meal, Tad wanted to explore everything and went off with his papa, Uncle Harrison and Supleen. Zoë sat sipping coffee while Nora and Clara cleaned up. Nora was anxious to get away from this strange household to her own place.

Everyone came with them when they went to their own home. Clara carried several small items to make things comfortable for Nora. Supleen went because his father insisted and Zoe because she didn't want to be left out. As they approached their new home, Nora and Angus clasped hands tightly. This was what they had traveled so far to see. The place was only about a mile from the Renfrew's.

As they pulled into the long driveway, Nora caught her breath. In spite of the obvious neglect all around, the house stood proudly. The two-story Colonial, with big windows and a veranda on two sides, was their first very own home, and to Nora it was beautiful. Angus took in the barn and outbuildings, both with doors hanging off the hinges, tall weeds growing across the entrances. A corral beside the barn had leaning and broken rails and its gate hung open. But, beyond that, he could see green pastures encircled by lush woodland. He felt the stirrings of pride that this was his. Rundown it may be now, but, he promised himself, he would make it into a fine farm. He looked at Nora, whose eyes were shining.

"Oh, Angus, 'tis so big and beautiful. Our very own!"

"And we'll make it into a grand place, love. C'mon now." Angus declared, as he jumped down from the carriage.

Tad jumped out the moment the wheels stopped. He ran over to where a few hens were pecking and scratching at the gravel. As he ran into their midst, they scattered, clucking and scolding. He laughed at them.

"Here, lad, you can't be scaring them like that or they'll not give us any eggs for our breakfast." Angus admonished.

"But, where did they come from?" Asked Nora, bewildered. Uncle Harrison laughed.

"They are a present from Clara and I, for your new home. We sent over a cow, too, so you can have some fresh milk. She is out behind the barn, I think."

Angus and Nora both thanked him for his kindness.

Angus took Nora's hand and they went up the stairs into the house, followed by the others. The large, carved doors opened into a spacious hall with doors on each side. Halfway down the hall a lovely staircase of dark wood led to the upper floor. Angus and Nora, with the others trailing and Tad running ahead, went from room to room. They went through the parlor on the left and into a room lined with bookshelves. Each of these rooms had a fireplace. On the shelves were some old-fashioned knick-knacks and old books. On the other side of the hall were a dining room, a kitchen, a large pantry and another room at the rear, apparently used for laundry and access to the back yard. The farm had been purchased with all the furnishings, but everything had been neglected for so long that it was difficult to tell, under so many coats of dust, just what condition they were in.

Upstairs there was one large bedroom and three others, one of them quite small. It was this one that Tad claimed as his own because he liked the seat that was built under the window with a hinged cover. It would be a great place to hide his toys. It was the closest to the largest one where his parents would be sleeping.

The large bedroom, to Nora's surprise, was clean and ready for them. She looked around with pleasure at the freshly washed windows, neatly made bed and newly laid fire in the tiled fireplace.

"Oh, this is lovely, Aunt Clara, you shouldn't have!" Nora exclaimed.

Clara protested with a pleased smile and flushed face that it had been no trouble at all. The men left to bring in the McDonald's belongings while the women went to the kitchen. There were boxes and cans on the counter that Nora discovered were filled with coffee, tea and other staples Clara had sent over.

"Just enough for a few days, until you can get into town to shop." She explained, while Nora thanked her profusely.

Zoë, who had been trailing along behind them, was brushing dust from her fashionable, brown coat.

"Well, if you ask me, it is a real mess! How will you ever get everything cleaned?" She spoke disdainfully.

"We can do it, it'll just take some time, that's all." said Nora. "It's our own and I love it."

After everything was brought in and the others left, it was too dark to do anything else. Besides, they were awfully tired. So Tad was put to bed and Angus turned to Nora, picked her up and swung her around until she was laughing helplessly. She clasped his head between her hands for a long kiss.

"C'mon now, my darling, we've got lots to do tomorrow, so its off to bed for us now."

They were both awake at dawn, and leaving Tad still asleep, went down to the kitchen. While Angus started a fire in the old range, Nora mixed up batter for bannocks, a kind of pancake. When the fire was going good, Angus put on his coat.

"I'm for looking around the barn and see what I need to start fixing. Tomorrow we'll plant our trees up on that ridge behind the barn. They will be a fine windbreak when they're grown."

"No, no, Angus, let's plant them along the driveway for all to see when they come to the McDonald's. We will name our farm Belltrees."

Angus considered this for a moment. "Alright, lassie, a fine idea. Now I'll be back in a bit for my tea."

By the time he came back, Tad was up and had eaten. After breakfast, Tad followed his papa outside, and Nora could take her time to explore her new home, She walked through each room downstairs, marveling at the space and making mental notes of what she would do to improve each one. She wrinkled her nose at the dust that rose from the draperies when she moved them to let the light into the parlor.

Leaving the dust and clutter behind for the moment, she went back the kitchen to see what Aunt Clara had left for them. She found plenty of food for several days, among which was a ham, some potatoes and many of Clara's home canned vegetables and fruits. There were three, delicious looking fresh baked loaves of bread, and in the icebox, a large chunk of ice to cool the milk, butter and eggs left there. Bless you, Aunt Clara! Nora thought, this is a wonderful welcome. Suddenly she thought of her mother so far away and she struggled with a few moments of homesickness.

Tad and Angus walked around the small building, which had housed a large family of hens. In the barn were several, somewhat rusted stanchions. The floor was littered with hay that had drifted down from the loft. The barn, though, was sturdily built of hand-hewn beams.

"A lot to work with here, me lad. We'll fix it good as new." Angus spoke out loud and Tad nodded solemnly, as though he understood.

The huge barn awed him. While Angus examined the tools, which hung neatly in rows against the wall, Tad grew bored and went outside. A moment later he shouted to his father.

"Papa, come here, see what I found!"

Peering out the door, Angus saw Tad patting a large, Jersey cow, whose udder nearly touched the ground.

"Look, papa, a cow. For our milk! She's a nice one."

As they were looking at the cow, a wild bundle of fur came charging at them from behind a bush. Horns down, the goat made a beeline for Tad, Angus swinging him out of the way just in time. The goat plunged past, striking the barn door with a good whack.

"That's not very friendly, now, is it?" laughed Angus.

He collared the goat and brought it over to Tad, showing him how to rub the goat's head and talk to him. Tad pulled some grass for it to nibble on, though it also tried the taste of Tad's coat and pants. They became fast friends, and often Spots, as they named him, followed Tad around the yard.

Angus returned to the barn for a scythe and mowed the tall weeds around the barn entrance. Then he found some screws and replaced the hinges on the barn door. He was standing back to admire his handiwork, when Nora called them in for lunch.

While they ate their ham sandwiches and Aunt Clara's chicken soup, Angus and Tad told Nora about the cow and the goat. She told them about her morning; she showed them the pantry, which was now clean and bright. Then it was time for Tad to have a nap, but Nora and Angus were eager to get back to their cleaning. Nora used pail after pail of hot soapy water to get the cupboards clean. Her back was aching before she finished. Angus was having a great time cleaning the rust off the tools and cleaning out the barn.

When Tad got up they decided to plant the Belltrees together. They put them in the semi-circle formed by the driveway because there the land was several feet higher than the rest of the lawn. In Scotland, Belltrees were always on higher ground. Angus carefully put the small trees in the ground and packed the Scotch soil around them. On top of this went more dirt until it was mounded up around them a few inches. After watering them, he built small cages around them to protect them from being trampled by animals as well as from the storms of winter.

"There you are, a bit of Scotland for us in our new country."

Tad clapped his small hands together, catching the importance of the occasion.

"Now, m'laddie, this is your chore every day, to water our Belltrees. Some day they will be taller than you are."

"I'll take care of them, Papa." The three-year-old's face was serious.

Just at that moment, Uncle Harrison drove his team of Bay's up the driveway. He had come to pick up Angus to take him to a neighbor about five miles away to look at a team of horses.

Tad stayed with Nora and followed her around while she got started cleaning the other rooms. She hardly knew where to begin. Everything was so dusty and neglected. She felt a twinge of pity for the former owners. It was sad to get old and not be able to take care of your home properly. I hope I never have to move from Belltrees, she thought. She went into the parlor, opened the windows to let out the dust, and took down the faded drapes. They were awfully old but maybe with careful cleaning she could save them. She dusted the tables and discovered that they were made of walnut and had a lovely sheen. The heavy chairs and horsehair couch were too heavy for her to move, so she would wait for Angus to take them outside with the rug, to be beaten and aired.

By supper time she was feeling shaky from hunger. While she was setting the table, with Tad "helping", she heard Angus' voice calling goodbye to Uncle Harrison. She went to the door.

"C'mon out, you two, and take a look at our magnificent beasts". He called to her.

He gestured toward a handsome pair of draft horses, who were blowing and stamping their huge feet. Nora and Tad went out to inspect them, praise them and smooth their silky coats. Tad's eyes were large.

"They are so big, papa!"

His parents laughed. Angus picked Tad up and sat him on the back of one of the horses.

"Now, do they look as big from up there?" he asked.

Tad crowed with delight. After the horses were bedded down and they were sitting at supper, Angus told her how Harrison had explained to him which seeds to plant now and which ones must wait a few weeks.

"But first, I want to look over the land and see with my own eyes what we have here. We'll be doing that tomorrow, for I want you with me."

Nora was pleased, because she wanted to be a part of everything on their farm.

The next morning Nora made up a big lunch for the three of them. An old blanket was thrown over some straw in the back of the wagon for Tad to nap on later. It was a bright, sunny day with everything coming to life after a long winter. They followed the perimeter of their land; going by a rough, hand drawn map that Harrison had given them. The pasture had been fenced in but in many places the fence was lying on the ground and some posts were rotted. They discovered a pond, which seemed to be fed by springs up high in the hills.

"We'll have some fishing, then." said Angus. "I'll make you a pole of your very own, lad." he told Tad.

They were pleased and excited by what they saw. They had lunch by the pond. Through the clear water they could see some fish swimming lazily. Tad was enthralled by them, running back and forth on the shore to get a better look. Nora and Angus laughed at him, admonishing him not to fall in the water.

They found that the western edge of their land was covered thickly with trees, as well as the northeast corner and continuing down the eastern side two thirds of the way. The rest had been cleared for planting. The Renfrew's property was their western boundary and, to the east a brook meandered southward to mark the line. Beyond the brook the land sloped upward to trees. They had not met their other neighbors as yet. Harrison had told them that one family had several young children. Nora hoped that at least one was near Tad's age.

During the next month both Angus and Nora were occupied from dawn to dark: Angus with fixing fences and preparing the land for planting, and Nora with getting the house in order. Her nausea was getting better each day but she felt constantly tired. When Tad took his nap in the afternoon, she would lay down, too. Most days when the weather was good Angus took his lunch to the fields, so no time was wasted. Sometimes Nora brought it out to him if he was near by and they could sit together and talk about what they were each doing and make plans for the future. They were still exhilarated with owning their own land.

As Nora watched Angus talking so earnestly she was filled with such happiness; she thought; this is all I could ever want, to be here on our own place with him. Angus saw the thought in her eyes, and gave her a squeeze and pulled her to her feet.

"Off with you, lass, I've had enough distraction for one day."

He sent her off with a playful spank. Nora picked up the lunch things and, holding her skirt high, ran, laughing, back to the house.

One morning, when Nora was kneading bread and Tad was playing nearby, she heard the sound of wheels on the gravel driveway. Her hands covered with dough, she grabbed the towel and went through the hall to the front of the house. As she got to the door she saw a women about her own age getting down from a wagon seat, followed by two children.

"Hello, there!" The woman called, "I'm your neighbor. Came to see how things are going with you."

She pumped Nora's flour covered hand, then they both laughed. Nora tried to wipe some of the dough off with the towel, while apologizing.

The other woman exclaimed; "Oh, don't bother with that, I'm used to it. I'm Mattie Carter and these two are Katie and Andy. That's a nice little fellow you've got there. I think they'll get along famously."

Tad, who had followed Nora to the door, was studying Andy, who appeared to be only slightly older than him. Andy was staring back at him.

Finally Tad asked, "Wanna see my goat?"

The two boys went off to find Spots, with Katie trailing behind. After warning the children to stay in the yard, Nora took Mattie back to the kitchen to finish the bread. Mattie had brought several jars of home canned goods with her, including some grape jam.

"We live on your east side, across the brook. I'm right glad to have a young neighbor. This house has been neglected for so long, since the McGowan's got too old to keep it up. We used to help them when we could. Then Mamie died and Samuel just seemed to give up. Anyways, tell me what I can do to help you get settled."

She was so friendly that Nora soon felt like an old friend. After the bread was in the oven, she showed Mattie around the house.

"I've been working mostly in the kitchen and parlor," she explained. "There is a lot more to do in here but I can't move the heavy pieces so I have to wait for Angus to help me."

"But it looks real pretty now." Mattie exclaimed. She admired the finish on the tables and credenza. "Looks to me like you've done a lot."

Nora flushed with pleasure. "It's been such fun. This is our first home, you know. Before, we lived with my mother and father."

She told Mattie about her home in Scotland, and as she spoke a wave of homesickness came over her. Being a perceptive young woman, Mattie noticed.

"Well, never mind now, maybe your ma and pa can come for a visit soon. Now, just tell me what you want done and I'll do it."

The two women worked together for several hours, periodically checking on the children. At noon, the little ones were called in for hot bread and jam washed down with cold, sweet milk. They acted as though they had always been together. Katie was telling Tad about their pony, asking him to come over and ride. Tad's eyes were shining at the prospect as he begged his mother to take him over to his friends' house. Nora patted his head.

"Maybe, laddie, we'll talk about it later."

Nora and Tad were both sorry when the three Carters had to leave in mid-afternoon.

"Now, remember, Nora, be sure to call on us if you need help. There are several big boys, by the name of Bates, who live about five miles down the road. My Andrew sometimes hires them for haying and such. Tell your husband about them. And, come over anytime."

"You, too, Mattie, and thanks for helping me." As the wagon started to move down the driveway, Mattie called back.

"If you feel like a walk, you can cross over the brook. Its about a mile to our house that way."

Then, waving cheerily, they drove off.

That evening, at supper, Angus smiled at Nora's bubbling account of the day. He was pleased that she'd found a friend nearby.

"I just might need one of those Bates boys." he said. "I have to start planting soon, and with everything else to do, I may need some help. Though I canna afford to pay much."

"But, Angus, I can help with the planting. The house can wait and Tad can come with us. He can nap in the wagon, or on the grass."

Angus' brows came together in a frown as he looked at his young wife.

"No, no, lass! You've enough to do with this house and getting ready for the new one. I don't want you getting sick on me."

He looked at her with such concern that Nora, impulsively jumped up and came around to him. She sat on his knee and burrowed her face in his neck. Tad, who was sitting on a stack of books placed on a chair so he could reach the table, decided he'd been ignored long enough. He slid off the books, dragging most of then with him; he threw his short arms as far as they would reach, around his mama and papa. It was a moment Tad often thought of long after he was a grown man.

33

After supper, Tad usually followed Angus to the barn to feed the animals and frolic with Spots for a while. The boy would go into gales of laughter when Spots would stand on his hind legs to eat the new buds off the trees or prance around bunting at anything nearby. Spot's horns had been removed for safety, but he acted as though he still had them.

The last thing each night before Angus went into the house, he carried pails of water to the tiny Belltrees. Sometimes, as tonight, Tad went, too, carrying a small pail of water, most of which had sloshed out by the time he had reached the trees.

Nora lingered for a few moments at the table; looking around at the room she had made a comfortable and pleasant place for the family to gather. She had a red-checked cloth on the table and hand made cushions of the same material for the chairs and the settee. So far, she had no curtains at the windows, but the plants Aunt Clara had given her filled the sills and hanging from the beams were bunches of onions, dried peppers and herbs. The old stove was shining. The kettle simmered on the back, filled with a soup stock she was making. Everything was perfect here, she thought, but most of the other rooms were still a mess. She jumped up, hearing Tad's laughter outside, and hurried to clean up the dishes so she could join her two "men" when they watered the trees.

A sudden pain in her abdomen caused her to cry out and clutch the edge of the sink for support. When the pain subsided, she waited for several minutes. Instead of going outside, she rested on the settee, until it was time to put Tad to bed. She didn't mention what had happened to Angus when they retired to their bedroom, but she was unusually quiet. As she sat at the dressing table brushing her long hair, Angus came up behind her and, cupping her chin in his hand, forcing her to meet his eyes in the mirror.

"Now, my lass, what is bothering my lovely girrul?"

"I-I was feeling just a wee bit homesick," she stammered.

She didn't think he needed another thing to worry about. As she spoke, a wave of longing to talk to her mother came over her. Angus was satisfied with her answer. He also had his own private worry. He had correctly deduced that Supleen could be a dangerous adversary, probably because he resented his father's obvious interest in Angus. That day, Supleen had ridden up while Angus was fixing fences and had stayed to talk to him about the land. Outwardly, he was friendly, but Angus didn't miss the way Supleen's eyes roved around the stand of hardwoods, with a calculating gleam. The thought crossed Angus mind; God help me if anything happens to Uncle Harrison before I pay off the mortgage. He, too, kept his worry from Nora. She had looked a little peaked lately and he was sure her pregnancy was dragging her down. She was doing too much. Maybe he could find someone to come in and help her. This was a big house to get into shape.

Now, he scooped Nora up and deposited her on their big bed. She lay back, wearily. Angus tucked her in.

"Now, m'lass you just rest. And you're not to get up when I leave in the morning, hear? I'll take the lad with me and bring him home at dinnertime."

Nora protested but gave in quickly. She really was feeling exhausted. The luxury of a morning in bed would be wonderful.

When she opened her eyes, the sun was streaming in through the lace curtains. She stretched luxuriously. She got out of bed slowly, washed and dressed. She felt rested for the first time in ages. This baby is making me so tired, she thought, or maybe it's because I never had so much to do before. She tied her big, white apron over her rust colored skirt and white shirt-waist, checked her self in the mirror, and went down to the kitchen. Her husband and son would be hungry when they came in from the fields.

By late May, Angus had plowed and harrowed most of the ground he needed to plant. He had already planted two early, hardy crops on the advice of Harrison, now it was time to plant the feed crops for the animals, as well as vegetables enough to see them through the next winter. The vegetable garden would be as close as possible to the house. Nora would be able to tend it or pick what she needed, without going too far from the house. Angus put up a swing for Tad in the back yard, near the kitchen door. While Nora was working she could easily keep an eye on him. Tad loved his swing. Sometimes his mother would hold him on her lap while they soared back and forth as high as they could go; or they would just swing gently while Nora sang to him.

Angus had gone to the Bates to see if one of the boys there could help him out. It turned out that the oldest boy, Cecile, had recently married and could use some extra money. Angus hired Cecile and his bride, Tansy, to come over to Belltrees each day for several hours. Tansy would help Nora and Cecile would work in the fields with Angus. As part of their pay they would receive their breakfast and dinner, as well as a portion of the vegetables grown.

Cecile was eighteen and had worked in the fields since he could be of any help, so his muscles were well developed. He had a square, sturdy build, sincere brown eyes and a cheerful grin. His eagerness to work impressed Angus, as well as his knowledge of the Vermont soil and when and how to plant each crop.

Nora and Tad liked Tansy on sight. At sixteen she was still half child and would giggle with Tad in games. She was plump, with a childish, round face framed by a fringe of unruly curls. She knew a lot about housework, too, having come from a family of eight children. With Nora's help, she learned to be a good cook as well.

CHAPTER THREE

With Tansy to help her, Nora was finally able to get the rest of the house in order. In the attic, they found a treasure of old clothes, packed in cedar. Tad and Tansy dressed up in some of the old hats and outfits and paraded up and down, to Nora's amusement. With Cecile and Tansy to help, Nora and Angus were able to spend a little time relaxing together. Often they would sit close together on the porch swing watching the fireflies sending neon signals to each other.

One balmy day in late June, Nora was hanging out sheets in the back yard when she heard the sound of horses in the front driveway. Thinking it was Mattie who had come to visit, Nora started around the corner of the house to meet her when she came face to face with Jack Bradshaw. Jack impulsively hugged her then stepped back, embarrassed.

Nora, flushing, exclaimed, "Jack! Where did you come from?"

"Well, it's a long story and you're looking at a starving man," declared Jack.

Nora took him into the house to give him some lunch. Tad was delighted to see Jack but Tansy suddenly turned very shy and found something to do in another part of the house.

Their words tumbled over each other as both Jack and Nora each began telling of their experiences. Jack had visited several towns in Massachusetts and Vermont looking for a place to settle. Then someone told him about a lumberyard in Morristown that was going bankrupt because of the owner's ill health. It was for sale, he was told, and so he had come to Morristown to investigate it. It was also a good excuse, Jack said, to see the McDonalds again.

While bustling about to make lunch for Jack, Nora recounted the story of their trip from Boston to Morristown; about Uncle Harrison and Aunt Clara. She said nothing of Supleen's antagonism. After Jack had eaten, Nora gave him directions to finding Angus where he and Cecile were working. Because of her condition, she didn't dare to ride out with him.

Jack found Angus easily from Nora's directions. He whistled shrilly to get his attention and when Angus realized whom he was, he came bounding over to meet him. The two were genuinely glad to see one another, pumping hands and clapping shoulders, as men do. They spent some time catching up on each other's news. Jack insisted on helping Angus with the planting, so they talked, laughed and worked together for the rest of the day.

When it was time for supper, Angus called Cecile, who had been working at the other end of the field. He introduced him to Jack and they all went to the house together. Cecile and Tansy left for their own home.

It was a happy group around the supper table that evening. Jack and Angus discussed their plans for the future; Angus for the farm and Jack for the lumberyard, if he could get it. Nora contributed her ideas while Tad fell asleep in his chair. Angus picked him up gently and carried him upstairs, Nora following to tuck him in. Jack watched them leave the room, enviously.

When Nora and Angus returned, the three sat over coffee and apple pie for long time. Then they took Jack on a tour of the house. Nora had prepared the front small bedroom for Jack. It was next to Tad's and cozier than the larger one.

"It'll be a pleasure to spend a night in a real home, instead of a rooming house." Jack remarked. "Just wake me in the morning, Angus, I'll go to the field with you."

Angus protested that Jack should just relax and enjoy his visit, but Jack was adamant. So in the early dawn, Nora and Tansy made breakfast in the cheery kitchen for the men before they went out to their chores.

Before the day was out Angus had nearly persuaded Jack to stay at the farm while he negotiated for the lumberyard. Then that evening, when Nora also insisted he stay, Jack gave in.

It was pleasant to have Jack there. It made every evening feel like a party to have company. Nora and Angus showed Jack the Belltrees and he exclaimed that they seemed to have grown already. He was shown the barn and listened to Angus' plans for buying more cattle the next spring. Then they sat on the porch after supper, talking and enjoying the twilight, fragrant with the scent of honeysuckle. Jack told them more about his parents.

"Dad was angry, at first, about my coming to America." said Jack, "But he seems to have mellowed a bit, from the sounds of his last letter. He just can't get used to the idea of my actually working."

"It was probably very hard for your father to have you go so far away. He must miss you a great deal. My parents didn't want Angus and I to leave, either, but they encouraged us because they knew it was a great opportunity for us." Nora said.

Jack nodded. "I realized that now. I am just sorry that we had some angry words before I left."

Angus then told Jack about his own misgivings about taking Nora so far away from her family.

Nora spoke up. "But now we are sure we made the right decision. We love it here, and Mother and Father have promised to visit us, perhaps next spring."

Angus nodded in agreement. "Aye, and if it wasn't for Supleen, it would be near perfect."

Then he had to explain to Jack about his cousin's attitude toward the family since they arrived.

Nora broke in to his explanation. "You know, I think Supleen feels that you are taking his place in Uncle Harrison's affections. Maybe if we try to be friendlier toward him, include him in more things on the farm...." She spoke without much conviction.

Angus looked doubtful.

Jack chuckled at his two friends.

"It sounds to me like this Supleen is a sour apple. Why don't you two just ignore him?"

Angus shook his head. "We can't do that because of Clara and Harrison. But, enough of Supleen! How about one of your scones with a cup of tea, m'dear?"

While Nora fixed the tea and scones for the three of them, she was thinking of their conversation. As she sat down she spoke.

"I think we should invite the Renfrew's to supper some evening so they can all meet Jack. Maybe tomorrow. Is that alright with you both?"

The men exchanged glances, and then laughed. Nora tried to look innocent.

"I see, we are being friendlier, now." Angus teased his wife. "Of course, love, go ahead and invite them. Jack will see for himself how it is with Supleen."

Nora ignored the men's amusement and went on with her plans. "I think I'll ask Mattie and her husband, too. You'll like them, Jack. And Mattie's sister from Burlington is visiting them. She will come, too. Great fun!"

Her eyes sparkled. She bustled off to start checking the larder for a suitable menu. She decided that Angus would have to prepare two of their hens for cooking. With them she would make a meat pie and dumplings. For desert, strawberry cake using some of Aunt Clara's preserves. And she would whip some cream for the top.

The next day, Nora and Tad rode to Uncle Harrison's and to Mattie's with invitations to supper the next day. Nora met Mattie's sister, Annie. She was a short woman with curly reddish hair and pretty brown eyes. Nora liked her. Mattie later confided to Nora that Annie's fiancé had been killed falling off a horse, about a year ago.

Tad was delighted to see his newfound friends, Katie and Andy, again. He begged his mother to let him stay when she said it was time to go home. So it was decided that Tad would stay at Mattie's for the night and go home with her family the next day. This was Tad's first time away from his home overnight and he and his mother both missed each other when it was time for bed. As it turned out, though, Nora had more time to prepare for the party than she would have had with Tad following her around every minute.

The next day being Sunday, the men could take more time off from their chores than usual, so it was a good day for them to socialize.

The party was a success. Nora and Angus felt they were re-paying Harrison and Clara, in part, for their hospitality, and Jack had a chance to meet their relatives and friends.

Nora had picked some wild flowers for a centerpiece and used her lace tablecloth. Her eyes shone with pride in her home and family.

Mattie and Andrew brought their children with them so a small table was set up for the three children near the grown-ups table.

The ladies took the opportunity to dress up. Nora wore her green sprigged taffeta, Mattie a gray and yellow plaid dress. Annie had a medium blue bombazine gown, which set off her auburn hair. Aunt Clara was in her usual navy blue with a white, lacy collar and her eyes sparkled with anticipation. Nora thought; this is the first time I've seen her look happy. Of course, Zoë was dressed in the latest fashion sent up to her from Virginia; a lustrous gray sateen, trimmed with black braid. She was her same old self, complaining about the Vermont weather and flirting with Jack, making Supleen more sullen than usual.

Mattie and Annie helped Nora to serve before sitting down with the others. The men were talking about the crops they had planted and about Harrison's new bull. Supleen took little part in the conversation until Jack started telling about his plans to purchase a lumberyard in Morristown. Then Supleen questioned him about its location and size. In Jack's enthusiasm, he failed to recognize the avarice in Supleen's eyes until he had already divulged many details of his plans. Too late, he attempted to change the subject by praising Nora's meat pie. The others chimed in with complements to Nora.

Supleen, though, was already planning the best way to get money from his father to beat Jack to the purchase of the lumber mill. He could never stand to have anyone do better than himself. Bad enough that Harrison had helped Angus to get this house, now he was praising Angus friend, Jack, on his business sense. Well, he would show them all, he promised himself.

Another decision made that evening was by Zoë. She had observed the genuine enjoyment Harrison seemed to have in the company of Nora, Angus and especially, Tad. Harrison was always bringing treats to the little boy and playing games with him now. Now, Harrison called Tad over to him and had the boy guess which pocket his treat was in. Watching them, one could tell they really liked each other. Tad threw his arms around Harrison's neck and gave him a big hug. The pleasure in Harrison's eyes was evident. Then and there, Zoë determined to have a child to regain Harrison's attention. She knew how delighted Clara and Harry would be to have a grandchild and would practically guarantee that she and Supleen would inherit the Renfrew farm. Zoë was aware of the animosity between her husband and his father, because of the son's laziness and disinterest in the farm work.

She couldn't take a chance on losing everything if Harrison should decide to leave his estate to these upstart cousins. She didn't really like children, in fact, thought of them as grubby little nuisances. She shuddered inwardly; I'll get a wet nurse, she thought.

One other person, whose life changed from the time of the party, was Annie Loftus. She had come to Nora and Angus' home as a guest because she was Mattie's sister. There she met Jack, the first man who'd interested her since her fiancé was killed about a year ago. She also noted that when his eyes were on Nora they had a special softness. Never mind, my lad, she thought, that one's taken and I'm free as the air, so look out. She was seated next to Jack at the table and had plenty of opportunity to show interest in his plans. Jack, being human, enjoyed talking about himself. Nora and Angus, at opposite ends of the table, exchanged a glance and smile. They would have a lot to talk about when their guests left.

At home, Supleen asked Harrison to join him in the library, while Clara and Zoë went upstairs to prepare for bed. When Supleen explained to his father his plan to buy the lumber yard before Jack could, he enlarged on how much they could make a year with a well run lumber yard and how he could easily run it himself. Harrison watched his son as he paced up and down before him while glibly explaining all the advantages of the scheme. Harrison felt a great anger rising in him. He jumped to his feet, startling Supleen, who stopped his pacing. Harrison, his face purple with anger and frustration, never the less spoke with control.

"Supleen, I will not be a party to hoodwinking a friend of my nephew's, who is also your cousin, remember? Not a cent of mine will go into an underhanded scheme like that." Then, in a gentler tone, "Son, I've been wanting you to take charge of your life, and I'll help you with any straight forward plan. But not this!"

He left the room, his heart heavy with disappointment.

Supleen slammed his fist into the palm of his hand. Damn! I should never have told him about it, he thought; He's an old fool! Supleen's mind was working. He thought of a friend who was in business in town. It was possible that Dick would lend him the money to buy the lumberyard if he could have a lien on the Renfrew farm. Supleen smiled as that thought occurred to him. Everybody knows that I will own the farm someday. Deciding to discuss it with Zoë, Supleen went upstairs. She, however, had her mind on her own scheme.

Zoë was more successful than Supleen in her planning. In September she announced the impending arrival of an heir. Harrison and Clara were delighted that they were to have a grandchild at last. Supleen felt more secure and even acted quite human for a while. This new hold on his future partly made up for his friend, Dick, refusing to lend him the money for the lumberyard.

The summer had passed quickly, as they do in Vermont. With Tansy to help her, Nora's health had improved. The house was gleaming and a bedroom upstairs was in the process of being prepared for the new arrival in December.

Hay had been cut and stored in the barn loft. The whole family had enjoyed the haying. Nora or Tansy would bring the men big jugs of cool, ginger beer to drink with their lunch.

Ginger beer was made with cool water, a little vinegar, sugar and some ginger for flavor. Then a large piece of ice was added to keep it cool. It was a very refreshing drink after hours of haying in the hot sun.

Tad often got a chance to ride to the barn on top of the hay. Sometimes even Tansy or Nora would climb on, too, while the men rode up front.

In the evening, after their supper and with Tad tucked away, Nora and Angus would sit on the porch or walk, hand in hand, to look at the Belltrees, which seemed to be thriving.

Jack had moved into town and lived in two rooms behind the office at the lumberyard. He was a frequent visitor at Belltrees.

One day, towards the end of July, he brought Annie Loftus with him to visit. He had hired her for three days a week, to work on his books. Nora was delighted to see her friend again. She was quick to notice how pleased Annie was to be with Jack. She was also intuitive enough to see that Jack was only thinking of Annie as a friend.

While the men were talking about the lumber business, Nora took Annie up to the attic to look at some of the old clothes she had discovered there. Annie had brought a Godys ladies Fashion book and they wanted to see if some of the clothing could be re-done in newer styles. When the women had left the room, Jack spoke in a serious tone.

"There is something I want to talk to you about, Angus. Can we go out to the barn?"

Surprised at the urgency in Jack's voice, Angus led the way outside, where Jack turned to him with a worried frown.

"I feel I have to warn you, friend, that Supleen is a more serious enemy than either of us thought. Bart, one of the men at the lumberyard, told me that he was in Snyder's bar one night a week back. Supleen was there with two of his cronies. Bart picked up his ears when he heard your name mentioned; he knows we are friends. Supleen had a lot to say about his upstart cousin and bragged that he'd make you sorry you ever saw Vermont."

Angus frowned, "Thanks' for telling me, friend. I knew he resented me, but I didn't realize he was so bitter. I'll be careful."

Meanwhile, Tad was playing with the wooden cows and horses that Claude had carved for him.

Sometimes, Nora would give him little chores to do, such as feeding the hens or the cats. She intended to bring Tad up with a sense of responsibility. She often talked to him about the new brother or sister that would be coming to live with them around Christmas time. Tad would listen, wide-eyed, considering the thought carefully.

By September, Nora was feeling a little awkward in her movements. She had let out the waists of her skirts and made two dresses to wear for the winter that would accommodate her increasing size. She copied them carefully from Godys fashions, simply adding pleats or elastic. She was very creative and the results were always attractive. Actually, Nora blossomed. Her complexion was glowing and her black hair was shining with good health.

Soon the harvesting would be completed. Already Tansy and Nora had canned endless tomatoes, in every possible way; just plain, stewed with onions and basil, pureed to use for soup. Peas, string beans, beets and cherries were also canned. Many of the root vegetables were put into buckets of sand and stored in the root cellar. It was all hard work but both of the women enjoyed seeing the results; row after row of glass jars of luscious looking fruits and vegetables. A great deal of food was needed to get through the long winter.

The kitchen was a lively place and full of delicious fragrances. Sometimes Mattie and Annie would spend a day helping Tansy and Nora do their canning, then the next day Nora and Tansy would go to Mattie's house to help. Many hands made the work go swiftly and it was more fun that way. The children could enjoy each other's company at the same time.

Nora noticed that Annie frequently brought Jack's name into the conversation. She thoroughly enjoyed working for him, although that seemed to be the extent of their relationship. But

Nora could see that Annie was willing to be patient. Annie talked a little bit about her fiancé, who she had cared for deeply. Nora liked both sisters and was grateful to have them for friends.

One day, when they were all in Nora's kitchen boiling peaches to can, Aunt Clara appeared in the doorway. It was extremely unusual for her to come over by herself so Nora was surprised to see her. Clara's face was drawn and grave. She put her arms around Nora, saying,

"I've got some bad news, love. I had a call from the telegraph office. Your father is very ill; I'm so sorry."

Her kind face reflected her concern. Nora had to sit down quickly. She felt sick but her thoughts went out to her mother. How would she be able to deal with this? If only they weren't so far away! she thought. I should never have left Scotland! Her thoughts scurried round in circles. Maybe she could go to them. Then her practical side surfaced and she knew she couldn't make the trip in her condition. Still she didn't speak. Aunt Clara shook Nora's arm.

"Are you alright, love?" she asked anxiously. Nora nodded. Clara went on. "I'm so glad your friends are here. I do have to get back home. Now, cheer up, lass, I'm sure your father will be all right soon. We'll be over later."

As soon as the peaches were finished, Mattie scooped up her children and took them home, leaving Annie with Nora. Tansy kept Tad busy so that he wouldn't bother Nora. Nora found herself telling Annie all about her childhood, her mother and father, and her sisters and how she missed them. She was hardly aware of what she said.

When Nora heard Angus coming into the yard from the fields, she ran out to meet him and blurted out the news. Angus held her close and comforted her. He berated himself for taking her away from her home. But Nora put her hand over his mouth.

"Shh, love, we both wanted to come here. It's going to be all right. I'm sure Father will get better."

She spoke more to reassure herself than Angus. She paused a moment, then her face lit up.

"I know, when Father gets well they can come here to Belltrees."

Angus let her go on with out answering. He could see that just saying these things made her feel better.

Though Clara had said her father's illness was serious, Nora pushed from her mind the thought of her father not getting well again. Everyday she wrote to her parents; her letters full of hope and plans for them to come to stay with them, for good if they wanted to or at least for several months. She kept busy by preparing a room for her parents to stay in. She received letters from her sisters Molly and Mairi saying that their father was in need of constant care. They wanted her to come, but understood that in her condition it was not possible.

Nora had been her mother's mid-life baby, a complete surprise to Victoria and Edward. Molly, the oldest sister, had seemed like an aunt to Nora, who had been only six when Molly was married. Mairi had been home longer so Nora had grown closer to her.

Harrison, concerned about his brother's health, decided to go to Scotland to be with Edward and Victoria. He and Clara had not been home for a visit since coming to America. Now he feared he would not see his brother alive again. He started to make preparations to leave immediately.

So Supleen and Zoë were left in charge of the farm while Harrison and Clara were away. None of the hired help had any respect for Supleen or his wife. They considered Supleen to be lazy and Zoë, affected.

Altogether, the Renfrew's had five hired help; Mrs. Curtin, who came in daily to help with the heavy cleaning, cooking and washing; three men who worked under Claude doing all the farm work and Claude, himself. Harrison trusted Claude and considered him a good friend, as well. Claude felt the same about his boss, though he had only contempt for Supleen and the latter was well aware of that fact.

As soon as Harrison had left, Supleen started his campaign to get rid of Claude. He saw his father's absence as an opportunity to take over the management of the farm, which would be his one day, anyway.

Claude soon realized that Supleen wanted to get rid of him. He also distrusted Chet, the slow moving slit-eyed hulk that, of late, had been coming to the farm with Supleen. Claude knew of Chet by reputation, which was not good.

"That couchon, he's up to no good, that one." Claude muttered to Dusty, one of the hired men, who was helping clean out the barn.

Dusty laughed to hear Supleen called a pig. He nodded his head in agreement.

"He's after your hide, that's for sure," he said.

Harrison had asked Claude to keep him posted as to how things were going at home. Not being able to write himself, Claude asked Mrs. Curtin to write a letter to Harrison for him. At the end of the letter he mentioned that Chet was often around. He knew that Harrison would understand the implication of the message.

On the day that Claude's letter arrived in Scotland, Nora received word that her father had died.

CHAPTER FOUR

Angus hurried to the house after Tansy had frantically run to fetch him. He found Nora in bed, shivering uncontrollably under several blankets. Angus held her tightly, tucking the covers around her, until her shaking subsided.

The next day, Nora was up early helping Tansy to make pickles. Her face was drawn and there was a heaviness in her chest, which was to stay with her for some time. She wanted to rush to her mother but it was impossible. Even if they had the money, a trip that long was dangerous at this time for Nora. She wrote to her mother and sisters asking them to come to America.

Nora went out with Tad each day to water the Belltrees, her only link to Scotland. As they carried water to the little trees, she told her son about his grandfather, who he was named after. Talking helped to ease the pain of her loss. As yet, she hadn't been able to cry, just felt a profound sadness.

"When I was a small lass in Scotland, we had big Belltrees on our farm. My sisters and I would take our dollies and play under them. It was so cool in the summer."

"And did you have a goat like Spots, Mama?" Tad asked.

Nora laughed, "No, but we had pet rabbits." It was good, Nora thought, that I have Tad. And having a new wee one on the way will keep me busy as well.

It helped, too, that her friends called more often. Mattie and Annie came and took her into town one day to have tea. Even Mrs. Dufrense, another neighbor, came to cheer her up. No one could stay depressed in Mrs. Dufrense's presence. She wouldn't allow it. She was a large Canadian woman with a hearty, take-charge manner. She brought preserves and stayed to show Nora how to make a batch of her own special bread recipe.

One day Zoë appeared, dressed in a fashionable gray suit with matching hat and gloves.

"Ah'm so sorry about your father, my deah." she drawled with a show of concern. But her eyes were on her own reflection in the hall mirror. "Ah'm going to town to have tea with some friends, won't you come along?" she asked Nora.

The last thing Nora wanted to do was spend time in Zoë's company. She thanked her for thinking of her but excused herself on grounds of having to look after Tad, saying Tansy was too busy with the canning.

"How are you feeling?" Nora asked Zoë, remembering that Zoë, too, was expecting.

"Sick every morning," Zoë answered with disgust. "Having babies is certainly no fun. I can't think why anyone would want more than one."

She patted her still flat stomach.

On her way out, Zoë offered as an afterthought, "I may stop at the lumber yard and see if Mr. Bradshaw can cut me some boards for the closet I want built."

Nora chuckled to herself. She knew Zoë was a natural flirt and enjoyed trying to attract any man. She was glad when Zoë left.

The next day, Claude came over with news that Harrison and Clara would be home in a few weeks and were bringing Nora's mother with them. Nora could hardly wait to see her mother. She had often looked forward to a visit from her mother and father. It had never occurred to her that her sturdy, robust Father would be gone so soon.

As she thought of it, memories flooded her mind of when she was small; how he would swing her up into his arms, calling her his "bonny lassie" and give her a ride on his broad shoulders. He was always there, a firm rock for her, her sisters and Mother to lean on. I don't know what Mama will do without him, Nora thought. She wiped the tears from her eyes, blew her nose and went out to tell Tad his Grandmother was coming to see him.

They walked hand in hand to the field where Angus and Cecile were preparing the ground for a crop of winter wheat. Nora couldn't wait to tell Angus that her mother was coming. He was as pleased as she was. She and Tad rode back to the house with Angus and Cecile.

As they arrived at the barn, Jack came riding up the driveway on his big black mare. While the men took care of the animals, Nora went in to help Tansy put supper on the table. She set an extra place for Jack. At the table, the talk turned to Jack's business.

"I've contracted to buy standing timber from several farmers around here, for the lumber yard. How about you, Angus? I'll give you a good price for any trees you let us cut?"

"I've considered it, Jack, but I wouldn't want to lose all of my good trees. The ones that grow down the east and west boundaries are good to have as shade for the cattle and the ones to the North will help to protect us when the cold winds blow down from Canada. Everyone tells me they can be pretty bad, sometimes." Angus replied thoughtfully.

"True, but you could hand pick the ones you wouldn't miss; we would just remove those." Jack speculated.

"Soon as I have the time I'll take a look and see if I have enough to make it worth your time, Jack."

"There is no hurry, Angus. I noticed that there is a thick stand of trees north of your land. Do you know who owns it? If the owners are agreeable, it would be a smart move for you to buy a few acres. I'd give you a good price for the lumber rights."

Angus looked thoughtful. "Why don't you contract with the owners yourself, Jack?"

"It would be easier and cheaper for me to be able to access that lumber from your lot, rather than making a whole new road from the other side." Jack replied.

Angus nodded, still considering the idea. "I wouldn't want to be taking on any more debts right now, Jack, I've got this farm to think of now, and feeling a little uneasy about it because of Supleen's attitude. Maybe in the future I'll think about it."

"I understand, Angus, it was just an idea."

Jack knew Angus well enough to respect his judgment, so he dropped the subject. Jack left soon after supper. Nora stood in the doorway with Angus' arm around her, watching Jack leave. Jack felt a pang of envy as he waved goodbye to them.

Later, when they went up to their bedroom, Angus touched a match to the previously laid fire in the fireplace. The nights were chilly and the warmth made their bedroom cozy. Nora sat at the dressing table brushing out her long, dark hair, lost in her thoughts. Angus watched her from the bed.

With an amused smile, he asked, "And what is making you so quiet, m'love? I've a feeling you are planning something. Am I right?"

Nora had to laugh; he knew her too well.

"I was just thinking about what you and Jack were talking about. Angus, I think we should try to buy the timberland. With the profit we make selling the lumber to Jack, we may be able to pay off the mortgage. Then we wouldn't have to worry about Supleen anymore."

"But, Nora, we don't have any money to buy anything right now. Put Supleen out of your mind; let me do the worrying about the farm. Right now you have enough on your mind, with another wee babe coming soon."

"What if we asked Uncle Harrison about it? Maybe he would help us buy the timberland and share in the profits?" Nora suggested.

"You've a good head for business, lass. We can talk about it again some other time. For now, let's forget it."

He kissed her gently. Nora relaxed and put the subject in the back of her mind, along with her foreboding about Supleen. As always, it was so pleasant to forget everything else, in the close circle of Angus' arms.

The days seemed to drag by as Nora waited to see her mother. At last, it was within days of the arrival of Harrison, Clara and Mrs. Renfrew.

Supleen was to meet them in Boston. Angus couldn't leave the farm right now even if he wanted to spend any time in Supleen's Company. Zoë refused to go on the long, bumpy ride. She considered it a bore. Her days were spent visiting friends or meeting them in town at a dressmaker or for lunch. Supleen left on October first; he would stay overnight in Boston, as the ship was due on the second. When the three travelers arrived the next day, Harrison insisted the two ladies rest for one night before the trip to Vermont. So it was the fourth of October, a crisp, fall day when Nora's Mother finally saw Belltrees.

Nora had been hovering around the front rooms and the porch since she awoke. Several times she ran up to the room she had prepared for her mother to make sure all was in order. She had picked a bouquet of orange and yellow mums to put on the bedside table. She smoothed the already smooth, woven, white bedspread; then downstairs again to make sure Tad wasn't playing in mud or dirt, she wanted him to be clean when his grandmother arrived.

Finally, at almost four o'clock, the sound of wheels sent her flying to the driveway, calling to Tad to come quickly and for Tansy to run for Angus. She could hardly wait for her mother to get down from the carriage before throwing her arms around her. As the tears for her father flowed, her mother patted her gently.

"There, now, love, its alright." she soothed, but her own eyes were glistening. "Well, so, who is this young man?" she asked in surprise.

Tad had come up to his mother's side. Her tears frightened him a little. He was soon smothered in a hug from his grandmother. He found her scent pleasantly comforting.

Supleen had left his mother and father off at their place, as Clara was too tired to go any farther. Then Supleen drove Victoria to Belltrees. Now he unloaded the luggage and deposited it on the porch.

In his usual ungracious manner, he said, "I've got many chores to do so I'll be leaving. I'm sure Angus will be along to carry these things inside."

As he spoke Angus came riding up and jumped down to greet his mother-in-law.

"Dinna worry, Supleen, I'll get the luggage and many thanks for your trouble. Tell Uncle Harrison and Aunt Clara we will be over soon."

Supleen merely touched his hat to the ladies and left.

Nora and her mother, arms entwined, went up the stairs in the house. Angus and Tad followed, carrying luggage.

"Mama, you must be tired, why don't I take you up to your room. You can rest for a while before supper?" Nora suggested.

Her mother was exhausted and followed her, gratefully. Her husband's death and then the long trip had taken their toll on the small woman.

"That will be good, lass, I could use a wee rest. I am anxious to talk to you all but a little later."

In the bedroom, Nora pulled back the spread and when her mother had removed her hat and shoes, Nora helped her out of her dress. Victoria lay back on the pillow with a weary sigh.

"Thank you, lass. I'll be good as new in a little bit. The room is lovely."

Nora kissed her and went downstairs.

"Why does Grandma have to go to bed?" Tad complained. "I want to show her Spots and our cow and everything."

"Hush, laddie, Grandma is weary, she came a very long way to see us. She'll be down at supper time. You can help me set the table, how will that suit you, laddie?"

Tad scurried about importantly trying to help his mother, while Angus went to finish his chores. Victoria came down for supper, her gray-streaked hair smoothly arranged in a bun, in a fresh black dress with a brooch at the neck. Nora was so happy to have her mother there! She vowed not to cry again, her job was to cheer up her mother.

After supper, Angus lit a fire in the large parlor and they sat around it, Nora and Angus telling Victoria about the farm and how it looked when they first saw it. Tad insisted on her coming outside to see Spots and Nellie, the cow. So they all went out together. They also showed her the Belltrees.

"Your father would like this, Nora, that you have a bit of Scotland here." Victoria said.

They showed her around the house before settling down in front of the fire again. Victoria praised the farm and what they had accomplished with it so far.

"Its a bonny place you have here. I'm happy for you. It's lucky, too, that you have Harrison and Clara near by. They're good folks. But that Supleen! He's a strange one. Didn't seem too pleased to see his mother and father. And acted very put upon the whole way here."

"He isn't very pleasant, I agree," said Angus. "I don't think he was in favor of Harrison's holding the paper on this farm. Don't worry your head about him, Mother, for we don't see very much of him."

"Thank the good Lord for that!" Victoria replied. "A little of that one goes a long way. How do you like his wife, Nora?"

"She's all right. Puts on a few airs, that's all. They'll be having a wee bairn next May. That may make nicer people of them both." said Nora.

"Humph! Don't you believe it! People don't change that easily. Take my advice, you'd better watch that Supleen."

Nora changed the subject then by asking her mother about her sisters and their families. Her father's farm had been left in care of Colum, Mairi's husband. He was a hard worker, loved farming and eventually hoped to buy the farm from Victoria.

There were a hundred things Nora wanted to ask her mother but seeing her start to droop a little, she insisted on her going to bed at ten o'clock. Talk of Edward and how he died would be postponed until Victoria had a good night's rest.

But Victoria didn't go to sleep for a long time. She lay in the sweet scented bed her daughter had prepared for her. She stretched her arm out to the opposite side of the bed that was so empty.

"I wish you were here, love, to see your daughter's new home. You'd be proud," she whispered.

She awoke in the morning to see Tad peering around her door.

"Are you awake, Grandmother?" He whispered hoarsely.

"No, I'm sleeping with my eyes open," Victoria said, seriously.

He laughed and came over to sit beside her and tell her about his farm, the goat and the hens, the ducks that swam on the pond and his new friends, Katie and Andy. Finally his grandmother interrupted his chatter.

"I think we'd better go down for breakfast, now, laddie. Run along while I get dressed; you can tell me the rest later. Tell mama I'll be right down."

It took days for Victoria and Nora to catch up on the news from Scotland. Nora told her mother about her new friends; Jack and Annie and Mattie, even about Mrs. Dufrense. There was so much to tell. They went up to the baby's room to look at the clothes Nora had made; many little dresses, sacques and nightgowns, all lovingly sewn with tiny stitches.

"And do you be wanting another son this time or a wee lassie?" asked her mother.

"It would be such fun to have a tiny lass to dress! But as long as it is strong and healthy, I won't complain, lad or lassie."

Nora hadn't told her mother of her illness early in her pregnancy. She'd felt well the last few months and the baby's movements were vigorous.

"I'm so glad you'll be here with me. I'd been dreading to be alone. Oh, I know Aunt Clara or Mattie would come, but it's not the same."

"I only wish that---" Victoria started but left the words unsaid. They both had the same wish; that Nora's father was there, too.

Nora took Victoria on a tour of the outside of the house, showed her the barn and the chickens. Tad followed, sometimes running ahead to find Spots, who often hid from him. Then, when Tad wasn't looking, Spots would run up behind him with a friendly bunt. Angus had clipped off Spots horns so he really couldn't do much damage. This day, when Spots saw Nora and Victoria walking toward the barn, he couldn't resist the inviting expanse turned toward him. He took one look and came out from behind the bushes, running full tilt. He made a direct hit on Victoria's bottom, sending her sprawling. He took off prancing while Nora threatened him with dire consequences as she helped her mother to get up. After the first shock, Victoria started to laugh. Seeing her unhurt, Nora joined in, both laughing so hard they had to sit down on the ground.

Victoria wiped her eyes. "That's the first good laugh I've had in a long time!" She exclaimed, breathlessly.

Tad, shocked at first by Spots action and then at seeing two grown-ups laughing on the ground, began cavorting around and laughing, too. Spots was smart enough to make himself scarce for a long time.

CHAPTER FIVE

The gorgeous, multi-colored spectacle of fall in Vermont gave way to barren trees and brown grass. When the whole world had become colorless, drab and dreary, suddenly one morning the household awoke to a white fairyland.

Tad shrieked with delight and begged Tansy to come out and play with him. Tansy, enjoying it as much as Tad did, pulled the sled with Tad on it around and around the house, then up into the apple orchard where there was a nice slope to slide down.

As they came to the edge of the orchard, where the bare trees stood like avenging goblins, Tansy suddenly spotted a dark shape at the other edge. It took her a few moments to realize she was looking at a huge black bear. He was standing on hind legs reaching for the shriveled apples that still clung stubbornly to the trees. For a moment, Tansy stood, frozen. Then, turning, she ran as fast as she could toward the house.

Tad held on to the sled for dear life and called frantically, "Tansy! Tansy! Stop! Wait! What's the matter?"

He hadn't seen the bear. Tears started to pour down his face. He was frightened. Tansy didn't stop until she was at the door where she scooped up Tad and flew into the house.

Nora and Victoria, who were having a second cup of tea, were startled by Tansy's sudden entrance, pulling a tearful Tad behind her. When they were finally able to understand her, they all rushed to the back window to look out at the bear. He was nowhere to be seen.

Later, Angus and Cecile found the bear tracks and droppings. They warned the women not to go far from the house for a while. The bear undoubtedly was looking for food to gorge himself before the long winter hibernation. Although the men didn't want to frighten the others, they both feared this was the same bear that had, last week, killed two small pigs at the Olsen's farm. Mr. Olsen had warned all the neighbors to lock their small stock up until the bear moved on or was caught.

For weeks, Nora was afraid to let Tad out of her sight. She had Tansy keep a close eye on him, but the bear wasn't seen again that fall.

Jack Bradshaw's venture in the lumberyard had proved to be a judicious one. He had expanded the original business by negotiating with area farmers to purchase their standing timber. He had hired two brawny, local men to work in the yard. With Annie Loftus doing the paper work three days a week, Jack was free to pursue new accounts. Jack was aware of Annie's interest in him and he had a great deal of respect for her. Also, she was a very attractive woman. He invited her for supper about once a month at the local hotel restaurant. It was a pleasant change from eating alone in his two rooms. One evening when they were having dinner together, he spoke of it to Annie.

"This is certainly an improvement over Sam's diner or eating my own cooking."

"Jack, a man like you shouldn't have to settle for either one. You should have a home of your own and someone to cook for you."

A flush stained her cheeks as she spoke. Jack settled back and lit a cigar.

"You are right, Annie, at least I should have a better place to live. Actually, I've been thinking of buying a piece of land and building a little house near town. Maybe I wouldn't have so much sawdust in my food. If you hear of a good place for sale, let me know."

Annie nodded while thinking; Good try, Annie, better luck next time.

Jack steered the conversation back to business matters. But when he took Annie home she stayed awake for hours thinking of possible ways she could get Jack too see the disadvantages of being single. She was not happy with her own state of aloneness. Nearly everyone she knew was married and most had a child or two. She longed for her own home. Loneliness overwhelmed her and her pillow was wet with tears when she finally fell asleep.

Jack let the horse walk on his way home, as he considered what Annie had brought up. He, too, would prefer to share his life with someone but, whenever he thought about it the someone was a lovely, graceful, young woman with black hair and wide, gray-green eyes. Unfortunately for Jack she was also married to his good friend Angus. Dismissing the thought, Jack slapped the reins on Sultan's back and went home at a brisk pace.

The next day was Sunday and Jack drove out to Belltrees for a visit. There had been a heavy snowfall during the night so he used a small sleigh. He often visited Angus and Nora on Sunday for dinner, after they came home from Church. Angus had invited him today, especially.

This day, their conversation turned to the bear. A local farmer had seen him. With this particular bear, it was impossible to predict what he would do. It was more likely that he had been wounded in some way, which made it harder for him to forage.

If there was no sign of the bear, they planned to pick out a tree to be brought into the house and decorated for Christmas. It was still several weeks off, but Nora wanted to be ready in case the baby should come ahead of schedule. She had become awfully heavy the last few weeks and found it hard to get everything done. Her mother was a very capable woman and it was so comforting to know she would be here to help her, when the time came for the baby to be born.

Dr. Belden told Nora that everything was going well and "She had a big baby there". He thought she would deliver the end of the month. Privately, he was a little concerned about the apparent size of the fetus and he was uncertain whether he had heard two heartbeats. Once he thought he had but it had been so faint and then seemed to fade out.

Nora and Angus had wanted to have a big Christmas party inviting all their new friends and the Murphy's as well, but because of the impending birth they decided to postpone the crowd until spring when they would have a barbecue to celebrate their first year here.

As Jack pulled up in front of the farm, Tad spied him from the window and went flying to get his mother and father. They were enjoying a relaxing Sunday breakfast with Victoria.

"Papa, Papa, Uncle Jack is here in a big sled! Can I have a ride, please! Papa, can I?"

Tad was jumping up and down in his excitement. Then they heard Jack stamping his feet at the front door and loud knocking. All three hurried down the hall to let him in out of the cold.

Jack never entered a room quietly; it was not in his nature. Now, he grabbed Tad and swung him off the floor.

"How are you, my lad?"

Tad squealed with delight. Jack clapped Angus on the shoulder than gave Nora a gentle handshake.

"So, will we catch a bear today, Angus?" Jack asked jovially.

They laughed at Tad's big eyes when he heard this.

Tad began to pull at Jack's coat, "Can I have a ride in your sled, Uncle Jack? I can shoot a bear, I bet. Can I go?" he begged.

"Tad, be patient, lad. Give Uncle Jack time to sit down and have some coffee." Nora gently admonished her son. "C'-

mon in Jack, before these two can cart you off." She led the way back to the cozy kitchen.

While Nora gave Jack coffee and some of Victoria's hot scones, she listened to the two men talking.

"There hasn't been a real sighting of the bear since Tansy saw him in the orchard." said Angus. "Mr. Dobbs only thought he saw him. I doubt that he's still about, most likely sleeping in some warm cave."

"I hope so, I'm not overly anxious to meet him." declared Jack.

"Well, then, Angus, why don't we all go and select a tree for our Christmas?" Nora suggested. "I'd like to go for a ride in a sleigh, wouldn't you, mother?"

Victoria, who had regained some of her color in the past few weeks looked interested.

"Why, that sounds like great fun!" she answered. "I haven't been in a sleigh for years."

It was decided that since the sleigh would only hold three persons comfortably, the two men would ride horseback, while Nora, Tad and Victoria rode in the sleigh. Angus reassured Nora who protested that neither she nor Victoria was very familiar with the horse or sleigh. He said that he would ride close by.

"I shall drive, daughter, it wouldn't be good to have you pulling on the reins right now." Declared Victoria.

Nora gave in, though she enjoyed driving. It was better not to take any chances. They all bundled up warmly; the women in long, woolen capes and Tad muffled up so that only his eyes were showing. The sun shone brightly on the snow, which stretched in all directions. The sleigh glided over the meadows with Angus and Jack riding on either side of it.

Feeling the wind on their faces, enjoying the movement of the sleigh flying them through the white world, they nearly forgot about the Christmas tree. They rode around the periphery of the grove of evergreens. They tied the horse to a small tree and all tramped into the grove.

Angus stayed close to Nora as she was heavy now and had some difficulty walking through the deep snow. The new fallen snow was clinging to the evergreens branches, creating a fairyland spectacle. Jack scooped up a handful of the sticky stuff and pelted Angus with it. This started a snow fight; everyone joined in. No one threw at Nora but she was soon sitting in the snow, laughing at the others antics. Tad shrieked with laughter as he made a direct hit on his father.

They found a perfect tree, deep in the grove; it was about ten feet tall and perfectly shaped. They all agreed it was the one and Angus tied his red scarf on a branch so they could find it easily again.

Walking back to the sleigh, Angus started singing a Christmas song, "Good King Weneslaus". Everyone joined in, happily, with gusto.

In the middle of a word, Nora felt a strange dull pressure in the small of her back. She didn't say anything to the others although she felt it several times on the way back in the sleigh. She, never the less, joined in the carol singing. When they got back to the house Tansy had some mulled cider for them and hot chocolate for Tad.

A few days before Christmas, Nora and Tansy were baking plum puddings and breads for the big day. Victoria had done the bulk of it the day before, but today she had persuaded Angus to take her into town for some last minute purchases so they had left about eight that morning. They took Tad with them as a special treat.

Nora had awakened, full of energy that morning. She felt frustrated by her awkwardness while trying to bake so she let Tansy do the difficult tasks.

At eleven o'clock, as Nora was putting the last loaf of bread in the oven, Cecile burst in the door. He blurted out that Tansy's father had an accident in the barn. Her mother needed her at home. Tansy flew to get her cape then remembered Nora.

"Will you be alright, Nora?" she asked, anxiously.

Nora reassured her. "Of course! You go ahead, I'll be fine. Go to your Mother!"

"Well alright. I'll be back as soon as I can." Tansy felt uneasy about leaving Nora but she followed her husband out.

The sudden quiet of the house struck Nora. This was the first time she had been alone since they had come here. In a way it was peaceful. She busied herself cleaning up the kitchen. She glanced out the window; soft white flakes were drifting down. How beautiful it was, and so still!

It occurred to her that she should get out the good tablecloths and her mother's cut glass serving dishes. The good dishes were stored on the top shelf so she dragged one of the kitchen chairs over and, lifting her skirt with one hand, she leaned on the chair back with the other. Putting one foot on the seat, she started to raise her other foot off the floor. Halfway up the chair toppled over toward her, throwing her backward. Her head hit the edge of the table before she fell to the floor. Blackness descended and Nora didn't see the snow flurries turn to a full-blown blizzard.

CHAPTER SIX

Angus was having lunch with Tad at the little teashop in Morristown. Victoria was making the rounds of the stores and would meet them when she was finished. She had also stopped in at the lumberyard for a visit with Annie, who was delighted to see her. Annie told her that Jack had gone to the Dufrense farm where he was negotiating with Henry for his timber. After that he would stop at the McDonald's.

As Angus stepped out of the teashop, holding to Tad's hand, he noticed it was not as bright as it had been. To the north he could see black clouds and the temperature had dropped. He hurried Tad along.

"C'mon, lad, we need to find your grandmother and get home."

As he rushed off, Tad protested, "But, papa, I thought we were going to look at the toys today." He complained.

Angus pointed to the sky. "Look up there, laddie, bad weather is coming and your mama may need us, so come along now."

They found Victoria talking to Annie. She quickly collected her purchases and they started for home. The wind was blowing some but they were a mile from town when the snow caught them. It dropped suddenly from the north and they could hardly see. Angus could barely make out the road. He didn't want to alarm Victoria so he tried to pretend he knew where he was going, but in reality he was depending on the horse to know his way home. The going was very slow; Victoria and Tad were huddled deep in their robes. The snow caught in Angus' eyebrows and stuck to his beard.

"We should be coming to the Carter's farm soon." He told Victoria, "The road is only a few feet from their door. I think we should stop there until this lets up. Tansy is with Nora for now and we'll leave as soon as the snow stops."

He didn't add that they might miss the farm in the blizzard. But he was saying a silent prayer that Paul Carter would have a light on. He strained his eyes trying to peer through the mass of thick, soft flakes but could make out nothing. After another half mile a dark shape appeared on their right, then a faint yellow glow showed.

"Thank the good Lord." breathed Victoria.

Angus pulled off the road toward the light. They were within a few feet of the house. Angus helped Tad and Victoria up onto the porch. He banged on the door and a surprised looking Ethel Carter opened it. Immediately sizing up the situation, she pulled Tad and Victoria inside.

"Lord-a mercy! What are you all doing out in this? Come in! Come in! I'll have Paul help you put away the team, Mr. Mc-Donald. We have a small shed to the side." She called to her husband.

When Angus and Paul came in they joined them. Talk centered on the storm; then Paul remarked that his brother, Andrew, had been by earlier and told him that Tansy's father had been in a serious accident. The Carter's knew that Tansy worked for Nora and Angus. Victoria and Angus were worried about this new situation and more anxious than ever to get home. But nothing was to be gained if they got lost in a snowstorm, so all they could do was wait for it to stop.

At the McDonald's farm, Nora opened her eyes. Her hands went to her head, which was throbbing. Then a more severe pain in the middle of her back made her groan. The room seemed dark and she glanced toward the windows. There was only darkness, expect for a faint glow from a small lamp in the corner of the room. She could feel the drop in temperature already and she knew the stove needed replenishing. She couldn't stay on the floor and get a chill.

She grasped a chair near her and gingerly pulled herself to a sitting position. If I could just get to the settee, she thought. Gradually she dragged herself over to the settee and climbed onto it. The pain in her head and back was excruciating. She lay very still for a few minutes and the pain in her back subsided. She pulled the warm knitted coverlet around her tightly and closed her eyes.

Just as she was about to fall asleep, another pain started in her back. This time it seemed to go through her body to her abdomen, which became ridged. She doubled over in agony. Now she was sure the birth pains were starting. This was not the way she had planned it, all alone, with no one to help. When the pain receded, she lay back and tried to think of what she should do. She didn't know how long it would be before the next contraction.

There were three lamps on the table that had just been filled and their wicks trimmed. They should be put in the windows to guide anyone who was within eyesight, although the chance of anyone being out in this storm was unlikely. At least, if Angus had started back, the light would help him to find their house. Nora managed to light the lamps and put one in each window. The glow made her feel better, as well.

It was a slow process with her head pounding; she held on to chairs to keep her balance. She looked at the clock to try to keep track of her contractions. She was back on the settee before another one came. Oh, please, she prayed, wait until Angus gets here. Tears ran down her face.

Jack, who had been about his usual business of visiting local farmers to buy their timber, had concluded his business with Mr. Dufrense. As he was taking his leave, the snowstorm started.

He had planned to stop at Harrison's before going to the McDonald's for the evening. He could barely see to cover the two miles to Harrison's. Luckily, he had an excellent horse and they understood each other. When he reached the Renfrew farm, he put his horse directly into the barn, thinking he would stay there until the storm blew over.

As Clara and Harrison shared their tea with Jack, they told him that Claude had seen Angus pass by with Victoria early that morning. Then, about an hour ago a friend of Harrison's had called and told them that Tansy's father had been injured.

"I had just decided to send Claude over to Belltrees to see how Nora is doing. If Tansy had to go home, Nora will be all alone." Harrison said.

Clara was wringing her hands nervously. "Oh, I hope she is alright! Harrison, do you think Claude could find his way over there in this?"

Her husband scoffed. "That man could find his way there blindfolded; he's like a cat in the dark."

Jack, listening to this conversation, spoke up. "Angus may not be able to get back here for hours, the way this storm is going. If you will let Claude come with me, I'll go over to be sure Nora is alright."

When Harrison summoned Claude and explained the situation, the feisty, little Frenchman was optimistic about finding his way to Belltrees, even in the storm.

As they prepared to leave, Clara paced about nervously, "If only Angus had a telephone over there." She said for the third time.

Her husband patted her shoulder. "Now, now, my dear, don't worry. Chances are that Nora is all right. And with Jack and Claude going over, we'll soon know."

The snow was still falling so thickly it was like a white wall, so that Jack would have had no idea of direction. But Claude set out confidently. He'd tied a rope between the two horses so they wouldn't get separated. It took them almost a half hour and Jack felt sure they were lost, when a faint glow was seen to their left. Claude waved his hand to Jack, pointing. With relief, Jack recognized the McDonald house as they drew nearer the light.

The two men tied their mounts to the railing and went up on the porch, stamping their feet and brushing snow from their clothes. Jack knocked loudly on the door. There was no answer. After a few moments, he knocked louder. No one opened the door, so he opened it a crack and shouted for Nora.

A faint voice answered him from the direction of the kitchen. Sensing trouble, Jack, followed by Claude, ran down the hallway into the kitchen. Seeing Nora lying on the settee, her face white and drawn, Jack felt fear and shock.

Taking her gently by the shoulders, he asked, "Nora, my dear, what is it? Is it the baby?"

Nora, tears coursing down her cheeks, clung to him with relief. Her voice was weak. "I fell, now the baby is coming. Please! Get Dr. Belden!"

Jack turned to Claude, his face reflecting his concern. "Go back to Harrison's, Claude, try to call the doctor and try to find out where Angus is, I'll take Mrs. McDonald to her room."

As Jack scooped Nora up and headed for the stairway, Claude was off. Upstairs, Jack pulled back the covers and lay Nora down carefully. He removed her apron and shoes and smoothed her hair back from her face. He could do no more. Nora was wracked by another pain and Jack held tightly to her hand.

"Just try to relax, dear, someone will come soon." He repeated over and over but he could feel the sweat pouring down his back. He was afraid no one would get here in time. He tried to speak calmly. "I'll time your contractions after I get a cloth to wipe your face."

He found a washcloth, wrung it out in warm water and placed it on her forehead. As he held her hand, he chatted to her about anything that came to his mind in order to take her mind off her situation. To his relief, the pains did not seem to be at regular intervals yet. He'd always heard that they would come regularly for some time before the birth.

The hands on his watch seemed to stand still. The pains remained irregular but Nora seemed to get weaker with each onslaught. At one point, while at rest, Nora asked Jack to leave the room so she could remove some of her clothing that was restricting her movements. The best she could manage to do was loosen her skirt and slip it off and loosen her petticoats a little and remove her other undergarments. It was a tremendous effort for her to do this much.

When Jack came back into the room he was shocked at the way she looked. He wiped her face again. Her contractions were now about twelve minutes apart. Between the pains, Jack tried to make her smile by telling her some silly things he'd done when he was a child. Nora actually managed to smile, but they were both straining to hear some sound that would tell them help was coming.

Jack went to the window. "The snow has stopped at last." He reported. "Someone will be here soon."

A cry from Nora made him turn. She half rose to a sitting position as a pain tore at her body. He went to her quickly, gently rubbing her back.

"There, there, love, easy does it." He soothed her.

Just then feet were stamping on the porch. They heard the front door opened. With relief, Jack went to the bedroom door and saw Aunt Clara toiling up the steps and Claude brushing himself off in the hall.

Clara was breathing hard when she reached the bedroom but quickly became efficient and took charge. She ordered Jack out and changed Nora into a nightgown. She chattered constantly in a cheerful voice and made Nora feel more confident that she could get through this.

Actually, Clara was appalled at the grayness of Nora's face and the severity of her pains. It seemed different to Clara than other birth's she had attended. But she spoke with reassurance to Nora.

"Don't worry, dear, Angus will be here soon with Dr. Belden. He called to see if we knew how you were doing and we told him what was happening."

Then, as Nora gasped and called out in agony, Clara grasped her hand and held tightly. She could see Nora was pushing and thought that the baby would come soon.

"My God, Nora, just hold on a moment, please!" She implored.

But an hour later, the baby's head still hadn't crowned. Nora was getting weaker and incoherent from the pain. Clara was beginning to fear for Nora's life and possibly the child's as well.

Downstairs, Jack and Claude were both pacing the floors. Claude made coffee to bring up to Clara. Nora could only sip a little water between contractions.

The two men went outside to try to clear away some of the snow to make a path for Angus. They were both relieved to get out of the house, where they felt so helpless.

Clara was becoming more and more nervous as time went by. Nora's pains became more intense. At seven fifteen, she was bearing down mightily with each one. With great relief, Clara saw the tiny crown appear.

"You're doing wonderful, love, just a little more."

One more push and Clara held the little girl baby in her hands. She expertly tied off the cord and put the glistening newborn on Nora's chest. The small rose-colored face was topped by dark hair. Nora put her arms around the soft bundle and felt the same surge of love well up within her that she'd felt with Tad.

"O, You're so beautiful!" She whispered.

As Nora gave the infant to Clara to be cleaned, she felt an excruciating pain in her back again. At her cry, Clara put the baby down and came back to Nora.

"What is it, love?" She asked.

"I don't know." gasped Nora. "It doesn't feel right."

Clara soothed her, saying. "It's probably just after pains, many women have them. I'll see what I can do."

But when Clara started to gently massage Nora's abdomen to help clean out the placenta, she knew something was not right. Nora's abdomen was still distended far more then it should be.

She felt around carefully, her face ashen. Trying to keep her voice matter-of-fact she said. "Well, love, may be that you have another wee bairn in there. Just think of that, now!"

But when she looked up at Nora, she was frightened. Nora was looking very weak and now this. What should she do? She'd never been present when twins were born. Please, please, let the doctor get here, she prayed silently. All she could do was wait. She couldn't bear to think of going through another several hours of this. She didn't see how Nora could stand it either.

Clara sponged Nora's gray face with cool water, chatting all the while about how blessed it would be to have twins. But Nora was too exhausted to respond. Pain wracked her body again and again. She wanted to just give in to it and retreat into darkness.

Clara felt herself on the verge of hysteria when outside they heard shouting. She ran to the window and saw two men on horseback starting up the driveway.

"Oh, thank you Lord!" She exclaimed. "It's Angus and Dr. Belden."

A moment later, Angus bounded into the room and went straight to Nora. "I'm so sorry I was not here! Are you alright?"

Nora tried to manage a smile, but tears started down her cheeks. She spoke, weakly. "We have a daughter, love."

Clara showed him the baby and he was awe struck, touching her cheeks, her hair.

Then he turned to Clara. "But what's wrong with Nora?"

The doctor had already thrown off his coat and taken charge of the situation. He confirmed what Clara had decided, that there would be another baby, soon.

Angus was shocked. "Twins! My god! Will Nora be alright?" He blurted out. "She looks so sick!"

The doctor took Angus aside, saying. "Now, my boy, everything will be alright. You get out of here now and let me do my job. Get something to eat." He gently pushed Angus toward the door and into the hall.

"I could use a cup of coffee, myself. And bring some hot water and some brandy for your Aunt."

Then the doctor returned to his patient. After examining Nora, Dr. Belden was very concerned. The infant was in the breech position, very dangerous to both Nora and the child. Nora was weak and he was sure that she had suffered a concussion when she fell. He hoped she would be able to stand the necessary procedure to turn the baby. He could also see that Clara had taken almost as much as she could stand.

He made sure the baby girl was all right and then turned back to Nora.

"I'm going to give you a little ether, my girl, because I have to turn this little one around so he can come out into the world."

Then, turning to Clara, he said, "I know you've been through a lot already Ma'am, but can you help me for a little longer? You've done a great job, so far."

Clara, exhausted as she was, took her place where he indicated at Nora's head to keep her eye on her reaction to the ether. Nora relaxed almost immediately and Clara averted her eyes as the Doctor struggled to turn the baby.

Nora moaned and it seemed an eternity before Dr. Belden exclaimed, "There we are, now, can you give a push, my dear, and we'll have your baby for you."

A few moments more and there was a second tiny body in the doctor's hands. But this one was still and bluish. Clara gasped as Nora fell backward onto the pillow; she had half raised to see the baby. When she heard the doctor trying to rouse the infant, she cried out in fear. Dr. Belden plunged the baby into the pan of water that Jack had brought and then he vigorously rubbed the small body. At last the three on-lookers heard a small cry and little fists waved in the air as though in protest at this cruel reception. But as Clara and the doctor cleaned and wrapped the baby, they exchanged sad glances.

When Clara gave the baby to Nora she exclaimed. "But she is so small, and blue. Will she be alright, Doctor?"

"We'll do the best we can, my dear. Now you need a long rest." He avoided her eyes as he turned to finish his job.

There was a knock on the door and Angus' worried voice asking to come in.

"Just a few minutes, Angus, and you can see your new daughters." called Clara. She quickly cleaned Nora and put on a fresh nightgown.

As Clara opened the door for Angus he nearly knocked her down in his eagerness. He first went to Nora and hugged and kissed her while at the same time she was saying, "Oh, love, look, we have two daughters, look!"

The color drained from Angus' face and he went to the cradle to stand staring in awe at his two minute daughters.

"Dear God!" he breathed. "They're so small. Are they alright?"

Dr. Belden reassured him but warned that they would need a lot of care because they were so tiny and had such a difficult time coming into the world. Finally, Dr. Belden and an exhausted Aunt Clara left the little family alone. They were both still stunned by having two babies instead of the expected one. Angus had to bring both babies to Nora so she could check them again.

"Angus, I'm so afraid for them, especially this one, she is so small. You must get Pastor McMillan as soon as you can to baptize them. We'll name them after Mama and your mother. This is Victoria and this is Abigail."

She touched each small nose. Then Nora lay back on the pillows, her face happy but wan. Angus kissed his wife and pulled the covers up to her chin. She was asleep before he reached the door. He quickly found the doctor, who was having some coffee in the kitchen, with Clara and Claude. The doctor told him what he couldn't tell Nora. He felt grave doubt that the smallest twin would survive and even the other one would need care night and day.

Angus put his hands over his face as the others looked on with sympathy. There was little they could say. Clara put her arms around him.

"We'll do all we can to help, Angus. It's going to be all right."

Tears were running down her cheeks. The doctor insisted that Clara go and lie down and get some sleep.

"I'll watch out for Nora and the babies until Mrs. Renfrew can get here."

It was nearly ten o'clock the next morning when Victoria and Tad arrived. The roads had been plowed and she had started out as early as possible, her mind in turmoil. She knew Nora was in labor but that was all.

When a distraught Clara met her in the hall and filled her in about all that happened, Victoria collapsed into the nearest chair, her hands clasped on her chest to still the wild fluttering there.

"My poor, poor gerril!" was all she could say, her Scotch burr taking over in her distress.

But she didn't sit for long. Tad was pulling at her and begging to see his mama.

"All right, laddie, now you just be very quiet and we'll see how everything is up there."

They went upstairs where she made him wait in the hall while she peeked into the bedroom. Seeing Nora asleep and Angus sitting in a chair beside her, Victoria let Tad come in. Angus held out his arms to Tad and hugged him while whispering to him to be very quiet. Then he showed him the cradle with the two sleeping babies. Tad's eyes widened.

"They're very wee babies. And both lassies, Papa?" The boy asked.

Angus nodded, then they all went out into the hall to talk so as not to disturb Nora. Tad was sent downstairs for Aunt Clara to feed and Angus explained to Victoria what the doctor had told him. His mother-in-law set her little jaw and took on a determined look.

"There'll be no more talk of dying in front of my lassie, and with God willing, the wee bairns will be all right." She declared.

From then on Tansy and Victoria took over the care of the babies. The doctor had to see to his other patients but promised to look in on them often. Tansy's father was still in poor condition so he also was in need of the doctor's attention. Angus tried to tell Jack, Claude and Clara how grateful he was that they had come to help Nora. He was berating himself for not being there when Nora needed him.

The babies were both put in the cradle; they were so small that there was enough room and Nora felt that they should have the warmth of each other's bodies to gain strength. Hot water bottles were placed at the top and bottom of the cradle to give added warmth. Nora spent a lot of time holding and talking to the twins. She thought that when she sang a soft Scottish lullaby to them that they seemed contented.

It was a week before she felt like leaving her room at all, but she had several visitors. Besides the doctor, Zoë and Uncle Harrison had been over to see the twins. Harrison was enthralled with his great-nieces but Zoë wasn't impressed.

"They're very small, aren't they"? she declared. She thought to herself that she would certainly produce a much better child than these puny specimens.

Nora was glad when Zoë left. She wasn't yet strong enough to cope with Zoë's cynicism. She had a lot on her mind with the twins and Christmas in just two days. She felt badly that she had not been able to participate in the preparations but Victoria and Tansy had taken on the full burden with the help of Angus.

Christmas Day was bright and beautiful with the whole world, it seemed, covered in a white blanket. Angus and Jack carried the twins' cradle down to the living room and placed it near the fireplace where they would be cozy. Then, with Angus' help Nora managed to walk slowly downstairs and be with her family for the first time since the twins were born.

It all looked so charming with the Christmas tree alight and the fireplace glowing. With Nora downstairs, Tad was so excited he could hardly stay still but kept running between his mother and the cradle. Angus caught him and tossed him up in the air.

"Come now, laddie, don't you want to see what you have under the tree now?" He placed his son on a stool at Nora's feet.

There were gifts under the tree for everyone, including Tansy and Cecile, who were giving up a part of their Christmas with their family to help out here. They would leave after dinner to spend some time at their home. The Christmas meal was a quiet one; Jack proposed a toast to the twins, which everyone drank to, prayerfully.

After the meal Nora suddenly felt very tired. Angus saw the color leave her face.

"C'mon, love, its up to bed with you for a bit."

He picked her up and carried her back to their room. Tad followed them up and climbed onto the bed beside his mother. She held him close for a moment.

"Mama's just a wee tired, laddie. I'll be good as new after a small rest. Run along, now, and play with your new toys."

Angus sat with Nora for a few minutes, holding her hand until her eyes drooped, then he went downstairs to bring up the twins.

Nora awoke to hear Abigail's hungry cry and Baby Victoria's thin, weak one. Her mother was just coming into the room with an armload of clean baby clothes. Nora went to the cradle and picked up the babies. She laid them on the bed to be changed and fed. As she lifted Baby Victoria's tiny arm Nora had to blink back the tears. How could anyone so small survive, she wondered. She quickly changed the two and held them both closely to her as if to infuse her own energy into them.

Baby Abby, as they all started calling her, seemed to gain every day but little Victoria didn't appear to get any larger or stronger. She would stop nursing after only a minute or two as though it was just too much work to eat. So Nora would feed her more frequently. While she held her, Nora would talk to her constantly, telling her about her father and her big brother and how happy they all were to have her with them. At times the dark eyes would open wide, seeming to understand what her mother was saying to her. Then Nora would stroke the satin soft cheeks and smooth the light fuzz that crowned the small oval head.

CHAPTER SEVEN

1901

Spring thaw came as usual in mid-march. It lifted the spirits of most of the inhabitants of Morristown but at Belltrees there were heavy hearts. Nora had not left her bedroom since February twelfth, when baby Victoria had given up her struggle for breath.

Nora had been rocking both babies and singing a lullaby when she felt the spasm shake Victoria's tiny body. Nora's anguished cries brought her mother and Angus but she was scarcely aware of them being there. For hours she refused to relinquish baby Victoria to them to be prepared for burial.

To make it more difficult for her there could not be an actual burial because the ground was frozen. The small coffin, lovingly constructed by Angus and Claude, was placed in a stone building in the back pasture for burial in the spring.

Nora had been lavishing all her time and love on Abby, who was thriving. All her relatives and friends had called to try to cheer her up but she had taken all her meals in the bedroom. She was terrified that something would happen to Abby.

After three weeks of watching Nora get more and more withdrawn, Angus decided to take matters into his own hands. One day, when Jack was visiting, he told him how concerned he was. Together they went upstairs to the bedroom. Nora was just tucking Abby into her cradle after feeding her. She looked up and smiled at them.

"How nice to see you, Jack, and what have you been doing with yourself? How is Annie? I haven't seen her either."

It was obvious that Nora was trying hard but her sad eyes and wan face showed the strain she was feeling. She smoothed her hair back with a hand that trembled. Angus put his arm around her.

"Jack and I have some business to talk over, dear, and he will stay for supper." As Nora started to excuse herself, Jack turned from admiring Abby.

"I'm looking forward to seeing you later, Nora. Angus and I want to ask your opinion on something, isn't that right, Angus?"

"That's right. Now, don't disappoint us, love. I will send Victoria up to help you."

Then, ignoring the pleading look on Nora's face, the two men went out. They actually did have some business to discuss but the main idea was to get Nora out of that room and back among them again.

When they reached the kitchen, Tansy and Victoria were hard at work; Tansy washing clothes and Victoria starting the evening meal. Angus told them that Jack would be staying and that Nora would be coming down. Victoria looked visibly relieved and said that she would have Tansy stay with the baby while they all had their evening meal.

When Victoria went up to help Nora she found her sitting on the edge of her bed with silent tears running down her cheeks.

"I can't bear it! I can't!" She covered her face with her hands.

Victoria, blinking back the tears coming to her own eyes, patted Nora gently.

"Look here, my girl, you've had a terrible blow and we are all very sad, but remember, Angus has to bear the same loss. He needs you now. By staying in this room you are hurting him."

Her deliberately matter-of-fact tone did more for Nora than anything else could have. She put a mirror in Nora's hand.

"Now here, you're looking like the wrath of God. Fix yourself up a bit and you'll feel better, too."

Nora looked with disinterest at her image. She didn't care that her once immaculate hair looked neglected or that her eyes were red-rimmed. But for Angus she made the effort. She put on a navy blue dress with white collar and cuffs, washed her face and fixed her hair.

When Tansy came up to stay with Abby, Nora was ready to go down. She took a last look at the baby and went down to the dining room where Angus and Jack were waiting. Angus was so relieved to see his wife downstairs once more that he was unusually talkative and the conversation was animated during supper at least between Angus, Jack and Victoria. Even Tad caught the spirit and chattered away about the animals, in particular about Mandy, one of the cows that was about to give birth.

Nora was the only one who said very little. She heard her husband and the others talking about the death of Queen Victoria, beloved monarch of Great Britain for sixty-three years. She had been Queen for all of their lifetimes and it seemed strange to think that she was gone and her son, Edward VII was now the head of the country.

It all seemed very remote to Nora compared to her own personal grief. She tried to be interested when Jack and Angus discussed the pros and cons of the new automobile that was becoming so popular in their new country.

She excused herself early. Angus walked up to the bedroom with her. But she felt a little stronger and from that day on she went to meals, often taking the baby with her. Her heart was still heavy but she could see how the others were affected by her sadness, so she made an effort to conceal some of her feelings.

Jack and Angus had come to an agreement wherein Angus would sell Jack the right to cut down a good share of the wood lot over a period of several years. The trees would be replaced with saplings each fall so as to guarantee that the woods would never be depleted. They also agreed not to cut the sugar maples, which Angus hoped would produce a portion of their income in the future.

Jack told Angus about Supleen's anger because the farmer who's land bordered Harrison's property to the north refused to sell his woodlot to Supleen. Jack sounded worried.

"That Supleen is a vicious man. He wants me to buy his woodlot on the east side but to tell you the truth, Angus, I hate to have any dealings with him at all. But, if Harrison wants the deal, I would have to consider it."

Angus tried to reassure his friend. "You can trust Uncle Harrison. He's a good man. He helped me a great deal when I needed to find a farm here. And as long as Harrison is alive, he is the boss. I'm just sorry that Supleen is so resentful of me."

"Well, it's no fault of yours, my friend, so don't worry yourself about it. Just be careful of him."

It was a constant source of concern for Angus that his cousin was so bitter towards him and he could hardly avoid the man or be curt with him because of his feelings for Aunt Clara and Uncle Harrison. But he knew that, if Supleen had his way, Angus and his family would never have come to America.

Angus and Jack, with Tad trailing behind, went out to see how Mandy was doing. She was a cow that Angus had paid more than usual for because of her bloodlines. Her calves would sell for a good sum and she would produce a great deal more milk than his other cows. This meant that they would have an ample supply of milk, cream and cheese for their own use and to help pay Cecile's and Tansy's wages. Then what the other cows produced could be sold to the creamery. This money would help to repay Harrison a little sooner.

Now that Nora was feeling better, Angus could concentrate on the farm, though the heaviness in his chest when he thought of his tiny daughter was always with him, as it was with Nora.

The first week in April, when the smell of spring was on the breeze, the minister came out and read the service as they put the small coffin in the ground under a large oak tree near the woodlands. Cecile and Angus built a white picket fence around the spot. Harrison, Clara and even Zoë and Supleen were there as well as all of Nora's and Angus' friends and neighbors.

Zoë was large with her child, which was expected, in another month. She was still as fashionable as ever, wearing a purple velvet dress and coat to match, with a large-brimmed purple hat placed squarely on her head, as was the style in New York.

On the first day of May, when Nora took Abby outside for an airing, she was acutely aware of her surroundings for the first time since baby Vicky had died. All around her were new beginnings. The crocus had pushed their colorful heads through the last remaining snow patches and new buds were unfolding on the bushes and trees.

Suddenly she felt that she could face the future and be content. The baby was sitting up, her round, serious face framed in a pink bonnet crocheted by her doting grandmother.

Nora walked over to where the small Belltrees were. Their winter burlap had been removed and she could see new shoots on the branches. She thought how pleased Angus would be. Tad came running over to talk to his baby sister who responded with a smile and gurgles.

At around the expected time Zoë gave birth to a baby boy, to the delight of Harrison and Clara. Supleen seemed almost human in his pride and Zoë was basking in the limelight. She had produced an heir. Now Harrison would be less likely to disinherit Supleen no matter what their disagreements.

Zoë had refused to have the baby at home and insisted that Supleen take her to the hospital in Montpelier, about fifty miles away. She had also employed a nurse to be with her at all times.

Although her delivery had been a normal one, she had complained constantly and harangued throughout the whole experience until the doctor, in self-defense, had given her ether even when he felt she could get along without it. He was glad to see the last of her.

The baby was named Harrison Findly II, after his grandfather. Because of the distance to the hospital, the doctor had made Zoë stay a little longer than usual. Clara had, with much delight, described the baby to Nora as being beautiful and strong. Nora was happy for them and thought it would be nice for her children to have a little cousin for a playmate.

The soft, spring days were getting longer and the buds were opening on the apple trees and the lilacs. The forsythia was already brightening the landscape with it's golden blooms. The spring work had begun on the farm and everyone was busy.

Nora decided to take an afternoon to visit the new baby next door. She took Tad with her in the buggy, leaving Abby with her mother and Tansy. Tad was delighted to be going with his mother and have her full attention. He was full of chatter and questions about his new cousin. Nora laughed at his enthusiasm.

She was feeling great and she looked it. Her eyes sparkled and she had dressed with care. She was still wearing her dark mourning but the black wool fitted her waist closely and was very becoming and her matching hat made her creamy skin glow.

At the Renfrew's, the door was opened by Aunt Clara, who greeted them with hugs. She happily conducted them up to the bedroom shared by Zoë and Supleen.

"They'll be so glad to see you." Clara said.

She knocked on the door. Zoë's voice called out to them to come in. To Nora's surprise, the new baby was not in his parent's room. Zoë explained that she just couldn't tolerate the baby's waking up in the middle of the night.

"I need mah sleep," she drawled, smothering a yawn. "And anyway, Mrs. Thorne is paid to take care of him. Well, come on, I'll show you."

Trailing her pink, silk housecoat, she led the way to a room down the hall where Nora was introduced to Sadie Thorne. She looked different from Zoë as one could possibly be. Her gray hair was pulled back smoothly from a round-cheeked motherly face. She smiled proudly as she showed them the baby. He was sleeping in a large, fancily decorated crib. Nora and Tad admired him while Clara proudly hung over the crib, adjusting the blankets.

"He's very bonny!" said Nora. "I believe he looks a little like you, Zoë. Of course, I can't see his eyes. Are they like yours or Supleen's?"

Zoë shrugged. " I don't see any resemblance at all. But the doctor said he's perfect, of course." She drawled smugly. "His name is Harrison Findly II, after Father Renfrew." She patted the baby's head. "You're just going to be the apple of your Granddaddy's eye, aren't you, sugar?"

They all went down to the parlor, where Clara served tea and cakes.

Tad complained. "He's little, too, just like Abby. There's nobody around here I can play with."

The ladies laughed and Clara gave him some cookies and suggested that he go to the barn, where his Uncle was looking at a newly arrived colt.

Then the women settled in for a long chat. Nora was amused by Clara's monologue about her first grandchild and dismayed with the new Mother's obvious boredom. Zoë's comments were centered on how soon she could get back to her normal activities.

Nora left as soon as she could, politely. She went to the stables to pick up Tad. She found him enthralled with the new colt, which was staggering around the stall on spindly legs, while the mother tried to clean her with long swipes of her rough tongue. Harrison, Claude and Supleen were all watching.

Claude and Harrison greeted Nora but Supleen grunted a monosyllable and turned and left the barn. Tad, his eyes round with awe, turned to his mother.

"Mama, Uncle Harrison says she is mine if you say I can have her. Can I, Mama?"

Nora looked at Harrison. He laughed heartily.

"That's right, Nora, I told him long ago that the next colt I had would be his. Every boy needs a horse of his own. When my grandson's ready we'll have one for him, too."

Nora expressed her gratitude to Harrison for his generosity. At the same time she understood why Supleen had been so uncivil to her.

When she could tear Tad away, they went home to tell the others about the exciting news. Tad even told his baby sister about his new colt. She listened with round eyes and gurgled and cooed in an appropriate tone of voice. She had no idea what he was talking about but loved having his attention.

Angus was surprised and pleased by Harrison's gift to Tad. Nora and Angus both noticed that from that day on their small son took on a new and more mature attitude.

Nora said to her husband, with mixed feelings, "He's becoming a person now, Angus, and not just our baby anymore."

Angus answered with a father's pride. "That's as it should be, love, you wouldn't want him a baby forever. It'll be very good for him to learn how to care for his horse. It'll be a while 'till he is ready to ride, alone."

"I know. It's just that it's happened so quickly. I have to get used to him being a person and not my baby any more."

Angus hugged her to him. Nora thought of the way Supleen had glared at her as he left the barn.

"I don't think that Supleen is very happy about Harrison giving the colt to Tad. He was barely civil to me when I saw him in the barn. I could tell he was angry about something. He seems to resent all of us so much. I hope his son doesn't take after him."

Angus frowned. "I know." he said. "I wish he didn't feel that way. It would have been better if Harrison hadn't given Tad the colt; it only makes things worse between Supleen and us. Anyway, don't worry your pretty head about Supleen; I'm thinking nothing's going to change him."

Neither of them had much time to worry about Supleen in the next few months. Nora was extremely busy with her children and supervising the spring-cleaning. And Angus had all of the spring preparations for planting and trying to improve the farm, which kept him more than busy. In Vermont the planting and growing season was so short that no time could be wasted. Whenever there was a good day, outdoor activities were pressing and on rainy days he and Cecile repaired harnesses and cleaned the outbuildings.

On the best, sunny days, Nora enjoyed taking the clothes out to the clothesline. Often she would bring Abby out with her and spread a blanket on the new grass for her to play on. Abby had reached an interesting stage now where she was aware of her surroundings. She would watch her mother and laugh and wave her arms in delight when she would see a bird fly by or the silly goat dance. Tad would sometimes play nearby and try to make her laugh.

Much of Tad's time now was taken with learning how to care for Pegasus, his colt. His father showed him how to brush and currycomb her. She also had to be fed and watered and let out to run and kick up her heels in the pasture. He loved the feel of her satin nose and how she would nibble at his clothes.

It seemed to Tad that the time would never come when he could actually ride the colt alone or when his little sister would be old enough to play with him. Sometimes, though, Andy and Katie would come over with their mother to visit. These times were the highlight of Tad's life. He could run and play and show off his colt and goat to his friends. He and Andy would often try to escape from Katie but she would refuse to be left behind and come puffing after them, red curls flying. Tad really didn't mind her playing with them. He was just happy to have playmates.

Nora, too, was always glad to visit with her good friend, Mattie. Although she had her own mother for company, it was through Mattie that she learned about their new country. Mattie explained to her about the two main political parties and how voting was done. Only men were allowed to vote, she told Nora. In Scotland, where this kind of thing had been mostly predetermined, Nora had never felt too interested. But now she drank in everything she could hear about how America was run. Mattie didn't know a lot about President McKinley but had heard a great deal from her husband about the newly elected vice president, Teddy Roosevelt, who was a vibrant man with definite ideas of his own.

"Do you think women will be allowed to vote someday, Mattie? It doesn't seem fair, when we are expected to obey the laws." Nora mused.

But Mattie had lost interest in the subject. "Oh, I don't know, but anyway I don't have time to bother about those things with all the work I have on the farm, and I think most women feel the same way. Of course, there are some women who are trying to get the vote for us. I heard about a woman named Elizabeth Stanton who spends most of her time trying to get other women to help her convince the country that we should be able to vote. I've heard that she has even been arrested for making speeches in public places."

Nora's eyes widened in amazement thinking that any woman would have the courage to call such unfavorable attention to herself. Yet she felt admiration for someone that would stand up for her convictions.

She asked many more questions of Mattie but her friend seemed disinterested. Mattie was far more excited about the latest Sears Roebuck catalog that she had brought with her and the two spent a lovely hour pouring over the latest fashions and furnishings for the house. Nora's mother joined them for a while until it was time for tea and Mattie had to take her children home.

Victoria had insisted on having teatime each day as she was used to do in Scotland and they all enjoyed it. As Victoria was about to pour that day, there was a knock at the door, and Tansy appeared followed by Clara and Mrs. Thorne, carrying the new baby. Clara looked proud.

"This is the first time he's been out and I am mighty glad to get out of the house, too. With Harrison out from dawn to dark doing spring work and Supleen always on business, it's just been Sadie and me in the house with little Harrison for days."

"Well, we're glad to see you, Aunt Clara! Please, you both sit down and have tea with us. And how is Zoë feeling?" Nora inquired.

"I don't see much of her really, she has so many friends in town, you know."

Clara quickly changed the subject and Nora and Victoria exchanged glances. They had heard that Zoë had been spending even more time with her friends in town since little Harrison was born. They both felt a great deal of sympathy for Aunt Clara but agreed that Mrs. Thorne was an excellent mother-substitute.

Actually, as they talked together that day, it became apparent that Sadie Thorne was well read and had great deal of experience with children. She had helped her sister bring up her seven children. In her own words, "I just missed having a baby to take care of so I decided to apply for this job."

It was also clear that she and Aunt Clara had become close friends.

CHAPTER EIGHT

Jack's lumber business was going even better than he had hoped for. He had contracted with many of the farmers in the area to purchase their timber and orders were beginning to come in from, not only the local people, but out of town as well.

Still, he felt there was something missing from his life. He was no longer contented to return to his one-room bachelor quarters at the end of the day's work.

One night he was more restless than usual. The sandwich he had fixed seemed tasteless. As he sat at the little kitchen table he thought of Angus and Nora and their comfortable home. A thought suddenly occurred to him and he jumped up to bring paper and pencil back to the table and began to sketch swiftly.

He sat at the table for four hours, measuring and drawing until, exhausted but satisfied, he finally turned off the lights and went to bed. His last thought was, "in the morning I'll see Bill Horton about that piece of land he was telling me about."

The next morning, after a meeting with Bill Horton, Jack rode out to Belltrees to share his plan with his friends. He found Nora outside hanging up the clothes, with Abby and Tad close by. Angus was still out in the fields. Nora was happy to see him and Tad insisted he go out to the barn to see Peggy.

"Angus will be here shortly for dinner, Jack. He'll be glad to see you," said Nora.

They all went to the barn and admired the colt who was kicking up her heels all around the stall.

Jack could contain himself no longer; he had to tell someone about his plan.

"Nora, I've decided to build myself a house! I brought over the plans. Perhaps you and Angus can help me with them, since I've never had a house of my own before."

Nora smiled, "That's wonderful, Jack, it'll be great fun! And what made you decide to build all of a sudden?"

She wondered if Annie had anything to do with Jack's sudden decision.

"Well, I guess I just got tired of that room of mine. I'd like to have a place where I can feel more at home." Jack replied.

When Angus came in from the fields with Cecile, they had dinner, and then Jack spread his plans out on the dining room table. Everyone had a suggestion on how to improve the plans. Nora thought there should be more room in the kitchen for cupboards and a closet in every bedroom. Angus was interested in the plans for the barn; he suggested that Jack have a separate building for his hay storage to prevent loss of the main structure in case of a hay fire. This was a common occurrence in the area due to combustion of the hay when it was tightly packed into haymows and the temperature soared in the summer.

Jack made a note of each suggestion. Angus and Cecile had to go back to the fields so as not to lose any daytime hours to prepare to plant. Jack stayed on for a while, poring over the papers with Nora, their heads nearly touching.

Jack was suddenly aware of her closeness and her fragrance. Abruptly he straightened up and started rolling the plans together.

"I think I'll give Angus a hand with the work for a while. I've nothing special to do today. Perhaps next week you will both take a ride with me and look at the property."

Startled by Jack's sudden shift in ideas, Nora stared at him. She could not read the strange look on his face.

"Of course, Jack" she said. "That would be great fun. We can bring a picnic." And, as he hurried from the room, she called after him, "Come back for supper, won't you?"

She stood staring after him for a moment before going to help her mother take down the curtains to wash. Jack, on his way to the fields, dug his heels into his mount's side to spur him to a fast gallop. "I'm some fool", he thought, "in love with my best friend's wife. I'll have to watch myself".

The following Sunday, they all met at Hooper's Mercantile Store to go with Jack to view the property. Jack had invited Annie to go along and Angus and Nora brought Tad with them.

Jack led the way, out through town for about two miles then turned off the road to follow a bumpy dirt lane where he came to a stop.

Everyone piled out and Jack proudly took them on a tour of the land. It was a very desirable plot. Actually there were ten acres in all but where Jack wanted to build was on a knoll from which there was a lovely view of the surrounding lands. Many large Maple and Elm trees circling the knoll would shade the house in the summer.

While the men strolled around to inspect the property, the women spread out blankets, and then sat down to have a visit since they hadn't seen each other for a few weeks. Annie was full of chatter about her sister, Mattie, and her family.

"Mattie said to tell you that, after the spring planting is finished, maybe we could plan some kind of a celebration party. What do you think?" Annie asked.

Nora was delighted, as always, to think of a party and they spent some time discussing the details to make it an enjoyable time for all the farmers in the area.

There was a lull in the conversation and it seemed to Nora that Annie had something she wanted to tell her. Annie was setting out salads and rolls for their lunch, but was obviously thinking of something else. Nora wondered if it had something to do with Jack.

Then Annie said, "I've seen your cousin, Zoë, in town quite a lot since the baby was born. She is always dressed so beautifully. Do you see her often?"

There was something else, Nora felt sure, that Annie wanted to say and she looked closely at her friend's face as she answered.

"No, really, I see her only rarely. Sometimes Aunt Clara brings the baby over, though, usually with Mrs. Thorne."

Annie's face was crimson as she shifted the subject to the baby, inquiring as to how he looked and whom he took after. Nora was puzzled by her friend's reaction but didn't pursue it.

Just at this time the two men returned with Tad. They were all hungry and so full of good spirits that Nora forgot about what Annie had been saying. Angus was impressed with the piece of property.

"When will you start building, Jack?" Angus asked. "You might have trouble finding enough men to help until after the planting season."

"Oh, I'm not in a big hurry, Angus, I still have to draw up the final plans and make a few other decisions. Maybe about August I can get started on the house."

When the last bite of fried chicken was gone, Angus and Nora had to leave so that Angus could help Cecile with the plowing. On the way home, with Tad tucked between them, Nora and Angus discussed the land Jack had purchased.

"Jack is a shrewd one, he is. That land will be worth a good sum one day, even if he didn't build on it." Angus commented.

Nora was thoughtful. "I'm wondering if he is going to propose to Annie and give her the house for a wedding present." She mused.

Her husband laughed. "Oh, stop with your matchmaking now, lass. Jack told us he is sick of living in one room, that's all."

"Maybe. We'll see." Nora responded.

That evening, as Nora was brushing out her long hair in front of the mirror in their bedroom, she suddenly remembered Annie's strange behavior at the picnic.

"Angus, what is going on with Zoë, do you know? Annie got all flustered today when we were talking about Zoë spending so much time in town. Do you know what it is?"

"Well, lass, you know I don't hold much with gossip, but I have heard that Zoë is spending a lot of time in town with that crowd of lounge-abouts and there is one fellow she has been seen with pretty often. I surely do feel sorry for her husband." Angus replied.

Nora's face showed the shock she felt. "What a fool that woman is! She has a beautiful little boy and a good home, though I don't envy her Supleen. Aunt Clara is the one I feel sorry for."

"Well, don't you be fretting about it, lass, it is naught of our affair. Besides it's only gossip as far as I know."

Nora still looked concerned, but she dropped the subject for the time being. Neither one could know the impact this situation would have on their lives.

That same evening, Supleen was confronting Zoë about the same subject. That day, in town at the grain store, he had overhead some banter between a couple of laborers. He heard a reference to "that group of idlers who play cards all day at the Deauveau's." Supleen knew that Zoë spent some time at Betty and Eliot Deauveau's house. A lot more than he liked but there was no way he could stop his defiant wife from doing exactly what she pleased.

Another phrase came to his ears. "That brother of Eliot's seems to have found himself a new playmate with that southern belle from---" the voice trailed off as the speaker caught sight of Supleen, who pretended he hadn't heard.

He left the grain store seething inside. He knew of only one person in the area who would be referred to in that way. He was furious at Zoë for causing him this embarrassment. He also loved his wife and was aware that she spent as much time away from home as she could, leaving many of her responsibilities for his mother to do.

Supleen's anger grew as he worked around the farm the rest of the day. He knew Zoë would not return home until about supper time. In the meanwhile, the animals and inanimate objects he came into contact with suffered for his bad mood.

Supper at the Renfrew's was a subdued affair that evening. Clara and Harrison knew something was going on between their son and his wife. From the look on Supleen's face it was not something good.

Zoë had arrived shortly before the supper hour in high spirits. She had even inquired about the baby for a change, but when she saw Supleen's face she had become pretty quiet. She knew something had happened and had an idea that it had something to do with her activities. She hadn't been very discreet about her card-playing friends, but she didn't think he could have found out about Larry Deauveau.

After supper, Supleen took Zoë's arm, none too gently. "I want to talk to you." He said angrily in a low whisper.

She had no choice but to go with him. Once in their room he turned on her, his face twisted in anger.

"What have you been up to with your fancy friends? Do you know you're being talked about all over town?"

His own pride prevented him from mentioning the Deauveau's brother.

Zoë, feeling a little safer, lounged on the bed. "Oh, what're you getting so fussed about, Honey? You know how bored I am here all the time".

She pulled him down to her. "I just have to get out some and the Deaveaus are very entertaining. There's no harm in enjoying myself, is there"? She wheedled.

She could always talk him out of being angry with her. But this time, Supleen, with the laborer's words ringing in his ears, was not to be put off. He sat up straight and grabbed her arm.

"Well, I'm telling you now that from now on you're to stay at home and act like my wife and take care of the baby! And you're not to see that Larry Deauveau again! Do you hear me?"

Zoë sat up. She hadn't thought that Supleen could have known about Larry. But from the look on her husband's face she knew she had better say something to placate him. She pretended to misunderstand him.

"Oh, what a fuss over nothing! Larry's just a friend, that's all. You know how dull it is around heah. Ah just have to get out and talk to people, if ah don't ah'll go crazy!" Zoë cried out, her drawl accentuated.

Supleen, for once, was not giving in to her wiles.

"Then you can take mother or the baby when you go into town. Go shopping or where ever you want, but act like a wife, for God's sake! If you don't you'll not get another penny to spend on your foolishness!"

Being deprived of money to spend would be unbearable for Zoë, who had married Supleen believing him to be a wealthy landowner. Her mind was racing. Hot anger rose in her. She knew she couldn't live here under the conditions he had described. She really hated the farm life and had little or no motherly instincts toward little Harry. But she would have to play for time and coax Supleen into giving her more freedom and money. She swallowed hard and reached for his hand.

"Oh, Suga', don't get your self all fussed. Ah'll be good and stay home more. Come here now."

She pulled him down beside her with a sweet smile. Supleen melted, as usual. He considered himself to have been very fortunate to win such a lovely southern flower. He thought that he had won today.

In the next few weeks Zoë played the part of wife and mother pretty well, fooling only Supleen, not Clara or Sadie Thorn, who knew her very well. At least once a week, Zoë, Clara and the baby would go into town for lunch or to shop. Clara, being a homebody, didn't enjoy being dragged around town by her daughter-in-law but she knew there was a crisis in her son's marriage so she went along to help keep peace in the family. She never mentioned to anyone that Zoe always found an excuse to leave the baby with Clara for an hour or two on each trip to town. Clara was concerned and would have been more so could she have followed Zoë.

After leaving Clara at a friend's or at lunch on the pretext of looking for something special, Zoë would meet Larry at the Deauveau's house. At first she was just trying to have some fun and at the same time to defy Supleen. But soon Larry was getting more serious and she enjoyed the little flirtatious games. He would be leaving town soon anyway, to go back to his work in South Carolina.

Zoë was impressed by the fact that he was working in the South and seemed to have plenty of money to spend.

Zoë's mother, who considered herself the epitome of a southern lady, had coached her daughter in "how to marry a rich man" since the day she was born. She was the daughter of a family that once had been wealthy plantation owners. She had been determined that Zoë would marry and help to regain the wealth they once had, regardless of whom she had to marry to achieve this goal.

So far, Mama had been disappointed in Zoë's marriage and let her daughter know it in no uncertain terms. Zoë also felt that she had married beneath her. That, and this little hick town she found herself in, added to her discontent. She couldn't wait for Harrison to die so Supleen could inherit the farm. It seemed a lifetime away.

One day, after Supleen had refused Zoë some money she had asked for, Zoë asked Clara to go into town with her. Leaving Clara and the baby with friends, she went directly to the Deauveau's where she knew Larry would be.

There was a card game going on but when Zoë came in Larry dealt himself out and took her into another small living room. They sat down on a green, velvet sofa. Zoë turned tear filled eyes to Larry.

"Oh, Larry, I just had to see you! That selfish pig won't even let me have a new coat or give me any money at all to spend. I might as well be a prisoner!"

The tears spilled over and she laid her head on his chest. He dabbed at her eyes with his handkerchief.

"There now, baby, you don't have to put up with that treatment. Now, look what I've got for you, honey."

He pulled from his pocket a velvet case and held it out to Zoë. At the sight, her eyes opened wide and she greedily took the case and opened it to see a lovely bracelet of rubies, her favorite stone.

"Oh, Larry, you are so good to me. I just love it."

She threw her arms around his neck. Encouraged, Larry put his arms around her and kissed her. Zoë didn't pull away. This was the first time she had allowed him to be so familiar with her. Always before she had made sure they stopped short of this kind of familiarity, being afraid he would think she was cheap, plus she was terrified some inkling of her actions would get back to Supleen. So, after a moment, she pulled back from Larry. He put his hand on her arm.

"I've been thinking about you, baby. I want you to come to Charleston with me. We can have a great time together. You can have anything you want. What do you say, baby?"

He caressed her face and shoulders. Zoë's mind was working furiously. This might be her chance to get away from this hick town and have fun as well as maybe getting a richer husband, or at least having the best of both worlds.

"But, Larry, honey, you know I'm married. I don't want everybody talking about me. You know what they say about divorced women."

"Well then," Larry said. "Just tell your husband you want to visit someone in Charleston. When you get there we can make plans. You can do what you want there and no one will know you."

Zoë's thoughts were racing. Could she convince Supleen to let her go away for a while? She did have an aunt in Charleston. Of course she didn't like her and had rarely seen her but Supleen didn't know that. She straightened up and looked at her watch.

"I have to go in a minute or I'll have lots of explaining to do. I really do want to go to Charleston, Larry. I'll think about it."

By the time she got home, Zoë had hatched a plan. She found a letter she had received a few days ago from her mother. She had barely scanned it before as she was never very interested in anything her mother had to say. She found a pen of the right color and added a postscript, carefully copying her mother's writing.

Zoë was especially sweet to her husband when he came in from the fields. Supleen congratulated himself on having put his foot down and his self-esteem raised several notches. At the supper table that evening Zoë produced the letter from her mother.

"Oh, Clara, Mama sends her love. Poor dear, she is so worried about her sister. You know, Aunt Charlotte, in Charleston." Zoë declared.

This was the first time any of them had heard Aunt Charlotte mentioned, except for Supleen, who knew of her existence, but had never met her.

"Why, what is the matter, Zoë?" Asked Clara, always sympathetic to anyone with a problem.

Zoë elaborated, with a worried look. "Poor Aunt Charlotte had a dreadful fall and can't get out of bed and mother isn't feeling too well herself. She just doesn't know what to do. Poor thing! I wish I could help!"

She sighed heavily and gave Supleen a look designed to melt. He would have given her anything at that moment and she knew the effect she had on him. The only two at the table who were skeptical were Harrison and Sadie Thorne. They each had their private opinion of Zoë and wondered what she was up to.

Ten days later, Zoë was boarding a train for Charleston. Accompanying her was a young woman; a friend of the family, who Supleen trusted and whom Zoë disliked intensely. Miss Frawly was a plain young woman, gentle and honest.

Zoë had won the argument that Mrs. Thorne and Baby Harry should not go on the trip with her. Supleen had proposed that arrangement, but Zoë had countered with the fact that it was too long a trip for a baby; that he might get sick. Clara and Mrs.

Thorne had agreed with her, so Supleen had to be satisfied with Miss Frawly going. She had relatives in Charlotte, North Carolina so she would be on the train with Zoë for most of the way and she planned to return at the same time that Zoë would.

CHAPTER NINE

Nora and Victoria were sitting on the back porch; Nora was folding the clothes fresh off the line and Victoria was shelling new green peas for supper. Nearby, Tad was carefully giving Abby a ride in his wagon.

Abby, at twenty months, was a chubby little girl who could twist her big brother around her tiny finger. Of course, she wasn't much fun to climb trees with yet and he had to wait for Andy to come over to have that kind of fun. But, in the meantime, Abby was an appreciative audience. She had her mother's straight, dark hair and her father's determination. The two women watched the children with amusement.

"I feel so lucky, Mama." Nora said. "Just look at my bonnie lad and lassie! I have a wonderful husband and this place that belongs to us. Two years we've been here and we will be able to pay our year's mortgage to Uncle Harrison on time. The crops are doing so well!"

"True, lass, you've reason to be happy. If my Robbie were here it would be perfect." Her mother replied, her eyes misting over.

Nora put her hand over her mother's. "I know, Mama, it must be very lonely for you without Papa."

Not one to indulge in self-pity for long, Victoria blew her nose and returned to the task at hand.

To change the subject, Nora commented; "Things aren't so good next door. Sadie tells me that Zoë doesn't show any sign of coming home and Supleen is very short-tempered. She was supposed to come back with Agnes Frawly this week, but

Zoë wrote that her Aunt still needs her. She is certainly a very strange woman."

Victoria shook her head; "A woman shouldn't leave her husband for so long a time, not to mention her small baby."

Little Harry was a lively toddler and kept his nurse and grandmother busy. Luckily, he was a good-natured child and Sadie Thorne was determined that he would not be spoiled.

Nora jumped in time to catch Abby from a headlong dive onto the grass as her brother took an enthusiastic turn with the wagon. Abby gurgled with laughter at the unexpected tumble as her mother held her closely. She struggled to get loose and continue the fun but Nora decided it was time to go into the house and get ready for their evening meal. Abby's glee quickly turned to howls when she realized she was being taken indoors. She was easily pacified with a little biscuit while Nora prepared the supper and Victoria made some hot scones.

When Angus came in an hour later he had more news of the situation next door. Uncle Harrison had told him that Supleen was so furious at his wife that he was talking about going to Charleston and bringing her back. He was making life miserable for everyone around him with his bad temper.

"I almost feel sorry for the man, with a wife like that." Declared Angus.

He looked around the table with satisfaction at his little family. He had a feeling of well-being. The crops were good this year, they had a good batch of canned food put up for the winter, and soon he would have a barn full of hay. He also had a substantial order for some timber from Jack, which would pay the mortgage for the year to Uncle Harrison. He was a lucky man indeed!

Jack was having quite different feelings. As he stood and surveyed his property where he planned to build his home, he felt a deep loneliness. The foundation for the house was already marked out for the men to start work the next day. But somehow the excitement he had felt when he had planned it had left him. There was no one to share it with him. Also, his father had written again expressing his disapproval with his son's lifestyle. He insisted that Jack come home and take on his responsibilities as a gentleman and heir to his family estate. Jack hated to disappoint his father but he knew he couldn't tolerate living that way.

From his parents, Jack's thoughts turned to Nora and Angus. He envied their life together and was aware that his feelings for Nora could never be acknowledged or acted upon. He then thought of Annie, who worked for him in the office. She showed in little ways daily how she felt about him. She was a sweet woman and nice to look at. He wondered if she would want him if she knew how he felt about someone else. Maybe she would take me on this basis, he mused. I need someone, but would it be fair to her?

He tormented himself with these thoughts as he paced around his land. When the sun began to set, he slowly mounted Blaze and rode towards the office. Although he had purchased a Ford Motorcar, he preferred to ride his big black horse when going outside of town.

Back in town, he put the gelding in his stall after brushing and feeding him. He changed his clothes and drove to the house where Annie lived with her sister.

Annie was helping her sister prepare the evening meal when he arrived. She invited him to eat with them but he asked her if she would go to the hotel to have supper with him. Annie looked at him thoughtfully. He was unusually serious tonight.

She went quickly upstairs to change, her heart beating faster. She had thought about Jack for so long now and hoped and prayed that he would start to think of her as more than just a friend and secretary.

Being an empathetic young woman, Annie was aware of Jack's feelings for Nora. She had been around the two of them often and had observed his facial expressions when he didn't realize that anyone was watching.

Now she hurried to fix her unruly, curly hair under a hat and snatched up her gloves. She struggled into her jacket on the way down the stairs.

During the supper, Jack didn't initiate any conversation, replying shortly to Annie's attempts to converse. This was not like Jack at all and Annie finally gave up trying to talk. After a few minutes of silence, she could stand it no longer.

"Jack, what's wrong? You aren't like yourself at all tonight."

Jack reached over and took her hand.

"I'm sorry, Annie, I've been trying to think of a way to ask you about something. I've never had trouble with words before but now, well, you know that I'm building a house and.." The words came in a rush. "Annie would you marry me and share it with me?"

This was not exactly what Annie wanted to hear. She had hoped for a declaration of love, and this sounded more like a business proposition. But she was never a woman to play at being coy so, with only a slight hesitation, she replied. "Yes, Jack, that would make me very happy."

Jack breathed a sigh of relief. He apologized for not having a ring and said they could go together and pick one out. They agreed not to tell anyone until they bought the ring, when they would announce it to everyone.

Back at Annie' house, Jack walked with her to the door and kissed her goodnight. They each had mixed feelings. Annie was terribly happy and yet felt deprived of something. Jack had a peaceful feeling that he had made a good decision, along with a nagging guilty feeling that he wasn't being honest. He rationalized this by mentally promising to give Annie a wonderful life and to devote his future to home and family.

On September first Maggie gave a small engagement party for Annie and Jack. All of their friends were invited. It was a beautiful summery day and Maggie had a table set up out-of-doors to accommodate everyone.

She was happy that her sister had found happiness after the tragic loss of her fiancé four years ago. Annie was fairly glowing today and had spent more time than usual to get ready. Her curly hair was under control and her brown eyes were sparkling. Maggie had helped her choose a lovely, filmy, yellow tea gown for the occasion. There was a matching yellow hat.

Maggie wouldn't let her lift a hand in the kitchen, in spite of her protests. Several other friends, including Nora, were helping to set tables and pass the small sandwiches and little cakes around. There were endless pitchers of lemonade as well as some homemade wine. This was mostly imbibed by the men folk.

There was a special table for the children, supervised by Lucy, one of Mrs. Dufrense' older girls. Jack was the target of many hearty handshakes, backslapping and the bachelor jokes. He seemed pleased with it all and, looking at his bride-to-be, didn't regret his decision.

He thought of his parents. They would undoubtedly think his whole affair very bourgeois, although he was sure his mother would be more open minded about it than his father. His letter to them would not reach them for a while, he knew, and it was quite certain that they would not make the wedding.

When Nora and Angus arrived, they went straight to the engaged couple to give them their good wishes. Although when Nora hugged him, Jack felt the familiar stirrings, they quickly passed. Glancing at Annie, he felt contented.

On their way to the engagement party, Clara and Harrison dropped Supleen off at the railroad station. He was leaving to bring his wife back home. At least that was his intention.

Zoë had written many times to say that her Aunt still needed her and she had ignored Supleen's letters, which had gone from pleading to ordering her return home to husband and child. He was beginning to feel humiliated before the whole town and imagined everyone laughing at him because his wife had gone away and seemed reluctant to return.

Then Supleen heard in town that Larry Deveau lived in Charleston. At that moment he decided that if she refused to return one more time, he would go down and bring her back. He also wrote her that he would not send her one more penny for spending. She hadn't bothered to answer this last time, so he packed and informed his father he was leaving.

Clara and Harrison were relieved to see him go because he had become impossible to live with in the last few weeks. He barely said a brusque goodbye to his worried parents.

As they walked back to the buggy, Clara took her husband's arm. "I've spoiled the lad," she said sadly. "'Twas from mourning so for the wee lost ones."

Harrison patted her hand. "May be, lass, but he is a man now and has to answer for what he does. You acted out of love and can't be faulted."

A sense of foreboding stayed with her during the festivities at Annie's house. Nora noticed her Aunt's preoccupation. She sat down beside her." Auntie, is everything all right? The baby?"

Clara forced a smile. "Oh, he's right as rain, lass, it's not that, it's, well, it's Supleen."

She told Nora what had happened. Nora tried to reassure her that everything would be all right, but she didn't convince either of them.

CHAPTER TEN

Supleen was gone for a month. He had found Zoë's Aunt Charlotte's house. That poor woman, frightened at the look on Supleen's face, stammered out that Zoë had only stayed with her for a week during which time a mustached man named Larry had called on her several times. Then Zoë had packed her bags and left, telling her Aunt that she was returning home. As to her own health, it was and had been fine.

As she put it, "Ah ain't had so much as the sniffles for two years now."

The truth was that she had been glad when Zoë had left. They had never cared for each other, and she had been quite surprised when Zoë had appeared on her doorstep, saying she had come for a visit. The only clue she could offer Supleen on his wife's whereabouts was that this Larry had talked about a riverboat.

After Supleen had stormed out of the house with not even a thank you, Charlotte hurried to write all that had happened to her sister, Zoë's mother.

When Supleen returned to Morristown, three weeks later, no one dared to ask him where Zoë was or what had happened. His countenance was dark and angry and no one heard him speak a civil word to anyone. He worked like a man possessed, more than he had ever worked on the farm before.

After a month he started going into town more and it was known that he was a frequent visitor at a certain house the other side of the tracks. Only there did he talk or laugh and no one cared about his past problems. He often returned to the farm in the wee hours swearing loudly to himself and bumping into the furniture.

Harrison seemed to stoop more than before and Clara lost much of the glow she had had since little Harry was born. Indeed, the only happy places in the house were wherever the baby was at the moment. Mrs. Thorne was determined not to let the gloom invade his small world.

Then one day, when Harrison was going over his books, he discovered that there were several hundred dollars missing.

Supleen had left for the evening, but the next morning Harrison asked his son to come into the library. Judging by the wary look that came over Supleen's face, Harrison knew that his son knew what was coming.

With the doors closed, he asked Supleen if he knew where the money was. Supleen, who was perched on the edge of the desk, admitted he took it.

"I work here, don't I" he blustered. "Well, I earned it! Do I have to ask for every penny I want?" He glared at his father.

Harrison tried to keep his voice normal.

"Of course not, lad, but we do have to live within the salaries that we have agreed on. If we don't, this farm will not make any profit. And it's mighty important that we write down in the books everything we spend over our salaries. It took me a long time to build up this place, and a lot of hard work. It will all be yours someday."

Harrison was always a patient man and now he also felt some pity for this son of his, whose wife had left him. But his tone only angered Supleen more.

He jumped to his feet and stormed toward the door, shouting, "I don't have to listen to this! I'll get your money back!

You didn't mind loaning that cousin of mine money but you're stingy enough with me!"

"Why don't you sit down and---" Harrison's words were cut short by the emphatic slam of the door as Supleen left.

He stomped down the hall and outside, slamming the door behind him. Harrison sighed heavily, his head in his hands. He was getting older and had hoped to put the farm in Supleen's hands very soon. He had gradually given him more responsibility. Now what could he do?

Clara, hearing the commotion, had come to the library door in time to see Supleen going out the front door. She went to the window and watched as he saddled his horse and left in the direction of the McDonald's place.

She went to sit with her husband. Although tired, when the regular time came for retiring, neither of them felt like sleeping. Clara finally insisted that they go up and get ready for bed.

Just as they reached their room, there was a loud knocking at the front door. Clara, with a sense of foreboding, watched as Harrison hurried to answer it. Claude was leaning against the door frame, breathing heavily.

"It's Angus' wood lot! It's afire. I'm taking the men over to help."

Harrison responded quickly to the situation. "Go on, then, man, I'll be along." As he turned from the door his eyes met Clara's. Neither one could voice the fear in their heart.

As Harrison approached the northeast section of Angus' land he could see the flames shooting high and licking out at nearby branches. Silhouetted against them were his men and Angus, with Cecile, armed with shovels to dig a back draft. Some were hauling water from the pond, but it looked like a hopeless task. Even if the firemen from town came, it would be too late to save most of the timber.

As Harrison drew closer, he saw a lone rider heading away from the McDonald farm toward the south. He was quite sure he recognized him. A hand seemed to close around his heart.

By dawn, the fire was partially under control. Every one of the neighbors as well as the fire department from Morristown was at the farm. The ladies were helping Nora and Victoria to serve coffee and biscuits to the men, who were all smeared with black soot. Although they could not stop the fire, they were keeping it under control and no sparks had been allowed to drift near the house or barn.

Still, Angus had lost his wood lot and the nearby cornfield, which had been ready to harvest. The smell of burnt corn pervaded the area.

About six o'clock, Angus missed Harrison from the group that was eating breakfast. He went out to the site of the fire, where several men were stationed to keep an eye on things. He still could not find Harrison. When he inquired about him, the workers said they thought he had gone to breakfast. One of the men suddenly called out, "Isn't that Harrison's horse over there?" pointing to a grazing mare.

It took them more than an hour to find Harrison. He was lying on his side, partly obscured by a charred tree, which had fallen close enough to knock him to the ground. He was unconscious. Doctor Belden was quickly sent for because the men didn't dare to move him without the Doctor's opinion.

Doctor Belden determined that there were no broken bones and that Harrison probably was on the ground before the tree fell. He had been protected from the force of the tree's fall because he had fallen into a hollow spot in the ground.

They gently put Harrison in a wagon, thickly cushioned with some of Nora's quilts and took him home. Clara, who had been sent for, rode beside him, too shocked for tears.

When Doctor Belden could give Harrison a thorough examination, he determined that Harrison had apparently suffered a stroke, fallen from his horse and hit his head on the ground.

The doctor and Clara stayed by his side until the following day, when he wearily opened his eyes. Tears of relief came to Clara's eyes.

He seemed to recognize his wife, but when he tried to speak, no sound came from his lips. Doctor Belden spoke to him.

"There you are, Harrison, don't try to talk now. There'll be plenty of time for that later. Right now, you need to sleep. We'll be right here when you wake up."

Clara patted his hand. "Don't you worry, now, love, the fire is out and everyone is fine."

He closed his eyes and slept. The doctor told Clara that her husband had had a stroke, that his right side was paralyzed as well as his vocal cords. He assured her that in most of these cases the paralysis was only temporary so she was not to worry herself into sickness.

When Supleen returned home, the day after the fire, he said he had been with friends and had only heard about the fire when he met some of the firefighters on his way back to the farm.

CHAPTER ELEVEN

At the McDonald's farm, the stench of the fire was everywhere.

Angus, Nora and Jack spent the morning surveying the damage. Two-thirds of the wood lot was gone as well as the corn. Both of these represented most of the money Angus had planned on to pay his mortgage this year.

Back at the house, when they had all sat down to Victoria's scones and tea, they discussed their plight. When Claude came over with news of the doctor's diagnosis, their depression increased.

"Poor Clara, I must go to her," said Victoria. "She will be beside herself."

She went upstairs to get ready to go to her sister-in-law.

"Give her our love and tell her we'll be over soon." Nora called after her.

After chores were finished, they all followed Victoria over to lend moral support to Clara. When they ran into Supleen leaving the house, he offered no sympathy on Angus' loss, nor did he seem overly concerned with his father's condition. There was a sly gleam in his eye that made Angus wonder what was behind it.

On the way back to Belltrees, Jack offered his opinion. "He may be thinking that with your woodlot gone and his father paralyzed he could be in control of the mortgage. Watch out for him, my friend."

At Jack's words, a shock went through Angus. That could very well be the case and if so, he would be in a tough spot. He had planned on his Uncle giving him an extension on the mortgage but if it was up to Supleen, he knew he would get no such consideration. He wondered again why Supleen hated him so much. The money he had brought with him from Scotland was running very low. The thought of possibly losing Belltrees now made him feel sick at his stomach. And what of Nora and the others?

He had to find a way around this. If necessary, he would plead with Supleen; he would do that for his family; though the thought made the bile rise in his throat.

Jack had been watching his face and had a good idea what was in Angus' mind.

"Well, old man, no sense in anticipating trouble." Jack said, trying to cheer up his friend. "The mortgage isn't due for a while, is it? And in the meanwhile, Harrison may get better, and you'll have nothing to worry about."

"Even so, I hate to put Uncle Harrison off, he has been more than generous as it is. I'll just have to think of something," replied Angus.

Each man had his own thoughts on the subject and neither one trusted Supleen.

The entire corn crop burned meant no fodder for the cattle in the winter, only the hay. That, combined with the loss of the timber, which Angus had planned to sell to Jack, was a heavy financial setback. He would have to buy extra feed for the animals, as well. The prospect seemed hopeless.

Angus was not a man to give up easily, though, and for now he had plenty to do. As they worked to clean up the debris blown about by the fire, few words were spoken. Each man was deep in his own thoughts. When it was time to return to the house for the evening meal, they each had some ideas.

Jack suggested, "I can buy the rest of the standing trees, Angus, that would be of some help."

"I would like to save the acre or so that's left." Angus replied, "It's going to look pretty barren out there for a long while, as it is. Thanks anyway, my friend. I have a couple of thoughts on the matter. It'll take me a while to mull them over."

"Well, don't forget, let me know what I can do to help." said Jack.

"I'm knowing that, and I appreciate it, too." Angus spoke with great feeling.

That evening, Angus and Nora walked together out to the Belltrees. The small trees were sending out new, soft branches.

"Well, they seem to be happy with the Vermont climate, don't they, lass?" Angus commented.

Nora slipped her arm through his, "I'm thinking we are all happy here, Angus, and we'll find a way. You know, Mama has some money she would be glad to help with, as a loan, of course."

"No! I will not let Victoria spend her money for the farm! It's my job to take care of this family." Then, more gently, "You're not to worry your bonny head about it either. You've plenty to think about with the bairns and the house."

Nora sighed. She had known what his reaction would be but she couldn't help worrying. She was well aware that Supleen disliked having them there and would do what he could to get rid of them. The coming winter would be a rough one. As they turned and walked toward the house, they could feel a hint of fall in the breeze that ruffled their hair and tugged gently at their coats.

Even Tad sensed that something was wrong. His grandmother wasn't humming as she usually did when she was getting breakfast.

"Are you alright, Grand mama?" he asked.

Victoria looked down at the anxious little face. She smiled.

"I'm right as rain, lad, now, eat up, it's almost time to leave for the kirk."

She put an extra dollop of cream on his bannocks and gave him a light kiss on the top of his head. Tad forgot his concern as he stuffed his mouth with the delicious hotcakes and in a moment was out the door to say goodbye to Peggy.

At the church many of their friends came over to sympathize with them about the loss of the woodlot and also about Harrison. On the way home, they stopped to see how their Uncle was feeling. The doctor was there and didn't have any good news. Harrison was still the same and Doctor Belden couldn't say how long it would be until he could talk. But he still felt that Harrison would fully recuperate, in time and with a lot of rest.

Aunt Clara begged them to stay for Sunday dinner; she seemed so forlorn that they agreed. Supleen was nowhere to be seen, to their relief.

They had to leave soon after the meal because Abby needed a change, but Nora promised to come back the next day. Aunt Clara seemed to feel a bit better when they left.

As they were getting out of the carriage in front of their house, they heard the sound of many wheels coming up the driveway. As they watched in amazement, six wagon loads of people pulled up and out piled their friends, with much hilarity and joking at their startled faces. It turned out that they had each brought along a part of their own supply of silage and hay for Angus' cattle.

Nora took the women into the house for some tea, while Angus and the other men packed the feed into his barn. As they worked Angus' heart was full. He would stay here, he thought, no matter what he had to do. It was his home now and these, his good friends.

The money for the mortgage was another story, however. Angus didn't really want to sell any of his animals, but it was the only solution he could think of. The two draft horses earned their keep and the chestnut mare drove them into town and to church every Sunday. No, it would have to be Mandy, his prize cow whose milk was sweet and which they sold to the store in Morristown. There was no other choice. It would cut down on their income some but would pay the mortgage.

Once he had made the decision, Angus went to call on some of the farmers he knew who might be interested in the cow. He wouldn't ask any of his close friends for fear they would buy her out of pity for his predicament. He finally made the sale to an older man, John Seymour, who, after haggling a bit, paid Angus' price.

A few days later, Angus rode over to the Renfrew farm. He wanted to check on his Uncle's condition and he wanted to hand the mortgage payment to him in person. He had been over at least every other day to spend some time with him. Though Harrison couldn't talk yet, he was able to make some sounds and write a little in response to questions. He seemed to be pleased whenever Angus was there.

As usual, Clara was in the bedroom with her husband, when Angus arrived. She looked pale and drawn. Angus kissed her on the cheek and patted her hand.

"I wish you could take a little rest now and again, Aunt, we don't want you getting sick now."

Clara looked at him gratefully. Her own son rarely showed his face in the sick room or showed any concern for his parents.

"You're a good lad, Angus, I'm glad you are near us now." Clara said.

Angus sat and chatted, as usual about the farm and news from town. Though Harry couldn't speak clearly yet, it was obvious that he was pleased to have Angus there.

Before leaving, Angus handed the bank draft for the mortgage payment to Clara, explaining to them both what it was.

"You both know how grateful we are to you for helping us get the farm." Angus said. Then he quickly changed the subject, not wanting to embarrass them with his thanks.

"You'll be up and about sooner than you think, Uncle Harrison. I'll be back to see you the day after tomorrow. Nora will be here tomorrow."

He took both of his Uncle Harrison's wrinkled hands in his for a moment before leaving. He was worried that Harrison didn't have the stamina to fight his illness.

At the door, he told Clara, "Make sure he sees little Harry every day, if you can, that's the best medicine for him. And you, too Aunt Clara, a little laughter helps everyone."

"I was trying to keep the little laddie away from him, afraid to tire him too much." Clara said.

"I think it's just what he needs, but, if you want, check with Dr. Belden first. Now, keep your chin up." Angus hugged her.

"Thank you, lad, it gives us a lift to see you and Nora."

When Supleen came home that night, he noticed the envelope on the big desk. When he saw what it was, his face turned crimson with anger. He had been looking forward to seeing Angus in person to gloat when he couldn't pay his mortgage. With his father incapacitated, he was in control and had intended to make full use of his power to foreclose on the farm and get rid of his cousin once and for all. He was well aware of what Angus had lost and had expected that he would default on the mortgage. Now that it was paid there was nothing Supleen could do, legally. He threw down the envelope and stomped out of the room to vent his anger on the foreman, Claude, who only remained on the farm because of his admiration for Harrison.

For the time being, Nora and Angus could relax and concentrate on their farm, but they each knew that a way had to be found to bring more revenue in to meet their obligations.

The following February of that year, 1902, Angus prepared to begin tapping the trees in the maple grove. He had already talked to store owners in Morristown and even in Hardwick. Several of them had agreed to buy some of his syrup out right and a few others agreed to take some on consignment.

The trouble was that this was Angus' first experience with making the syrup so it was difficult to say how much it would benefit him in the long run. Luckily, he had Cecile to help him. Coming from a big farm family, who had been in Vermont for generations, he had been involved in making maple syrup since he was a child.

He and Angus spent hours inspecting the trees in the grove and marking the ones that would be suitable for tapping. Then they had to determine how many buckets they could hang on each. The older trees could have three or four pails, while some of the younger ones could only handle one pail. Cecile had learned from his father that if you over-tap a tree and drain off too much of it's sap the tree would die.

After all this, they had to decide how many pails and spouts they would need and set up a place where they could boil the sap until it turned into syrup. Angus had to spend some of his small savings to buy these supplies as well as wood to construct a strong sled on which to haul the syrup to the boiling shed.

They had to be ready by March first, in case of an early thaw. As soon as the days turned warm enough for the sap to flow and the nights stayed cold, they must start, because one never knew how long these ideal conditions would last.

Cecile found some used equipment that they could buy from an older farmer who could no longer use it himself.

The man's name was McFarland and he even proposed to Angus that if Cecile and Angus would tap his maples for him he would give them two-thirds of the profits made. Angus decided to first see how it went this year with his own maple grove and consider it for next year. It would certainly help his income if it all worked out.

In late March, when the thaw began, they were all ready. It was time to collect the first batch of sap. In the early morning, before the sun was up, the two great workhorses were hitched to the heavy sled in the barnyard. As Cecile secured the harnesses, there was the sound of creaking leather and the snorting and stomping of the horse's feet. The sled had been loaded the night before with the freshly washed and scalded pails, covers and spouts.

Now, Nora came out of the house with a large parcel of food for their lunch, because it would save time to eat in the grove. She was bundled up against the chill of the dawn and she was excited to be a part of this adventure. Angus had not wanted her to at first. She had convinced him that she would enjoy it and that it would leave him and Cecile free to collect the sap if she drove the team. Cecile agreed with her, so Angus gave in.

They started out with Angus driving until they reached the grove. There was a hard crust on the snow in places where it had melted in the day and frozen again at night. Sometimes the heavy horses would break through the crust so the going was slow. As the sun rose, they could see the shadows of the woods creatures coming alive through the trees. The pungent smell from pine trees drifted to them. Nora thought she had never seen a more tranquil scene.

The freeze/thaw cycle continued long enough for them to harvest all the trees. Now the sap was boiling furiously in the big vats that Cecile and Angus had constructed in the log sugarhouse.

They were all busy watching the boiling sap, which had to be tended day and night. The finished syrup then had to be drained off and put into containers to be delivered to the stores.

A couple of times Nora brought Tad out to the log house for a special treat which Cecile had showed her. She would scoop up a bowl of fresh snow, pack it down and then dribble over it a dipper full of syrup, which was boiled longer than the rest, so it was thicker. Then, with a fork Nora would roll up the golden candy and give it to Tad to eat. He couldn't get enough of it; never had he tasted anything like it before.

At suppertime they would sometimes eat in the log house, heating their coffee on the little pot-bellied stove in the corner. It was a cozy, comfortable time, not to be forgotten. Nora was sorry when it came to an end.

Angus sold all the syrup they made, expect for what they kept for themselves. Most of the merchants ordered more for the next year. Now they could start to hope that they would be able to pay the mortgage on time next year.

The news from the doctor about Uncle Harrison was not encouraging. His progress was much slower than had been expected. He could speak but only with hesitation and it was difficult to understand him. He could move his fingers some on the affected arm but the arm itself as well as his leg still did not respond.

Clara was getting worn out by the prolonged worry about her husband. She spent much time rubbing Harrison's arm and leg in the hope that it would stimulate the blood flow. She had taken Angus's advice and had Sadie Thorne bring little Harry in for a while every day. It did seem to have a positive effect on Harrison. His mouth would twist into a half smile and his eyes come alive. The baby was crawling all over and would attempt a few steps with the help of anyone's hand. He had a ready smile and would pat the bed as he hung on with his small hands. Harrison would try to stroke the child's head and beckoned Sadie to put him on the bed.

Sometimes, Claude would help Harrison to sit in a bedside chair. It was a change for Harrison and it helped to prevent bedsores from lying too long in bed. Often, when Angus came over, they would play chess, it didn't require much talking. Sometimes Harrison was too tired to finish the game, but the effort was good for him.

Supleen rarely visited his father, only when he needed to ask something about the farm, or at his mother's insistence.

Supleen's relationship with his own son was only slightly better than that with his father. Although he would sometimes brag about him to some of his friends in town, little Harry seldom saw his father. Mrs. Thorne and Clara had tried to foster a closer relationship but the child was very small and Supleen seemed to be uncomfortable around him. He did, occasionally, take him on his knee if one of the women handed the baby to him. At these times he appeared to like him, patting his silky blonde hair that was more like fuzz.

Clara hoped that, as his son grew, Supleen would be closer to him. At this time, though, his anger at Zoe was carried over onto everything and everyone. That, and his jealousy of Angus controlled his emotions.

Jack and Annie planned to be married in June. Their home was nearly completed. The winter weather had held it up somewhat, but now the workmen were at it daily.

The women had pored over Gody's Magazine to copy the latest fashions for Annie's trousseau. Annie herself did not have much fashion sense, but her sister and Nora gently guided her to the most becoming styles and colors.

Then there was the wedding itself to be planned. This was mostly Annie's province, with some help from Maggie. Nora had been so busy all winter, with the sugaring and her family that she hadn't been visiting often. But Jack brought Annie sometimes when he visited Belltrees.

When she came, Annie would tie on an apron and work beside Nora and Victoria, as she knew they had their hands full. Besides, she seemed to enjoy it.

Tansy was expecting her first baby so she wasn't at the farm as often as before. She hadn't felt well and she was also busy preparing her baby's layette. Both Nora and Tad sorely missed her. She had always loved to joke with him and join in his games. Nora hoped she would be all right with the baby's birth.

Tonight, Victoria had a fruit dumpling bubbling on the back of the stove and the aroma of beef pies permeated the cozy kitchen. Abby was seated in her high chair, watching the adults and playing with a small wooden cart that Harrison had made for her.

When they all sat down to eat, the talk was light-hearted, about the coming wedding and the new house. Jack was proudly explaining how he was going to have a washroom by the back door where he could clean up before going into the house. "To save Annie some work."

Annie described some curtains she had ordered from Sears, Roebuck catalog. Tad, who wanted to be a part of the conversation, piped up. "Uncle Jack, will you make a barn, too, with horses and cows and a goat like Spots?

The others laughed, but Jack answered him seriously. "Well, not right away, Tad, but for now we will have a shed for the horses."

Tad was satisfied and didn't mind the laughter; he was used to it. He often laughed at his little sister, too, and he had a good sense of humor.

It was not an evening for serious concerns, so the two men didn't discuss the farm problems until they could be alone. While the women were cleaning up, Jack and Angus strolled about the yard checking the Belltrees and watching Tad cavorting with his dog.

"You know, Angus, if you have some time on your hands next winter, I could use some help at the lumber mill. Orders are always coming in and we like to catch up with them during the winter." Jack said.

"I might just do that, Jack, things will be slow here after November. I'd really like to get a head start in paying off the entire loan to Uncle Harrison. A man doesn't feel too secure with someone like Supleen in the picture."

"I know how you feel." replied Jack. "I've watched men like him before. They are never happy if someone else is making a success of things. Best not to give him any hold on you."

"Don't worry, my friend, I'm keeping my eyes open."

Both men were thinking that Harrison didn't seem to be getting any better and each day more of his responsibilities were being turned over to Supleen.

Angus also was fearful for his Aunt's future, if something happened to her husband. There was no doubt in his mind that the Renfrew farm wouldn't last long under the management of Supleen.

Angus didn't have time to spend on worrying, however; the snow had melted and the signs of spring were all about, the busiest time of year for a farmer. And Angus had to make up for his losses of the fall.

CHAPTER TWELVE

1902

The first of June dawned clear and sunny. It was Annie and Jack's wedding day. It was a little cool, to be expected in Vermont.

That didn't detract from the day for Annie. She was up early, with butterflies in her stomach. She could hear the sounds of her sister's family getting ready and Mattie's voice admonishing the children to hurry so Aunty Annie could have the bathroom to herself.

Annie looked at herself in the mirror over her dressing table. Her curly auburn hair was sticking out in different directions. She smoothed it down with her hands, thinking "Jack won't like me much in the morning. I'm afraid this mop is impossible. I hope I can make it behave for today."

She stroked the sleeves of the creamy lace wedding dress that was hung on its padded hanger. Her sister had worn this dress on her wedding day and with slight alteration it now fit Annie. She hoped it would bring her good luck as it had Maggie, whose marriage was a happy one.

Everything was ready now. The wedding was to be at eleven at the little church in the center of town and then the party was to be held at the hotel. The ladies from the church would help serve. Annie had insisted that her sister not work on this day. Of course, she would be Annie's attendant. Angus would be Jack's best man.

It was a short but moving ceremony and drew many a tear from the ladies. Annie had coaxed her curls into a bright halo and she had never looked more beautiful. Maggie wore a dress in a soft shade of blue. They both carried white lilacs. The churchwomen had decorated the church in the fragrant purple and white lilacs that were in abundance this time of year.

At the hotel, even Aunt Clara was there, with Harrison, who was in a wicker wheel chair with Claude attending him.

Harrison had insisted on coming as he was very fond of Jack and, with Claude's help, he had managed it. His speech had improved greatly so most people could understand him. He didn't stay as long as the others as he tired easily. He thought Clara should stay but she wanted to leave with him.

Supleen, who had been invited out of respect for his parents, did not show up, to the relief of both Angus and Jack.

The bride and groom left by three o'clock as they planned to drive to Burlington, spend the night, and take the ferry the next morning across Lake Champlain to New York State. From there, they planned to go to a hotel in the Adirondacks. The couple was pelted with rice from their well-wishers as they drove off. Annie looked radiant in her gray traveling suit with black velvet collar and cuffs and a gray hat with black plumes.

As they rode home from the wedding, Nora slipped her hand into Angus', remembering their own simple, little wedding in Scotland with only family and closest friends in attendance. She had worn a blue suit and matching hat with a frilly white blouse. Angus' father had died a few months before and they didn't want to have a big party. They had spent a perfect week at the Haawood Inn. Neither one had any regrets. Their eyes met over Tad's tousled head, love and contentment in their glance.

When Mr. and Mrs. Jack Bradshaw came back from their honeymoon, they took up residence in the house outside of town. There were still many things that were not quite finished but there was plenty of time to do that. Annie went back to helping Jack in business, although Jack thought she should stay home and enjoy being a housewife.

He was really pleased with her decision to go back to work. She was good at keeping the books and declared she would be bored silly staying at home all the time.

Jack hoped for children soon. He had enjoyed Tad and Abby and in general liked children.

Annie got into the habit of coming home in the early afternoon to start their supper because she knew Jack hated eating in a make shift way.

Nora and Maggie wanted to hear all about Lake Champlain and New York and Annie was most eager to tell about it all. It had been her first trip anywhere and she had thoroughly enjoyed it, though the best part had been being with Jack. She felt so lucky to be his wife and she, too, wished she would soon have a child.

That fall the crops were good, to the relief of Angus and Nora. They were able to pay their mortgage on time and felt safe from Supleen's animosity for a while.

Supleen was barely civil when they met now. His rage at Zoë had made him a bitter man as well as a selfish, insensitive one. He still spent much of his time with his gambling cronies in town and very rarely saw his little son.

Fortunately for little Harry, he had the loving care of Sadie Thorne and Clara. He also had his Granda, who liked nothing better than to read to him and laugh at his antics. Harry was too young, as yet, to realize the place his father should have been playing in his life. He was surrounded by people who loved him and for the time being was contented.

As Nora and Angus took their usual stroll after the evening meal one night in October, the moon was just coming over the horizon. It was a real harvest moon, dark yellow and full. They were looking at the Belltrees and reminiscing about their arrival in America and their stay with the Murphys.

"I would really like to see the Murphys again, wouldn't you love?" Nora said, longingly. "They were so kind to us when we needed a friend. Hannah writes that three of their boys have left home already to work elsewhere and how she misses them. Oh, Angus! Let's invite them for Christmas! We can have a real party and celebrate Abby's birthday at the same time."

Angus looked down into his wife's lovely eyes, sparkling with anticipation. He laughed and stroked her dark hair.

"That's a bonny idea, lass, though where we'll put them all if they come in full force, I don't know, but there is always the barn for the bigger boys."

"Oh, don't worry, Angus, we'll make room and if I know Hannah she will bring enough food to feed that army of hers. I can't wait to write to her about it."

That very evening, Nora wrote a note to Hannah outlining her plans and begging her to come and bring her whole family. The one time she had met Hannah they had formed an instant friendship and they had corresponded ever since. Nora was sure that Victoria would feel the same about the Murphys. In making the preparations, perhaps she wouldn't dwell on Scotland and the other family she had left behind. For all that she was happy with her youngest daughter's family, Nora had noticed of late that her mother had many pensive moments.

Clara, too, was delighted with the idea. Hannah was her cousin and she hadn't seen her for several years. They were all anxious to hear if the Murphys would be able to come for the Holiday.

Angus worked part time for Jack at the lumberyard after the hay was in and the farm ready for the winter. He wanted to have some extra money saved in case the next year was not as productive as this one had been. He couldn't stop feeling uneasy about the situation, knowing Harrison's state of health and Supleen's attitude.

In the first week of November, they received a letter from Hannah saying that they would be there and not even wild horses could keep her from coming. Two of the boys had married since she saw Nora and they would be spending the holiday with their own families, but the others would be there. In the letter, Hannah said "not to worry, dearie, I'll bring plenty of food". Nora laughed when she read this part; it sounded so much like Hannah.

The next few weeks were filled with frenzied activity. The whole house must be thoroughly cleaned, as usual in the fall, but with extra care. The week before the guests were expected, the house was filled with the aroma of Victoria's cooking.

Snow had started falling in October and the freezing weather of a typical Vermont winter had set in. Nearly everything could be cooked ahead and stored in the cold pantry in crocks, to keep out inquisitive mice. The shortbread and current cakes were in tightly closed tins.

One day, the first week in December, as Nora and Victoria were making more goodies for the party, there was a knock at the front door. When Nora answered it she thought at first that the woman on the porch was a stranger. Then as the woman spoke she realized, with a shock, that it was Zoë.

She was dressed in clothes that once had been stylish but were badly in need of cleaning. Her hair was awry, no longer in the meticulous coiffure that Zoë had always had. She spoke in a breathless voice.

"Nora, I need your help. Supleen refuses to let me in the house and I really need some money. Could you talk to him for me, please?"

For a moment, Nora was speechless. Then, drawing Zoë in out of the cold, she tried to think of a reply. Zoë was still arrogant and selfish, apparently, thinking only of herself.

"Why, Zoë! Come in! What has happened to you?" Nora exclaimed.

Zoë shrugged her shoulders, impatiently. "Nothing! Nothing! I'm fine. But I do need money and Supleen won't even let me in. He's cruel Can you talk to him, Nora, please!"

The nerve of her, Nora thought. Not a word about her child.

"You know he would never listen to me or Angus, Zoë. I'm sorry. I know Supleen is very angry with you," said Nora. "Is there anything else I can do?"

"Never mind, then, I'll be going. A friend is waiting for me. Could you talk to Clara about helping me? I'll be back to find out what she says. Will you? Please, Nora?"

"All right, Zoë, I'll try."

As Zoë turned to leave she asked, as though suddenly remembering him, hesitantly. "Is little Harry alright?"

Nora replied that he was right as rain and growing. Without answering, Zoë continued out the door and walked to the closed carriage and left without another word.

Nora stood for a moment, scarcely believing what had happened. When she told her mother about it, Victoria was shocked.

"What is the matter with the woman? She acts very unnatural! What could she expect from a husband when she just left without a word. She's a strange one, all right!"

Nora shook her head. "I still feel sorry for her. She doesn't realize what she has lost. And some day she may wake up when it's too late."

Zoë didn't return or get in touch with them. It was the last anyone saw of her until young Harry was old enough to want to find out for himself what had happened to his mother.

A week later, when Angus was in town, he heard that Larry had dumped Zoë and she had taken up with another man who had been with her when she was in town.

Anyway, Nora had very little time to worry about Zoë. She still had a great deal to do before the guests arrived. She was hoping that no big snowstorm would prevent the Murphys from coming. But they arrived, as planned, just two days before Christmas. They had five of their boys with them and the house was full of fun and laughter for the next few days.

The older boys and Tom helped Angus with the chores so that they could have their evenings free to enjoy. True to her word, Hannah had brought enough food for a small army, including a leg of lamb and two turkeys.

That evening, they had a birthday cake for Abby. She didn't know what was going on but they all had a good laugh when she took the piece of cake on her tray and soon had her entire face and some of her hair smeared with the icing. She had laughed along with them.

The smallest Murphy boy, Mikey, was good company for Tad, though he was a few years older. In spite of the cold weather, the children were outside nearly every waking moment, running with Spots or the dog or brushing Peggy.

Abby was not lacking for attention from all the ladies and even the older boys. A girl baby was a novelty to them.

The day before Christmas, most of them went into the woods to pick out a tree, making a party of it, singing as they tramped through the trees.

That evening Jack and Annie came over to help trim the tree. The children did the actual trimming while the adults caught up on the news. Tad was held up high to put the star on the top of the tree. Someone started singing "Silent Night" and even the littlest ones chimed in while staring at the lighted tree in awe.

Christmas morning the children were awake at dawn. They could hardly contain their excitement, but the parents insisted they eat breakfast before the presents were given out. There were mostly home made gifts for the children; sleds, carved wooden toys and clothes. The grownups gave each other gifts of home made preserves, special pickles and knitted items for the house.

That evening, the Victrola was wound up and the grownups danced a little while. Everyone was pretty tired, so it was early to bed.

The Murphys left the next morning amid a great hubbub. The house seemed awfully quiet after they left and Tad wandered around acting bored for a day or so until things went back to normal.

Nora and Angus were well pleased with the visit and Clara had been very happy to see her cousin. The Murphys had invited them to come to their home next Christmas but they would be writing before then.

Tad was now five years old and could hardly wait for spring when he was to start learning how to ride Peggy alone. Up to now he had been allowed to sit in the saddle and led around the corral by one of his parents. He had learned how to take care of the colt. He couldn't reach very high yet, so his father would brush the back, while Tad brushed the parts he could reach. By now the colt knew him well and would welcome him with whinnies and big licks of his tongue when Tad came within reach.

A few days after Christmas, Clara came over to visit with Nora. Although she and the others of her family, except Supleen, had been there for Christmas, she had not wanted to bring up the subject of Zoë in front of the Murphys. Now, alone with Nora and Victoria, she told them how upset she was about what had happened. She recounted what had taken place the night Zoë came home.

"I could hardly believe my ears when I heard Zoë's voice at the door and Supleen shouting". Clara went on to say. "I'm so glad that little Harry was upstairs with Sadie. Before I could get to the door she was gone. But I heard Supleen tell her never to come here again and that he was going to divorce her."

"Poor woman, she has carved a hard row for herself," said Victoria.

"And the wee laddie does need a mother." Clara bristled. "I don't think he needs that sort of a mother. For once, I agreed with Supleen. I doubt if she could change her way of thinking."

"She did ask me to ask you to intervene with Supleen on her behalf, Aunt Clara." said Nora, tentatively.

"Well, consider the question asked; but I have no intention of talking to Supleen about her again." Clara declared.

Then, seeing the look on Nora's face, she added. "Don't mind me, love, but I get very ornery when I think of all the heartache that woman has caused, I don't care if I never see her again."

Tears welled up in Clara's eyes. Victoria patted the distraught woman's arm.

"Come now, dearie, we'll have a nice cup 'o tea, we'll feel a lot better. We don't have to talk about this any more. Tell us how the wee mannie is doing these days."

Victoria knew this was one subject that Clara never tired of talking about. Her pride in her little grandson was boundless. He was now toddling all over the big house, making everyone in it smile a little. And smiles were badly needed in that house to counteract the surliness of Supleen. But, even, he, on the rare occasions when he was home, came close to smiling when his little son would throw his arms around his father's legs and say

"Dada". Though Clara was "gramma" and he called Harrison "papa" his grandmother had trained the boy to call his father "Dada."

Though Harrison had to be confined to his wheelchair, his health had improved enough so that he could sit at his desk and manage his large farm, at least on paper. He had daily conferences with Claude to discuss what had been done each day and to plan for the next day's work.

Supleen disliked Claude because he could not browbeat the sturdy little Frenchman. Supleen liked to control those around him. But Harrison had made it clear that he had to do his share of the work in order to share in the profits, so he grudgingly worked, as far from Claude as possible.

Harrison and Clara had finally realized and admitted that their son was an uncaring, selfish person. Each of them privately vowed that their little grandson would be brought up differently. They sadly acknowledged that their overindulgence of Supleen when he was a child made him what he was today.

As for Supleen, his anger and frustration with Zoë were all consuming. When she had appeared at his door, for one second he felt glad. Then he saw the silhouette of a man in the waiting carriage and a red-hot rage engulfed him. He had raised his fist to strike her but instead satisfied himself by slamming the door in her face after cursing her and telling her never to show her face here again. Then he had stalked out of the house to be with his cronies and try to forget.

A few of his friends had heard rumors about Zoë and what she was doing in South Carolina but would never have volunteered the information or even mention her name, for fear of Supleen's rage.

Supleen had gone to a lawyer to talk about getting a divorce and was told he wouldn't have any problem since Zoë had abandoned her family. He had not gone through with it. As he had no desire to remarry, he didn't want to spend his money on a divorce when he could use it to gamble with.

Gambling had become his favorite pastime, accompanied, of course, by his ever-present glass of whiskey. However, his short temper caused most of the other men to want to avoid playing cards with him after he punched out a fellow just because the unfortunate man was winning.

The only one who wasn't afraid of him was Genevive, one of the hostesses at the "club" where Supleen spent his time. He put in the required time on the farm but the rest of the time he could be found there. Often he spent a good share of his time with Genevive, who had become his sounding board for all his troubles. And, on her part, Genevive had become really fond of him. In fact, it was understood by the other men who came to the "club", that they were to stay away from her.

Supleen called her Genny, and the name stuck. Genny was a tall, buxom woman several years Supleen's senior, with a mass of hair bleached to an almost white color. Her features were even and she would have been very pretty, if not for the steely, blue eyes which had seen about every evil thing that could be seen in the world and were surprised at nothing any more. For some strange reason Supleen appealed to her maternal instinct, maybe because he was like a pouting, little boy who always wanted his way.

And for him, she was an indulgent mother figure, though he would have been the first to deny it. She listened to his complaints about Zoë, his father, mother and Angus and she commiserated with him, always taking his side. So with her, he could assuage the damage to his ego. Although Genny had some true feelings for him, she was also well aware that he was the sole heir to a very substantial farm worth a good deal of money, especially since he often bragged about it.

Clara was not sure about where Supleen spent his time away from the farm, but Harrison, through Claude, was well aware of Supleen's activities when away from home. Being a smart man, he had already had a long session with his solicitor from Morristown. His disappointment in his son was severe, and he was realistic enough not to believe that he would change. He had to protect the farm for Clara.

CHAPTER THIRTEEN

Jack and Annie had long since settled into their new house. Annie had added all the feminine touches that make a house a home. She covered their couches and chairs in the parlor in a bright chintz print, hung plants around and decorated Jack's study in a masculine red and black plaid. He was pleased and contented with the house and with his wife.

They worked together most days in the lumber mill office, then returned home to eat a pleasant meal that Annie had partially prepared the night before. Jack had tried to get Annie to hire a woman to help with the housework, but she laughed at the idea.

"But there is hardly anything to do here with just the two of us. Think of the work Maggie does with her family and no help." She protested.

"It's up to you, my dear," Jack replied. "But with your work at the mill and this, too. I thought it would be too much."

"But I'm only working three days a week. That gives me two days to clean here and spend the weekends with you." She argued.

Jack gave in. Annie sat on the side of his chair and tousled his hair. He pulled her down in his lap and mussed her already unruly curls.

"Take that, my girl."

She laughed and tickled him, then they both subsided and relaxed, arms entwined. Annie thought she could never be any happier than she was at that moment. It was a perfect moment; the light from the fireplace was dancing on the walls and she could see the snow falling gently outside the window.

Jack's business was doing very well. He was thinking of expanding and opening a store where he would sell precut boards and other items that were needed when working around the house or barn. He had talked it over with Annie and also with Angus. They both thought it was an excellent idea. The local emporium carried only a few household items and for larger items people had to go to the town of Hardwick. Jack planned to stock saws, hammers and other small tools as well as a variety of paint, stoves and planed lumber. He would hire another person to work in the store; perhaps one of Maggie's children when they got older. He planned to start working on building a new storefront in March.

Harvesting and preparing the maple syrup for sale kept Angus and his family busy during the month of March. Tad went along, too, and got his treat of sugar on snow. Abby was still too young to join the others, so stayed home with Victoria. She was old enough now to want to follow her mother or grandmother around and "help" with the household chores. Victoria would give her a apron which covered her from head to toe, put a pan of water on a chair and let her wash some small items. She had a special bond with Victoria. They enjoyed each other and Abby would often hug Victoria and tell everyone that this was "my Gammy." She was an engaging child with a ready smile and large alert eyes. She already had definite likes and dislikes. She much preferred to play outdoors wherever her brother was to staying in the house. She loved to play with her cousin, Harry, too, but an adult had to be on hand to encourage sharing, without hair pulling. Sometimes they would give each other big hugs, but if one or the other held on too long the other one would end up crying. They were entertaining to watch.

That year the trees yielded more syrup than before. Angus also tapped Mr. McFarland's trees so his profit was nearly doubled. The money was very welcomed. Every dollar had to be saved for the mortgage.

After the syrup making was finished, Angus helped Jack with building the storefront for the new addition to the lumber mill. Jack knew that Angus was constantly worried about paying off the mortgage before anything should happen to Harrison.

As they were working together one day, Jack ventured to make a suggestion. "Listen, old man," he said. "Why don't you let me lend you the money to pay off the loan to Harrison and get you out from under being possibly obligated to Supleen? I for one wouldn't like to have anything to do with that man."

Angus replied, thoughtfully. "I'm much obliged to you, my friend, but if I did that I would have to explain to Uncle Harrison where I got the money. He knows I don't have any. It would hurt his feelings to think I don't trust his son. I'm going to try to do it my way."

"You're a mulish Scotsman." Laughed Jack. They had become such fast friends they could say most anything to each other.

In early April, there was another sighting of the big bear in a neighbor's apple orchard. For a while Nora warned Tad to stay close to the house or barn. Angus, Cecile and Claude spent two days following the huge bear's tracks until they had to get back to their work. The bear had become more than a nuisance since he started preying on any small farm animals that strayed a bit from the vicinity of a farm. Two farmers had lost a calf each and one man's hunting dog had been found torn to bits by the beast.

So the men had planned another hunting trip in two weeks. There would be a dozen or more men, which would improve their chances of success. To mitigate the danger, they would hunt in pairs. But the hunting trip, as before, was unsuccessful. The clever beast knew what was going on and made himself scarce as long as the men were in the forest. Then, he seemed to have moved on to other areas.

Spring, in all its glory, had burst out the first of April. Soon the forsythia, daffodils and jonquils created a cloud of yellow punctuated by the delicate purple of the crocus and hyacinths. New buds popped out on the trees and the air had a balmy, soft feel to it.

Nora came out the back door with a basket full of wash and just stood there, breathing deeply of the fragrance of spring. This was her favorite time of the year in Vermont, with fall a close second with its gorgeous panorama of color. But spring meant many months of nice weather when they could all be outdoors often. It meant clothes drying on the line without freezing, light clothing for the children, summer picnics and picking berries and seeing the vegetables grow in the garden.

Behind Nora the storm door opened. She turned to see Abby's tousled head. "Where Taddie is?" she asked. "Me want play ball."

For a two year old her vocabulary was pretty extensive, although she said some things backward. Her mother scooped her up with a hug.

"You must put your coat on, lassie, then I'll take you outdoors for a while. We'll find Taddie."

She nuzzled the soft little neck. Abby had started to wail on being brought inside but she changed to giggles at being tickled and with the promise of going outside.

In the kitchen, Victoria was doing the washing up after breakfast. Nora tried to get her to leave the chores for a while and come out with them but her mother insisted on finishing up.

Nora and Abby went out to the clothesline. While Nora pegged the clothes out, Abby kept busy with Checkers, the cat, trying to give him a ride in her little wagon. But checkers had other ideas and ran off to the barn. Abby contented herself with filling the wagon with her dolly and the extra clothespins and pulling it around.

When Victoria came out they all walked around the yard, checking the Belltrees to see how they fared during the winter. Then they went to the barn, where they found Tad with Peggy. He was brushing her down. Her coat had become thick and shaggy during the winter to protect her from the cold and now it was coming out in handfuls when Tad brushed her.

"Me ride Peggy, Taddie?" pleaded Abby to her big brother. She knew Tad couldn't refuse her anything.

Nora and Victoria exchanged amused glances. "In a minute, Abby, if Mum says you can." The little boy told her. He was still not allowed to leave the corral himself. Abby was jumping up and down impatiently.

"Patience, love, wait till Taddie finishes brushing Peggy, then we'll go out in the corral for a while," said Nora. When Tad had finished the brushing, Nora helped him to saddle the young horse, then they all went outside. Tad led Peggy around while Nora walked beside with her arm around Abby, who laughed and chattered all the while.

It was there that Annie found them as she followed the sound of their voices. She rarely came to visit on a weekday by herself, but today she had felt restless at the lumberyard, and anyway, as the men were working on the new storefront, everything was in a mess. She had suddenly thought of going for a nice, long ride in the country to enjoy the spring weather. Also, there was something she wanted to talk to Nora about. As she approached the corral, Abby caught sight of her.

"Auntie, auntie! Looka me!" Abby cried.

Nora turned and seeing Annie, called out to her, without loosening her hold on Abby. "Annie! What a surprise! We'll be through here in a minute."

Completing the circle around the corral, they all came to a stop in front of Annie and Victoria. Ducking under the fence, Annie came inside.

"You have a rest, Nora, I'll have a turn."

Nora moved aside and Annie took her place. Once more around the corral and it was Tad's turn to ride. Under protest, Abby was lifted down and Tad was helped into the saddle. He could walk the filly around by himself as long as there was a grownup watching.

Abby went back to playing with the wagon, while the women leaned on the fence to chat and watch Tad, keeping and eye on Abby as well.

"It's so nice to see you, Annie, you've been pretty scarce around here lately." Nora chided her friend, with a smile.

"I know," Annie replied. "It's been busy at the mill lately; this time of year everybody needing lumber, too. But I just couldn't resist taking a ride in the spring air."

"I'm glad you did. Can you stay for dinner?" Nora asked.

"I'd love to and I told Jack to meet me here when he could get away. Hope you don't mind."

"It's perfect. Angus will be happy to see him and it will be a change for Mama to have company." Nora responded.

At this point, Victoria excused herself, saying she would start dinner. For a while the two friends watched Tad in silence. Nora felt that Annie wanted to tell her something, and she looked at her thoughtfully.

"Everything alright, Annie? There is a pensive look about you."

Annie gave a short laugh. "Oh, yes, everything is fine. The business is going great and we are really enjoying the house. You must come and see it, now that we are settled. It looks so nice."

"I'll be out soon, when you can take a day off." Nora replied.

"I'm off every Saturday and Sunday." said Annie. "I know. Why don't you all come to dinner next Sunday?"

"I'll ask Angus if he can take the time off and let you know. But you're looking a mite peaked, Annie, sure you are all right?" Nora looked closely at her friend.

Annie colored slightly. "Oh, Nora, you know me too well." Annie hesitated. "You know, I want a baby so much; so far nothing has happened. I've begun to worry there is something wrong."

Nora could see that Annie was deeply concerned. She answered lightly. "Is that all? You must stop worrying about it. After all, you haven't been married very long. Just relax and enjoy your time alone with Jack. Believe me, after the children come, it's hard to find time to be together. C'mon now, let's see what mama is cooking up."

Annie felt relieved for the time being. Annie and Nora helped Tad down and waited while he led the filly into the barn and gave her water. Afterward they all went in to see what delicious things Victoria had made. She loved to cook for her family especially her Scottish dishes and breads.

On the Fourth of July that year, they all went into town to watch the parade. It was a very warm day and there were some dark clouds that threatened a thunderstorm, but it didn't dampen the spirit of the crowd.

Angus and Nora felt very American as they waved flags and cheered while the band played some patriotic songs. The town band was made up of some of the local citizens who practiced religiously all year long for these occasions. If they were not perfect, the watchers were not aware of it and clapped with enthusiasm. The drums were loud, causing Abby to grab for her mother's legs and hide her face, but Tad loved it. He ran around with some of Maggie's children, having a wonderful time.

After the parade there was a baseball game between two teams of the local men, some of whom had never played before. Angus and Jack joined in for the fun, as well. Oscar, who owned the haberdashery, coached them all. The end result was everybody enjoyed watching the game whether or not they were quite sure of who was winning.

Then there was a picnic on the town green. The ladies had outdone themselves in packing delicious meals for their families. Mouthwatering aromas rose throughout the picnic grounds.

After everyone had eaten and rested for a while there were some competitive games. Tad participated in a bag race with his little friends. They each put one leg into a bran sack, then had to race to see who reached the big tree at the other end of the green. Tad started out fine, hopping his way along when he collided with another boy who got too close to him. They both collapsed, laughing.

It was a tired but happy group that drove home at the end of the day.

Angus turned to Nora, saying, "Well, love, we have just celebrated America's freedom. Does it make you feel that you belong here?"

"I do feel at home here now. What about you?" Nora asked.

"I feel the same way. Not that I could ever forget Scotland, but perhaps we should be thinking about becoming citizens. What do you think, lass?" Angus asked. "Of course we'll always love our homeland but if our children are going to be brought up here we should consider that they should really belong. We will never let them forget their heritage and who they are, though."

Nora bent her head to kiss Abby's dark hair. From the back seat Victoria spoke. "For you, I think it is a wise thing to do but for me I am too old to change my allegiance."

Victoria often thought, with longing, of Scotland, for it was there she had lived with her husband and brought up their children. She was thinking that some day she would go back and finish out her life there. But right now she felt that Nora needed her. She also loved her two other daughters but their children were somewhat older than Nora's and their lives well established. Perhaps they would come for a visit, she thought.

In August, Nora began to have a problem keeping her breakfast down and soon realized the reason. She hadn't said anything to her mother as yet, but one morning, as she left the table in a hurry, Victoria gave her a searching look.

"So, daughter, I guess we can expect another wee one before too long." Victoria said.

"I guess so, mama, but not until next spring, for sure." Nora replied.

She didn't really feel ready to have another baby. She was just enjoying Abby who was finally toilet trained. With all the demands of family and home, her days were full.

CHAPTER FOURTEEN

On Mayday, 1904, Lydia Pinkham's Vegetable Compound was widely used for female ailments, the Russians and Japs were fighting, men's suits were selling for ten dollars and Miss Caroline Janet McDonald was born at five twenty five A.M. on that bright, sunny spring day. She was not concerned about Lydia Pinkham, the Russians or men's suits; nor was she bothered by the fact that her mother had labored for fourteen hours to bring her into the world. She did complain lustily about the coldness of the outside world, which was a great relief to her mother and Dr. Belden, who had been with Nora for most of the night.

"A healthy and noisy little daughter." He said to Nora. "She's calling for her mama."

He put the small bundle on Nora's chest. She smiled weakly and put her arm around the baby, who stopped her crying when she felt the warmth of her mother's body.

Angus came in to see her, having spent a sleepless night also. He was relieved to see Nora was alright as he had been more worried about her, if the truth were known, than about the baby. He had insisted on coming in the room to see her and encourage her several times during the difficult night. Now he encircled them both in his embrace.

"It's a brave lass you are." He whispered to Nora. "And another sweet lassie you've given me."

In spite of the long labor, perhaps because her mother was there to help, Nora recuperated more quickly than she had after Abby was born. She was able to come down stairs and took some care of Caroline within a week. Tad and Abby were delighted to have her about again as it had seemed lonely with her confined to her room.

Both children were intrigued by the newcomer and vied to see who could rock her cradle. Tad soon tired of it and went about his normal play.

To prevent Abby from resenting the newcomer, Nora made much of her daughter and told her she needed her help with caring for the new baby. As well, her doting "Gammy" made her special treats and let her help making scones.

It was an unusually hot summer that year and Nora seemed to get more tired than before, as she did her work. Of course, there was more work with one more little one to care for and washing endless diapers made her back ache. She didn't mention it to Victoria for fear she would insist on doing it. She would have liked to get Tansy to help but that young lady had her own hands full with her second child. Anyway, there was no extra money to pay anyone, so there was no use thinking about it.

Unlike Abby, who had been a happy and contented baby, this little one never seemed to be contented for long, keeping her mother jumping all the time. She had the colic for the first month, and then she seemed to want company constantly. The exact opposite of Abby, Caroline had reddish fuzz covering her small round head and her eyes seemed a grayish blue.

Sometimes it seemed to Nora that she would never again have any leisure time to spend with Angus. But like most things, this period passed and her strength returned.

By the end of June she was feeling quite like her old self. She and Angus resumed their evening walks around the farm, enjoying the lovely summer sunsets.

One evening, Nora slipped her hand into his and squeezed it, saying, "It's so good to feel like myself again, love, I was beginning to think I never would!"

"And you're as bonnie as ever!" Angus exclaimed, with admiration. "After all you've been through! And with three wee ones to look after!"

"I could na do it wi'out the help of Mama. But I know she is getting lonesome for Scotland and to see the other girls. The other day she spoke of going for a visit. Do you think she could stand the trip over and back?" Nora asked.

"Maybe. She is a strong lady and sometimes it is worse to be pining than to make an effort to do something." Angus replied.

Nora was thoughtful. "I was thinking maybe we should invite the girls to visit here rather than have mama make the long trip. What do you think about that?"

"I'm thinking you should talk to Victoria about it and see what she really wants to do." Adam stated. And then he put his arm around her waist and pulled her down onto a big rock beside him. "Now, stop worrying about everybody and let's enjoy our time alone. You're due for an outing, I would say. Do you think we could get away together for a day soon?" He asked

Nora sighed. "Oh, that would be so lovely, but not quite yet. I hate to leave the whole burden on mama."

"I know. We would have to get someone to help her. Perhaps Annie would like to take Abby for a day, she loves the children." Adam suggested.

"True, but I haven't seen her much lately. I think sometimes she is resenting us for having all these bairns and she still has none."

"Yes, I know," Angus mused. "Jack speaks about it often. He sometimes brings Maggie's son to help around just because he likes little ones so much. It's too bad. Some have so many and others none at all."

"Well, don't worry, I'll think of a way to have that day together soon." said Nora.

She slipped her arms around him beneath his jacket. As he bent to kiss her they both lost their balance and slid off the rock, sprawling on the ground, laughing.

The following Sunday, they did have their day together. Annie, as Angus had said, was more than happy to take Abby for the day and Jack insisted that Tad come as well. So Victoria was left with only baby Carrie, as she had soon become known.

Nora made sure that there was a good supply of clean diapers and everything else that would be needed. Also, Sadie Thorne was going to come over for a while during the day in case of any other needs that might come up and to keep Victoria company. So it was with free minds that Angus and Nora set out on their first day alone together in years.

There was a fair in the next township and that was to be their first stop. Nora wore a dark brown suit she had brought with her from Scotland. It had a tight waist and flared out a little over her hips. The skirt was only slightly flared at the bottom. With it she wore a brown hat with a light yellow ribbon and a yellow shirtwaist of the same shade.

Angus thought she looked beautiful and told her so, bringing a rosy color to her cheeks. She'd had very few occasions to dress up and it made her feel young and frivolous.

They were to go to a restaurant for their evening meal. Jack had recommended one he knew to be reasonably priced and had good food. To save money, they packed some sandwiches for their lunch. They left at seven in the morning, taking sleepy Abby and Tad with them to drop off at Annie's house.

The fair was fun, if only for the fact that they felt carefree for the day. At the animal pens, Angus found a bull he greatly admired and had a long chat with the owner, who, it turned out, lived only a few miles from Belltrees. His wife was there as well and she and Nora took a liking to each other right away.

The couple was Hans and Rica von Stubin and they convinced Nora and Angus to stay for the evening dancing outdoors, to the music of a couple of fiddlers. There was a covered dish supper served by the local grange women. It sounded like more fun than ordinary dinner at a restaurant, to the McDonald's. They were not disappointed.

As Nora was swung around in her husband's arms, she kissed him under his ear, making him squeeze her tighter.

"I'm having such a good time, I almost feel guilty." She said.

But Angus said, "Shush, I don't want to hear it! You needed the time off and we'll both be the better for it tomorrow. Now, just enjoy yourself."

It was with some reluctance that they said goodbye to the von Stubins and started for home. In spite of being tired, they managed to sing several choruses of "Annie Laurie" most of the way home, until Nora fell asleep on Angus' shoulder.

They both felt a new zest for life the next morning and Nora insisted that her mother take a complete day off and go into town with Mrs. Thorne.

That same evening, in their comfortable kitchen, Jack and Annie were having their supper together. It had been a busy day for the lumberyard and they were both looking forward to the weekend.

"So how are we going to spend Sunday?" Jack asked. "How about going out to the Belltrees and visiting with Angus and Nora? We haven't seen the newest addition yet. What do you say?"

"I don't think so, not this Sunday. Why don't we take a picnic down to Lake Crystal?" Annie answered, without looking at him.

"Well, I haven't seen Angus for some time, and I really think we should view the new baby. What do you say?"

Annie threw her napkin down, saying, "Oh, bother the baby! That's all they think about out there. Babies, babies, babies! I'm sick to death of it!"

Jack, astonished, looked at his wife's face. This was the first time he had ever heard her use a tone like this. What could be wrong? As he stared at her, her face suddenly crumpled. Tears ran down her cheeks. He was at her side in a second.

"What is it, Annie? What's wrong, my dear child! I've never heard you speak this way before. You must be working too hard. I knew you shouldn't come into the office to work. We don't have to go anywhere at all, just stay at home and rest, if you like."

Annie only cried harder, her hand over her eyes. When she could talk she lifted her tear stained face to him.

"No, no, I am just being mean and jealous. I've longed so for a baby since we were married, but Nora seems to have them so easily. What is wrong with me, anyway?"

"Oh, is that all! Aren't you happy with just me?" He tried to make her smile.

She made a feeble effort. "Of course, Jack, but I know you want a child and I'm not getting any younger and---".

"And nothing," interrupted Jack. "The babies will come in time. You are just too anxious. How would you like to have ten crawling all over each other like Mrs. Magee, eh?"

The thought of the Magee children, who always had runny noses and shrill voices, like their mother, made Annie laugh, as Jack had known it would. The crisis was over although neither one forgot it.

The next morning found them on the way to the McDonald's farm. Annie was once more her good-natured self and looking forward to the visit. It was an unusually warm day for June and Annie wore a white dimity dress sprinkled with tiny blue flowers.

They had planned to arrive at the farm soon after the noon meal so that Nora would not feel obligated to cook for them. They found the whole family, including Victoria, sitting on the porch in the white wicker chairs.

That is, the adults were sitting; Abby and Tad were playing some sort of ball game, oblivious to the heat. Baby Caroline, was in her pram on the porch beside her mother and father.

While Annie and Jack admired the baby, Nora went inside and brought out a large pitcher of lemonade for everyone. Annie felt the familiar twinge of envy as she observed the small hands and feet of the infant, but she quickly put it away from her mind.

"Can I hold her, Nora?" Annie asked. "She is so sweet! And that reddish fuzz is so cute!"

She caressed the small cheek and, as Nora smiled her consent, picked up the baby and sat down in a rocker.

Her husband smiled at the picture they made together. He thought to himself that Annie had got over her despair but he could not see the tight, little knot that formed in her chest. And she would try to conceal it from him because she felt ashamed of her actions of the night before.

Jack looked at the older children in amazement.

"It's hard to believe that Tad is going to be six next week and Abby is already three. You'll soon have some good workers for the farm, Angus."

The two men laughed at the idea, then Angus said, "Tad's already a help but he'll be starting school soon. I want to be sure my children have a better education than I had."

Tad, bored with trying to play ball with his little sister, called out to his father. "Papa, why don't you and Uncle Jack come out to the barn and I can show him how I can ride now?"

He took his Uncle Jack's hand and the two men strolled with him to the barn, Abby dancing along beside them.

Watching them Nora said to Annie "That Abby is such a little tomboy! She stands on her head almost as much as on her two feet. I'm thinking of making her some overalls like her brothers. Her dresses are always so bedraggled."

Annie laughed. "That's a good idea. But don't worry about her. I was just like that until I turned eleven and discovered boys."

"Surely, not at eleven!" Nora exclaimed. "I don't want to even think about that. It's a long way off."

"Spoken like a true mother," Teased Annie.

Victoria joined in the laughter, saying to her daughter. "O, yes, daughter, I seem to remember a little lad named Paddy who you were moony about when you were eight or so."

They all laughed at that. "All right, all right!" Nora said. "I just won't worry about it yet. Come on, let's go and watch the riding, too."

They all stood around the fence while Tad proudly rode Peggy in the corral to show them how the filly could walk, canter and back up, all to his commands. He was very patient with his horse. His father had spent many hours with the two of them to master these moves.

Angus watched proudly now, and when Tad reined to a stop in front of the little group, they all applauded. Tad laughed with delight.

Then Abby insisted on being led around the corral while sitting on Peggy's back. Everyone clapped for her as well and she took a little bow, amusing them all.

Carrie was demanding to be fed so the women went back to the house.

While the men were helping Tad remove Peggy's saddle and brush her down, Angus told Jack that tracks of the old bear had been seen recently at the Renfrew's. Judging by her prints, the bear had lost a part of one paw years ago, either in a trap or shot by a hunter. Because it interfered with her hunting game, she had turned to the more easily captured farm animals for food. The whole community was concerned that she might one day attack a human.

The farmers had decided to organize a massive hunt, including all available men in the county.

"I'll let you know when it will be, if you want to go with us." Angus told Jack.

"Of course, count me in! I've never hunted for bear, but I am a pretty good shot."

A week later Angus was notified that the hunt was scheduled for the first weekend in October, after the major haying and gardening were completed.

CHAPTER FIFTEEN

The big day, when Shawn Edward McDonald was to start school and enter into the all-new (to him) world was, fast approaching. Tad would have preferred to stay home in the comfortable world he was familiar with but his mother and father had explained to him all the reasons for going that parents all have been explaining since school was invented. But the most convincing bit of information to Tad was that his friend, Andy, was going as well. In fact, they would be taken to school each day by one of their fathers. This fact made the whole idea acceptable to Tad.

The one room schoolhouse was about two miles distance from the McDonald's farm. It was a small building situated on a slight rise off the road. It was painted a dark red.

Inside, the focal point, especially in the winter, was a large, round stove set up on two layers of bricks. This stove was in the middle of the room and on either side were several rows of desks all facing the front of the room where the large wooden desk for the teacher was placed. On the right side of the room were many hooks in the wall for the student's coats. Beyond that a door led outside to the path to the outhouse.

The first two rows of desks up front were smaller, for the first and second graders. On the periphery would be seated the bigger children, with the middle sized ones in the middle. The reasoning was that it was colder in the winter further away one was from the stove and the older children could tolerate it better.

The first day of school the smaller ones were very quiet and well behaved, being intimidated by the whole experience. Tad and Abby were no different that the others. There were only four children in the first grade.

After the first few days they relaxed and were as rowdy as the rest at recess time. During recess the smaller children played in their own group while the older ones played "king of the hill", "pump-pump-pull away" or "run, sheep, run."

It was a wonderful, new world for Tad and Andy. They were full of news when they returned home. They were especially impressed with Mr. Paton, the schoolteacher; he was a young man with a bristling mustache, red hair and a no nonsense air about him.

Abby listened avidly when Tad talked about his day at school. She was lonesome without her brother and wanted to go with him. She couldn't understand why she had to stay home and miss all the fun.

Nora understood how her little girl was feeling and she decided to have a talk with Aunt Clara about the possibility of little Harry and Abby spending more time together.

It was decided that the two little ones would spend three days a week together. Sadie Thorne was delighted to have Abby come there as it would keep Harry occupied to have a companion his own age. It was a pleasure for Clara and Harry to hear the little ones at play.

It was difficult enough to find lightheartedness in that house with Supleen's gloomy countenance around. He was at home as little as possible still and his relationship with his father was as strained as always. To his credit, though, when he did happen to come upon his son playing, he would stop and talk to him.

During these times he was a different man than with anyone else. Perhaps it was fortunate that Harry didn't look like Zoë at all. He was a softened version of Supleen. So there was nothing physical about the boy to renew old hurts.

It did Clara's heart good to see how he was accepting his son now where before he had ignored the little fellow. It gave her some hope for the future.

Any changes for the better in Supleen could be attributed to his liaison with Genny. She was tough on the outside but she had a soft heart. A fact she kept hidden from most people.

She had spoken with Supleen many times about his son. In fact, she encouraged him to do so.

Another thing she had not told, even Supleen, was that she had once had a son who had died when he was two years old. She had vowed never to be hurt like that again.

Genny was very fond of Supleen, though she recognized his weaknesses. She was a good influence on him, though he would be the last one to admit it.

The arrangement for Abby and Harry was a good one and served the purpose of keeping them both contented while giving Nora a little more time to do her house work.

Then one day, in the first week of October, Abby couldn't go to Harry's because he had a bad cold. She played with her doll in the morning, then after lunch her mother went upstairs with her and tucked her in for a nap.

Usually she would get up and call for her mother when she awoke. But when two o'clock came and Abby had still not called or come down from her nap, Nora went up to get her. She was not in her bed.

Nora went into Victoria's room to see if she was there; Abby loved her grandmother's room. But she was not there, either. So Nora went down to the kitchen, where Victoria was peeling potatoes.

"Mama, have you seen Abby? She usually calls me when she wakes up but she is not in her bed or anywhere upstairs."

Victoria looked up from her chore. "No, I haven't seen her since you took her upstairs. Do you suppose she went out doors?"

Without answering, Nora went through the screen door to look around the yard. She walked around the yard and out to the barn, calling to her little girl. Then she went back through the kitchen and checked the rest of the downstairs. Victoria followed her. They were both getting concerned now. Abby was only allowed to play close to the door if she was alone.

"Maybe she is playing hide and seek," said Nora, hopefully. She ran back upstairs and looked under the beds and in the closets the entire time calling to Abby. But the house was quiet. She hurried downstairs.

"Mama, maybe she went to Clara's, she has been so lonesome since Tad went to school. I'm going to look. Mama would you watch Caroline? I'll hurry! Oh, I wish we had a telephone!"

She grabbed her shawl on the way out the door. Noticing Abby's coat hanging beside hers she took it with her. She circled the house and barn once more, calling loudly to Abby, but there was no answer.

Soon she found herself running in the direction of the Renfrew's. Her heart was filled with dread. Abby might be outdoors somewhere alone and the old bear had not been caught!

The only times she had walked with Abby to the Renfrew's they had gone cross lots, as it was quicker. There was no sign of the little girl on the way though Nora scrutinized every bush and tree she passed.

Arriving at the Renfrew home, she burst in without even knocking and startled Clara and Sadie, who were both in the parlor. Breathlessly, she explained what she was doing there.

Aunt Clara, shocked at the way Nora looked, tried to persuade her to sit down and have some tea, but Nora was so distraught that she burst into tears.

"Please, dear," said Clara. "Sit down a minute, I'll get Harrison and Claude and they will help you look for Abby. Where is Angus?"

Between sobs, Nora told her Angus was helping Jack that day.

"I'll call Jack's store, too." Clara soothed. "He will want to know."

She left the room to go to the telephone. Sadie had run out to fetch Claude and now the two came back into the room, followed by Harrison in his wheelchair.

Harrison patted his niece's shoulders. "Don't worry, girl, we'll find the wee lassie in no time." To Claude, he ordered, "Hitch up the buggy, Claude, you can take Nora by the road since she has already checked the cross lot. Also, get the other men to help us look."

Clara had called Angus and two close neighbors. Soon there were about twenty people combing the countryside for the three year old.

Back at the McDonald's house, Victoria was watching out the window, holding baby Caroline in her arms.

Claude brought Nora home to check around the place once more, but Nora had insisted on going out again.

Angus arrived home with Jack and they, too, joined the search.

Meanwhile, it was Andy's father's turn to pick up the two boys at school. He was about two-thirds of the way there when he noticed an unusual dark lump under a tree just ahead. When he was close to it he saw at once it was a child lying there.

Stopping the buggy, he went to investigate. He was shocked to see Angus' little girl curled up on her side, her face tearstained, sound asleep. He touched her shoulder gently, at which she opened her eyes. She immediately smiled at him.

"Did you come to get me? I couldn't find Tad, and I was losted." Abby said.

Mr. Harris swung her up in his arms. She clung to his neck. "C'mon, baby, we'll get the boys, then I'll take you home." He covered her with a lap robe and she promptly went back to sleep with her head in his lap.

While the other men combed the surrounding woods, Claude took Nora down the road toward the schoolhouse. So they met Mr. Harris coming back from the school with the two boys. As they both stopped, Nora saw Abby, asleep on Mr. Harris' lap. She was out of the carriage in a flash.

"Oh, it's Abby! Where did you find her?"

Abby woke when her mother touched her.

"Abby! lassie, where did you go?" Nora asked.

Abby looked up at her with sleepy eyes. "Mama! I went to school, only it was long way. Mr. Harris came to get me."

Nora was laughing and crying at the same time. She hugged her daughter tightly.

"Well, let's get you home quickly! We have to tell everyone you are all right. She held Abby close to her all the way home.

Mr. Harris rang the dinner bell loudly to let everyone know Abby was found. Victoria had made stacks of roast beef sandwiches and coffee to serve the searching party and everyone stood around laughing and talking about the tot's adventure.

No one mentioned it out loud but the fear of the old bear had been uppermost in all their minds. Each one of the men had thought it could have been his child out there.

Angus and Nora could hardly take their eyes off their little girl as she ate her supper. Both of them went upstairs when it was time for her to get a bath and go to bed. Abby was so tired she didn't protest about being put to bed as she usually did.

The following Saturday twenty-four men gathered in Angus' yard with their guns, ready to go on the bear hunt. In the first early rays of the October sun the mist was still rising over the meadows. They each had a lunch with them as they expected to be gone most of the day. They had decided to begin around the Renfrew's place because the "old one" had last been sighted in that area.

The younger men in the crowd were excited and anxious to get started, but the older ones, who had been on bear hunts, were a bit apprehensive. They knew that an angry bear was capable of anything. Unlike a normal one, who could often be frightened off by a loud noise, a bear who had been wounded or was sick was a dangerous adversary.

The men decided to break up into groups of four and stay in their assigned territory to guard against accidents. In the group with Angus were Jack, Claude and Andrew Harris. Claude and Andrew had both hunted bear before but it was a new experience for the other two.

They had been assigned the thick woods north of the McDonald farm. They moved slowly and warily, checking often for sight or sound of the "old one."

When the sun was straight overhead, the four men stopped to eat their lunches beside a large outcropping of rock ledge.

They had finished eating and were picking up to leave when a deep growl startled them. Looking up they saw the old bear coming around the ledge. As they grabbed for their guns, she rose on her hind legs, flailing out with her front paws. Claude was in the front and before he could get his gun up, she caught him with her right paw. She lifted the short man off the ground. Claude screamed. Angus, close behind Claude, swung at the bear's face with his gun. With a roar, she dropped Claude and raked her claw down Angus left side as he tried desperately to jump away. At that moment, Andrew shot the bear directly in the face. Temporarily blinded, the "old one" dropped to all fours, blood streaming from her head. She turned to amble away, when Andrew got off another shot, hitting her behind her left front leg. The bear took one more step and dropped.

The four men all fell back onto the ground with relief. Claude was bleeding from his shoulder, his coat torn. Angus' left sleeve was in tatters and pieces of his skin were also hanging out. He had a glazed look in his eyes. His arm was numb.

Jack tore off a piece of his own shirt to wrap around Angus' arm. They both knew that when the numbness wore off it was going to be unbearably painful.

"We're going to get you home as fast as we can, my friend. Just lay back while we fix a travois."

Jack tucked his coat under Angus' head. While Claude, who was trying to shake off the shock, sat beside Angus, Andrew and Jack looked for wood to make a travois.

As they returned to the clearing, they could hear, at some distance, the shouts of the other hunters. They had heard the shots and were calling to the four men to answer them. Jack yelled out to give them the direction. It was several minutes before some of the other hunters arrived. Only four of them had been within hearing distance of the shots.

They were dumbstruck at the scene, as they came crashing out of the woods. The huge bear lay full length only a few feet from their friends.

Cecile's father was one of the new arrivals, along with his son. He knelt beside the two injured men. He tried to reassure them.

"Don't worry, we'll get you out of here in no time." said Mr. Bates. Then to Cecile, he said, "You run as fast as you can to the McDonald's. Get on your horse and get Doc. Belden out here as quick as you can. We should be there by that time. If we aren't there when you get back, come after us with the wagon."

With his father's first words, Cecile had turned and started back. He could see that Claude and Angus were in grave danger.

Nora was hanging out some clothes when Cecile came running toward the house. She knew instantly that something was very wrong. She ran to meet him. He explained what had happened, while he caught and saddled his horse. He was gone in a moment.

Nora hurried to the house to tell Victoria. Together they prepared some clean cloths, hot water, and iodine and turned back the bed, which they covered with an old, clean blanket. Then, unable to stay still, Nora went back outdoors to watch for the men to come into sight.

It was another thirty agonizing minutes before she sighted the group coming over the rise. She ran to meet them.

At about the same time she heard horses driving in to the yard. As Nora neared the men she could see there were two men on a travois, being pulled by three of the other men. Nora walked along beside her husband, occasionally touching his shoulder. Inside, the sight of his bloodied arm sickened her.

The injured men were taken directly into the house, where the doctor was already washing up. They put Claude on the lounge in the kitchen and took Angus directly to his bed. The doctor barked out orders.

"I need to attend to Angus right away. One of you help Mrs. Renfrew clean up Claude. Someone should go over to tell Harrison what's happened."

Then he hurried to Angus' beside. He yelled over his shoulder. "I'll need a man to help me with Angus, too."

Jack came to help the doctor, while Cecile assisted Victoria with washing Claude's wounds. Then they could see that the scratches weren't as bad as they had feared. It was possible, they thought, that he had a cracked rib or two, because his chest hurt but he could breath all right.

When Doctor Belden examined Angus' arm he tried not to betray to Nora and Angus just how serious his injuries were. Nora had already guessed. Angus was half unconscious from shock and loss of blood. As the doctor began to work on Angus, Nora turned ashen.

Without looking up, the Doctor ordered. "Nora, you go down and help with Claude. Send your mother or one of the other men up here." Near fainting, Nora left the room and did as she was told.

It was more than an hour before the doctor came downstairs. Nora took his arm.

"How is he, Doctor Belden? He'll be all right, won't he? Can I see him?"

"Now, now, girl one thing at a time. You can see him, of course. But, he won't be all right for a long time. I've done my best to clean his wounds and to sew up the tears in his arm. He's lost a lot of blood and, if we are lucky, there will be no infection. His muscles have damage, too. Mind you don't tell him too much. He needs to keep his spirits up."

Nora was halfway out of the room before the doctor finished talking. She found Victoria sitting in a chair by the bed and Jack cleaning up the cloths the doctor had used.

"Mama, you and Jack go down and have some coffee and sandwiches. I'll stay here."

She sat down beside Angus who was still asleep from the ether. Only then did Nora allow the tears to flow. Her heart was filled with fear. He looked so white and still. She stroked his hair. His eyes fluttered half open.

He whispered, "Nora, love, what is it?" Nora forced a smile. "Nothing, dear, I am just so glad you are alive. Now, you have to rest and get all better."

He started to form a word but fell back asleep. Nora stayed with him until Jack came up. He squeezed her shoulders, affectionately.

"Nora, Angus won't want you to wear yourself out. I will ask Annie to come over to help you and Victoria. With the little ones and now this you will need someone. And it won't help if you get sick, too."

Nora gave him a grateful glance. "Thank you, Jack. That would be a big help. But from what the doctor said we might need someone for a long time: I know you need Annie in the store."

"We'll solve that problem later. You go now and have a rest or something to eat. The doctor has patched up Claude and Harrison's men are bringing him home. The doctor will stay the night here to keep an eye on Angus."

As Jack was speaking, he gently propelled her to the door.

Nora asked Cecile, who had stayed to help, to move a cot from Tad's room into the room where Angus was, so the doctor could sleep near his patient.

Then Cecile had to get home to his family and Nora and Victoria were alone with the children. By the time they had fed Tad and Abby and put them to bed, they were exhausted.

The doctor was asleep on the cot with his shirt and pants on. Nora sat for a few minutes by the bed and stroked Angus forehead. He didn't wake up and still looked white and wan.

A week later, Angus was sitting up in a chair by the bed. Nora was changing the sheets.

"Nora, has Doc. Belden told you anymore about my arm, that you aren't telling me?" Angus searched her face for an answer. "Will I ever be able to use this arm again?"

"He thinks that you will, in time." Nora answered. "As soon as your arm is healed, he said you could start to exercise it a little at a time. You have to be patient, love."

Angus shook his head, angrily. "Patient! With no one to help on the farm? And you looking more and more tired with each day?"

Nora leaned over and kissed her distressed husband.

"Now, stop stewing. We can manage for a few more days. And you will be about by then and feeling your old self. If you feel up to it you can come down to supper tonight."

He did go down to the supper table that evening; his legs felt like rubber. The children were excited to have him at the table once more. The smell and taste of Victoria's meat pie gave him an appetite. He complimented her on the supper.

"Mama, the smell of your cooking could bring a dead man back to life."

He had to eat with his left hand, which caused him to drop a few bites. He laughed at himself, though, and the whole family felt better than since the accident.

"Papa, is your arm dead?" questioned Abby.

"Course not, silly goose," laughed Tad. "It's just hurt that's all. That old bear hurt papa, but he killed him, anyway."

Angus shook his head. "That's not quite the way it happened, lad. The old one surprised us and I didn't have my gun ready so I hit him with it to make him let go of Claude. Andy's father actually shot him."

"Wow! You hit her with your gun? Weren't you scared?" His son asked.

"We were all scared, lad, he was a dangerous creature."

Nora cut in. "That's enough talk about the bear for now. Papa is very tired. He needs to rest."

At the look of disappointment on his son's face Angus said, "Mama's right, wee ones, your Papa will go up to bed now, and you two can help me. Alright?"

At the idea of being able to help their father, Tad and Abby brightened. With his son and daughter on either side of him, Angus went back to the bedroom.

Nora looked after them, not offering to help. She turned to Victoria, who was starting to clear the table.

"You know, Mama, I didn't think that they were so grown up. I think they can both help out a little from now on. It will be good for them."

Victoria replied, with the wisdom of age, "They are still just babes, but even babes need to know they can help. It makes them responsible in later life."

"What will we do if he can never use his arm again? He couldn't bear it. And I can't run this farm without him."

Her mother chided her. "Here, none of that, lass. We all bear what we have to. The best thing for your man is to start working as soon as possible. He'll learn to work the best way he can."

Doctor Belden agreed with Victoria's prognosis. He ordered Angus to start walking around out of doors right away. He knew that as soon as Angus looked around his farm he would find the incentive to start using his arm again.

The next day, after their noon meal, Nora urged her husband to come for a walk with her. He still felt weak but to please her he went.

With the children running about them, all excited, they walked out to look at the Belltrees. From there it was a short walk to the barn. Looking around the unkempt stalls, it struck him what a burden had been put onto Nora. He picked up a shovel and started to clean out the stall when he realized he was awfully tired. The shovel hung awkwardly from his left hand. He dropped it on the ground.

Nora's eyes reflected his despair. But she quickly reassured him. "Give yourself a few more days. This is your first time outside. You'll be as right as rain soon. C'mon outside and look at the horses."

With the autumn sun warming his tired body and watching the horses grazing contentedly, Angus felt more optimistic.

Each day after that Angus went out and worked around the barn and corral. Frustrations were many, trying to work with one arm, but he devised new methods of doing his chores. He used a rake instead of a shovel to clean out the stalls, and found he could lift a fork full of hay with his left arm, although it was clumsy.

He tried to hide his frustrations from Tad, who started to come out to the barn after school to help his father. Angus was glad for his help and it made a further bond between the two.

One day, about three weeks after Angus' injury, Nora and Victoria were working in the kitchen cleaning up after the noon meal, when they heard horses stomping out front and a loud voice shouting orders. They both looked at each other and smiled. They recognized the strident tones of Mrs. Dufrense.

Nora went to the door to greet the big Canadian woman. She had two of her children with her. She engulfed Nora in a bear hug, as usual. She was a good-natured woman who ruled her brood of ten with an iron hand and lots of affection. She treated the rest of the world the same way.

"Nora, ma petite, I heard about your man's accident. I brought him some of my strawberry preserves. And where is that little mother of yours? And I haven't seen your little baby yet!"

Over her shoulder, she shouted at her two sons. "You two go to the barn and give Angus some help!"

Nora took her guest out to the kitchen where Mrs. Dufrense greeted Victoria heartily and swept Abby up from her chair.

"How are you, young lady, and where is that new sister of yours, eh?"

Abby, taken aback, was speechless, but she pointed to the cradle in the corner. Surprisingly enough, the small girl was not afraid of this loud woman, but rather awed by her. Abby found her voice and said, "That's her. She's only little and she cries a lot, too."

Mrs. Dufrense roared with laughter at this. But when she talked to the baby, it was in such a dulcet tone that Nora and Victoria stared at each other in amazement.

"Ah, ma petite enfant!" She turned to Nora, rolling her eyes heavenward. "Oh, there is nothing like a baby! And I'm the one should know!" She laughed heartily at her joke. She slapped the table smartly. "Now! I've come to see if I can help your man. I heard he has no use of his arm, oui?" She questioned Nora, who nodded. "Well, two years ago my brother, he was hurt badly when a boulder he was trying to move rolled back on him. The Doc said he would never walk, but I took care of him and he walks as good as me now."

Nora, who was pouring a cup of coffee for her guest, nearly spilled it in her eagerness to hear more. She sat down abruptly. "How? What did you do?" Nora asked.

Victoria, too, sat quietly, waiting.

"Well, my meme' taught me long ago what to do. Now I tell you."

As Mrs. Dufrense explained how she used a combination of massage and exercise to heal her brother's leg, Nora was so excited that she could hardly wait to start on Angus' arm.

When Angus and Tad came in for supper, they both looked tired and Angus' face was drawn and white. Nowadays, he expended twice the energy to accomplish half the work. He listened with interest as Nora recounted what Mrs. Dufrense had told her.

"Well, it won't hurt to try it. I can't be any worse off. We can start tomorrow. Right now I'm for the bed."

His eyes didn't hold much hope but Nora felt a new optimism. She stayed awake a long time thinking about what her friend had told her.

They started the massage the next day. Angus suggested that they do it at noontime before he ate. Nora made him lie down on the lounge in the kitchen while she started at his shoulder and gently worked the flaccid muscles. When she reached his hand she worked the fingers in an up and down motion and flexed his wrist. She felt awkward at first doing it but in a few days she became more confident in what she was doing. If her arms got tired Victoria would take over, until a half hour was over. This was how long Nora thought they should do the exercises.

After a few days they both thought it would be even better if they also massaged the arm at night. Angus had caught Nora's excitement and he would try to move the muscles of his arm a little on his own. He took a small ball that Tad often played with and tried to squeeze it. At first it would just rest in his palm but gradually he could curl his fingers around it a bit. The first time he managed to do this, Nora and Angus were both ecstatic.

After that, Angus would attempt to pick up his tools in the barn. He couldn't as yet, but he felt that there was life in his arm still. He was glad that this had happened in the late fall when there were fewer pressing chores to be done. If only he could regain the use of his arm before the maple trees had to be tapped.

One day, in mid-November, Angus was just finishing his noon meal. Nora, who was by the sink, suddenly exclaimed "Angus! Supleen is out there by our barn with a stranger! What could he be doing?"

Angus quickly put on his coat and went out. As he approached the two men, he heard Supleen discussing the boundaries of his farm, with a possessive tone.

"Is there something I can do for you gentlemen?" Angus spoke in a louder tone than usual.

The man with Supleen turned to him, saying, "Oh, are you Mr. McDonald? I am Mr. Spaulding. Mr. Renfrew was showing me your farm. I am interested in buying in the area."

With a baleful glance at Supleen, Angus answered, "I'm sorry, Mr. Spaulding, but my farm is not for sale. Who told you that it was?"

Mr. Spaulding looked embarrassed and stammered. "But-but, Mr. Renfrew--" he looked helplessly at Supleen, who was standing there with a smirk on his face.

He glanced pointedly at Angus arm, hanging by his side. In a disdainful voice he said, "You'd better sell now, while you can. A cripple can't run this farm."

Mr. Spaulding was already leaving, stammering apologies to Angus. Furious at his cousin's highhanded action, he turned to Supleen and, through clenched teeth, told him, "Get off my land!

And don't ever do a thing like this again!" His left hand was a tight fist.

Supleen, fear in his eyes, backed off, then turned and walked quickly away not answering. Angus found himself shaking.

Nora came running out of the house to find out what had happened.

Angus explained, adding, "Supleen is hoping to be able to foreclose on the farm because I can't use my arm. I just wish I hadn't lost my temper. I don't want to upset Harrison and Clara."

Nora, upset by the look on his face, replied, "Don't worry, that coward won't mention this to Harrison, he knows how angry his father would be at his doing something like this."

"Aye, but if something happens to Harrison, Supleen will foreclose in a minute."

They both fell silent. Nora took her husband's arm and they started to walk toward the Belltrees. It always comforted them to see this connection to their homeland. The little trees had grown a lot since they had brought them from Scotland, helped along by the manure Angus introduced in the ground around them each spring and fall.

As they stood there, Angus felt a renewed determination to keep the farm no matter what he had to do. Now he put his arm around his wife's waist.

"Don't fret about it, lass, we won't let him spoil our day. But I'm thinking seriously about getting a loan from the bank to pay off our mortgage so we won't have to worry about Supleen's whims. I just have to think of a way to explain it to Uncle Harrison, so he won't think I don't trust him."

Nora scoffed. "I'm thinking that Uncle Harrison knows all about Supleen and what he's like. He'll understand without you telling him the reason. But do you think we could get the money from the bank?" Nora said, doubtfully.

"I think they would loan it to me. We've been here now for several years. And I know Mr. Patterson at the bank. He's a fair man."

But Mr. Patterson, besides being friendly, was a good businessman. And he had to answer to his superior's, too. They would be concerned that a man with only one usable arm might not be able to fulfill his obligations. If Angus would sign over the farm as collateral, he could consider the loan. But Angus would not put any lien on his home, so he left the bank empty handed.

After that encounter, Angus became more determined than ever to fully restore the use of his right arm. Besides the massage twice daily, he would have Tad assist him in the afternoons while he would try to saddle one of the horses to encourage his muscles to respond.

CHAPTER SIXTEEN

By late March, when it was time to start the sugaring, Angus had regained about seventy percent of the normal use of his right arm. His spirits had risen one hundred percent. He was confident he would have complete control and full use of his arm by late spring. Nora and Tad went with him into the woods to help with the "sugaring off." They all enjoyed it; the crisp air, the sound of their boots on the snow, the horses breath curling upward in steam and, above all, tasting the finished product.

On the last day, as they were getting ready to leave the house after a quick breakfast, Nora noticed that Tad was less enthusiastic than usual. He didn't finish his porridge, which he usually loved. Nora peered closely in to her son's face.

"Are you feeling alright, laddie?"

She put a hand on his forehead to test his temperature. "Why don't you stay home today and rest. You may be coming down with a cold."

But Tad was so proud of helping out that he begged to go and, in the end, Nora gave in and let him go with them. By the time they stopped for the noon lunch in the sugar shack, Tad's face was flushed and he felt hot to Nora's touch. Angus put him on the sled and they took him back to the house. Nora fixed him a hot lemonade and tucked him up on the lounge in the kitchen, where Victoria could keep her eye on him.

That evening he was still warmer than normal and he couldn't eat his supper. During the night Nora was awakened several times when Tad called out. He was chilled and shivering. Later he threw off the covers saying he was too hot.

In the morning Angus had to go off by himself to finish the sugaring off. It had to be finished before the weather turned warm or the syrup would be of inferior quality. But instead of eating his lunch in the sugar shack, he decided to go back to the house and check on Tad, as he was worried about the little fellow.

Angus found Nora preparing to go to Harrison's to call Dr. Belden. Tad was worse and she was afraid that he had pneumonia. When she saw Angus, tears welled up in her eyes and she clung to him.

"Oh, Angus! I'm so scared. I've never seen him so sick and he looks so small. Come up and see what you think."

They went up to the bedroom where Victoria was sitting in a rocking chair holding Caroline while Abby played on the floor beside her.

Tad, on the bed, peered at his father out of feverish eyes. In a hoarse whisper he spoke to Angus.

"Papa, I want to help you."

But his listless, little form did not move. Angus put his hand on his son's forehead.

"Now, laddie, don't you worry about that. You helped me a lot already. Now, you just rest while I go get the doctor. You'll be right as rain in no time."

He bent and kissed him, then turned to Nora. "You stay here, love, I'll go to telephone the doctor."

While Angus was gone, Nora took Caroline and insisted her mother go downstairs and have some tea. Lately she had been concerned because Victoria was looking tired. Nora felt a guilty twinge about having left her with the two younger ones while she and Angus were working outside. She thought that from now on she would make sure that her mother was not allowed to do quite so much.

She looked down at Caroline, who had fallen asleep. How sweet and innocent she looked with her long lashes laying on her cheeks, totally relaxed. She stood up to put the baby into her bed. Tad, too, had fallen into a restless sleep, his breathing audible in the quiet room. As she turned over the cool cloth on his forehead, Tad murmured and moved restlessly but he didn't wake.

The bedroom door opened and Angus came in with Doctor Belden, who nodded at Nora and went directly to Tad. Very gently, he took Tad's pulse and touched his forehead. Tad opened his eyes. He coughed with a deep, rattling sound.

"Hello, young man." said the doctor. "Not feeling so good, are you? Well, we'll fix you up in no time. I'm just going to look at your chest, now, alright?"

Tad looked at his mother for reassurance. She smiled at him.

"It's alright, love. Dr. Belden wants to find out what is wrong with you."

When the doctor had completed his examination, he tucked the covers around Tad and motioned to Nora and Angus that he wanted to talk to them.

To Tad, he said, "You're going to be fine, young man. I want to talk to your parents for a few minutes. Now, you take a nice nap."

Before she followed the doctor out of the room, Nora gave Tad a drink of water from the carafe on the bedside table and kissed him gently.

"C'mon down and have a cup of tea, Doctor Belden." said Angus. "We can talk as well down there."

On the way downstairs, Doctor Belden explained, "This is not pneumonia, it appears to be the croup, at this point. It can turn nasty sometimes, but he's a healthy young man.

The doctor went on to explain that Tad would need to have a steaming kettle of water in his room at all time. They were to mix the equal parts of honey and lemon and give Tad a spoonful every three hours.

"Adding a few drops of brandy to the mixture would be beneficial, too." The doctor added.

Nora, relieved to have something concrete to do, set about preparing the cough syrup while Victoria poured boiling water in the teapot and set out cups for them all. Angus and Nora first brought the prepared syrup and a steaming teakettle of water upstairs. Angus arranged the kettle on a table at the head of Tad's bed, being careful to put it far enough away to prevent accident's from occurring. Nora gave Tad the medicine and changed the cloth on his forehead.

"You go down, love, and have some tea, I'll stay with Tad a while." Nora said.

She was worrying about the possibility this might turn into something worse. It was so frightening to hear Tad's raspy breathing and deep cough. She prayed that the croup would get better.

Tad fell asleep again. Then she heard Caroline fussing. She thought how different her two girls had been as babies. Abby had always awakened with a smile while Caro usually woke up complaining. As she picked her up from the bed, Caro stopped crying. Nora took the baby downstairs, where Dr. Belden was still sitting at the table talking to Victoria.

"Well, daughter, sit down and have your tea now. Angus went to finish up with the sugaring. The doctor was telling me about the Spring Festival the townsfolk are planning." Victoria said.

Nora sat down with Caro on her knees. She looked at her mother's face. There was a new note in Victoria's voice, at least one that Nora had not heard for a long time. She glanced at Dr.

Belden. Why, she thought, these two have found a friend, or could it be more? Why not, she told herself, after all, mother is only fifty-eight; and she had been awfully lonely since Papa died. Nora sat back and listened to the conversation while holding Caro in one arm and sipping tea with her other hand. The other two seemed oblivious to her presence as they went on with their conversation. Nora heard her mother agreeing to help with the Spring Festival. She thought, it will be good for her to get out a little instead of housekeeping and cooking all the time.

The doctor rose to leave and Victoria got his coat from the hall. He went up to look at Tad once more before leaving. When he came down, he reported that Tad looked a little better already.

"His breathing is easier and if you can keep the steam going steady and with the cough medicine, I think he'll be alright. But call me if you need me."

While Victoria cleaned up the tea dishes, Nora finished feeding Caro.

"Dr. Belden is an awfully nice man, isn't he, Mama?" Nora asked.

Her mother gave her a sharp look. "He is that, for true. But don't you be getting any ideas in that noggin of yours, daughter." She rapped Nora gently on the head with the wooden spoon she was holding.

Nora laughed. Her mother knew her too well. Victoria changed the subject.

"Oh, while you were upstairs, Jack came by to give Angus a hand. They'll be famished when they come in. I'd better make a hefty supper. What about a meat pie?" She asked Nora.

But Nora was thinking of something else. She answered Victoria absently. "I'm sure they will like anything you make, Mama. I was just wondering why it is Annie hardly ever comes out here with Jack anymore. I miss her."

Victoria gave her a sharp look. "Well, maybe she doesn't like to see the light in her husband's eyes when he looks at you, my girl."

Nora was startled. "Why, Mama, shame on you! We are all just good friends, that's all." But her cheeks turned a rosy shade.

Victoria chuckled. "Oh, I know you love your husband, I'm only telling you what I observed and perhaps Annie noticed, too."

Nora protested. "But I know Jack loves Annie and he's a good husband. I don't think it's that at all. No, Annie has been disappointed about not having a baby, and when she was here last, she seemed almost jealous about Caro. Perhaps it hurts her to see others with babies."

Victoria, ever practical, said, "Well, I feel sorry for the lass, but she will be seeing them everywhere, so she will have to get used to it. She is still young enough to have a wee bairn. If it's not to be then there are many a poor orphan that needs a good home."

"I feel sorry for her, too, and I miss her coming here. Maybe I could let her take one of ours overnight more often. It might take her think seriously about adopting."

At that moment, Tad could be heard calling for his mother so Nora went upstairs to find that her son was looking a great deal better and was asking for his supper.

Nora was pretty accurate in assessing Annie's feelings. But Annie had decided not to inflict the pain of watching other people's children on herself. She started cultivating only those people who had no children or whose children had already grown. As the wife of one of the most influential men in town, as well as having an engaging personality, she had no trouble making new friends. So she always had an excuse when Jack wanted to go out to Belltrees. And she even avoided going to her sister's whenever she could. She couldn't stand the total quiet in the house, either. She would finish her housework as quickly as possible and then go to the office and work or visit one of her new friends.

Annie also started to spend a lot of time shopping for clothes. Realizing that her sense of style was sometimes not flattering, she depended on the local dressmaker, Mrs. Landry, to choose materials and patterns for her. As they spent a lot of time together discussing these important details, it was natural for Mrs. Landry to confide in Annie her dream of moving to a larger establishment. She would then hire someone to assist her with the sewing so she could expand her clientèle.

A few weeks after that conversation, Annie brought up the subject while she and Jack were having their supper one evening. She explained what Mrs. Landry wanted to do. "Mrs. Landry really is an awfully good seamstress and everyone likes her. I think she could make a good deal of money, especially if she has an assistant and moves to a nicer place."

"I'm sure she could." Jack replied. "But don't a lot of women buy ready made dresses now?"

"Some of them do, for everyday wear. But for special occasions or if women have trouble getting a good fit, they still go to a seamstress, especially if they have the money. Mrs. Landry is awfully busy all the time and sometimes has to turn down an order or postpone it."

"Well, it does sound as if it might pay for her to expand her business. You seem to be really interested in this. Now, tell me, what do you have on your mind?" He had a twinkle in his eye as he looked at her serious face.

Annie laughed. "You know me too well. I was thinking that, if I loaned Mrs. Landry enough money to expand her business, I could be her partner. She would pay me a percentage of her profits. It would be a little business for me and something to keep me busy, too."

Her husband scrutinized her face. It had changed some since their marriage. Her brow, which had been smooth, was now often deeply furrowed and she had lost some of the happy-go-lucky attitude she had before. Jack was sensitive enough to know how deeply she felt about the fact that they hadn't any children as yet. He didn't like to see her unhappy and this venture seemed very important to her. He didn't have the heart to discourage her.

"I see you have thought a great deal about this, my dear. I think you have good judgment and would make a fine businesswoman. But I have a suggestion. Find out exactly what Mrs. Landry needs and then offer to match what she puts in. With you matching her funds, the bank would be willing to loan her what she needs."

Annie jumped up from the chair and for a moment Jack saw the old Annie again. "Oh, thank you, that's a splendid idea!" She gave Jack a big hug.

He laughed at her enthusiasm.

"But since it will be your money, really, do you want to be a partner, too, or just get your money back?" Annie asked seriously.

"I'll settle for you being happy and getting our money back, hopefully with interest." Her husband replied.

"Oh, I'm sure we will. But, of course, I have to talk to Mrs. Landry about it, first."

That lady was actually quite surprised when Annie explained her plan to her. No one had ever paid any attention to her dreams before and she could hardly believe that there was a possibility of them coming true. Once she realized that Annie was serious, Agnes Landry was elated. She had faith in her work and her client list. With the backing of Mrs. Bradshaw, she felt it would be a success.

The following Monday the two woman met at the bank at ten o'clock. They were both feeling pretty nervous. Agnes was going into debt with no real promise of being able to pay it off. If the business was a success, it would mean financial independence for her family, but if the hoped-for clients failed to materialize she would be worse off than before. Her two children depended solely on her for support.

She was on the verge of telling Annie she had changed her mind, when Annie squeezed her arm and whispered. "Don't worry, it's going to work out."

Mr. Patterson, the bank manager, motioned to them to come into his private office.

"It's nice to see you ladies. And what can I do for you today?" He asked, rather expecting them to ask for a donation for some charity.

Agnes explained their plans to him and showed him a prepared statement of expenses they had put together. Mr. Patterson was impressed by the thoroughness of their preparations.

"I can see that you've put a lot of thought into your plan. How can I be of service?" He asked.

He really didn't think too highly of women going into business, but Jack Bradshaw was one of his best clients so anything Annie was connected with deserved respect.

Agnes went on to say that she hoped to borrow five hundred dollars from the bank and that Mrs. Bradshaw would match it to make a thousand dollars.

She continued, "And as you can see we have listed our total expenses to get started as nine hundred and seventy five dollars. This is only for the new location rental and starting salary for Mrs. Small, who will be assisting me in the actual sewing. We have also allowed a certain amount for the purchase of carpet and a few chairs for our waiting and fitting rooms. We expect to attract more of the elite clientele."

Mr. Patterson studied the expense account again. The two women both had butterflies in their stomach's waiting for his decision. Finally he spoke.

"I've known you for several years, Mrs. Landry, and I believe my wife is one of your customers. And since Mrs. Bradshaw is willing to put up some money, I guess we can help you out. I'll have the necessary papers drawn up and you can come back any time tomorrow to sign them and pick up your money."

He stood up and extended his hand to each of them. They both thanked him and Annie gave him her best smile. The two women left the bank with dignity, but once outside they hugged each other with excitement.

"We did it! We're in business! Cried Agnes. "Let's go look at out new store again now we are sure of it."

They spent the rest of the afternoon picking out the carpeting and chairs for the small waiting room and the fitting alcoves. They decided on a soft shade of blue for the carpet with chairs of a darker blue. These were the only items they had to purchase. Annie had two side tables and a library table she would bring. They would use the library table to hold patterns from which the ladies would make their choice of style. Mrs. Small was to bring her own sewing machine with her and everything else needed was brought from Mrs. Landry's former shop. The only other item to pay for was a new sign to hang over the door. It would read "The Ladies Fashion Shop." They were to sell accessories to compliment their fashions, such as parasols, gloves and scarves. If the shop proved a success, they would then include hats as well. Annie was to set up the book keeping system since she had experience with the one at the lumberyard.

From that day on, Annie spent every other day at the shop and the others at the mill helping Jack. There was a lot of time spent on the decorating and preparing the shop so that Annie was often late coming home.

At first, Jack was pleased that his wife was once again her happy self and had stopped brooding. As time went on, however, she seldom had time to prepare the cozy dinners they had shared together before. Sometimes she didn't arrive home until Jack had already eaten a cold meal, reminiscent of his bachelor days.

One evening, when she was late coming home, Jack brought up the subject. As she placed a cold sandwich in front of him, he caught her and pulled her down on his lap. He tried to make a joke of it.

"Now, I have a complaint to make. I miss seeing my wife every evening and I don't like being here by myself. How long before you and Mrs. Landry will be finished with your decorating?"

Annie tousled his hair and laughed. "I miss you, too dear. I'll make it a point to be home from now on. We should be able to finish in a couple of days, then we will just have regular work hours."

She snuggled closer "Mmm, this is nice. I'll just stay right here."

"Fine, but you'll have a starving husband on your hands."

After that, Annie was careful to be home for supper. In spite of his jocular attitude, she recognized that he was serious and she valued her marriage highly.

Getting involved in the shop had served its purpose, though, in that she seldom had time to dwell on her childless state. She didn't realize that it was only a temporary solution.

CHAPTER SEVENTEEN

Nora watched from the kitchen door as Angus, loaded down with milk pails, walked to the barn. A soft spring breeze played around the edge of her long nightdress. She lifted her head to enjoy the fragrance of lilacs in bud and new grass. How she loved spring! It renewed her spirit each year. Just when she thought she couldn't bear to see one more flake of snow or button up one more heavy coat for the children, it happened. The sun would take on new life, the snow melted, all the living things started to come awake. The frogs started croaking from the pond and the horses kicked up their heels in the corral.

And this was the best time of the day for her. She and Angus were the only ones up. The sun was just peeking over the horizon to chase away the night. In a half hour, Victoria would be up and about.

Impulsively, Nora took down an old shawl from the hooks by the door, pushed her feet into some house slippers and went out side. Her black hair hung loose making her look like a little girl. She curled up on the big swing Angus had hung on the porch and tucked the shawl around her. The swing moved gently to and fro.

For minutes she just relaxed and let the spring sounds and smells flow around her. But soon her thoughts turned to all the things that had happened to them since coming to America. How frightened I was, she thought, to leave my family and all the familiar things I had grown up with: my dear sisters, and father.

I never saw him again. A deep sense of loss pervaded her soul, it seemed. She put her head down on her knees as the tears flowed. Into her mind came regrets; I'm so sorry, Papa, that I didn't tell you how much I loved you, that you never saw my children, that you had too short a time, that I'll never see you again.

For a few moments Nora gave herself up to the sadness that had come over her. Then, as quickly as it had overtaken her, Nora's sad mood left her.

She raised her head and looked out over the farm she and Angus had created out of the mess that they had found when they arrived. She thought her father would have loved it here. She smiled at Spot's antics as he attacked a grain sack that had been left hanging over the back of the wheelbarrow.

Then, hearing little voices upstairs; Nora went back into the house. Victoria was already up and about. She had stoked up the fire in the kitchen stove and was mixing up a batch of scones.

Nora scolded her. "Mama, why don't you sleep late on Saturday? The children don't have to go to school and I can make the breakfast."

"I guess I'm just a creature of habit, daughter. My eyes pop open at six every morning. They don't seem to know whether it's Saturday or Sunday or Monday. So there I am. Canna stay in bed with my eyes open, can I?" Victoria said, laughing.

She beat the scones vigorously. Nora shook her head. "I'll run up and change and be right down. I hear the wee ones, too."

Upstairs, three year old Caro was sitting on her big sisters bed and watching Abby as she dressed. Her blond hair was tousled and her big blue-gray eyes took in every move of Abby's. When she saw her mother she squealed with joy and held out her arms. Nora swung the little girl up in her arms. Abby was concentrating on her dressing.

"Good morning, little lasses." said Nora, with amusement. "And what are you dressing up for Abby?"

Her oldest daughter had one of Nora's own aprons tied around her waist and what looked like a white rag tied around her head. She was struggling to adjust it just right.

"I'm a nurse, Mama, like Miss Nightie. I'll take care of Caro and everybody when they get sick." Abby declared.

"Who? A nurse?" Then, trying to keep a straight face, Nora said. "Oh, do you mean Florence Nightingale?"

"Yes, that's what I said, Mama. Miss Peale read us all about her. She wears a white cap and apron, too. But I can't fix this cloth. Can you help me, Mama?"

She leaned on her mother's knee as Nora adjusted it for her.

"I'll help you make a nurses uniform when the work is done. We really need a good nurse around here. C'mon downstairs now. Grandmama has some nice hot breakfast for you."

With the two girls skipping ahead of her, Nora went downstairs where Tad was already eating his crowdies and cream, his favorite. He took seriously the chores he helped his father with every morning when there was no school. Nora smoothed his hair as she passed his chair.

"And how are you this morning, my laddie? As soon as you finish, run and tell your Papa to come for breakfast." Nora told her son.

Gulping his last bite, Tad threw on his jacket and raced out the door.

Nora winked at her mother who was looking askance at Abby's new hair adornment. "See, Mama, we'll have someone to care for you."

"Oh, I see. Well, it's a great relief to know that. And here is a good, hot breakfast for the nurse and her little sister, too." Victoria declared.

While Abby regaled her grandmother with her knowledge of Florence Nightingale, Nora had her morning tea. She watched her oldest daughter as she was talking. Nora was remembering how, whenever one of the animals was injured or under the weather, Abby was always the one to hover around them to help. Even when everyone was well, Abby often did helpful things around the house, without being asked. She has the spirit for it, thought Nora, and it is a worthy thing to be doing. Of course, she may change her mind many times before she is grown, but if she wants to be a nurse, I would be all for it.

After breakfast, finding Caro an uncooperative patient, Abby went out to the barnyard to find Spots and bandage him. Spots let her know how he felt about it by pushing her into a lilac bush.

Nora, who was watching from the kitchen window, laughed so hard that she had to sit down. Victoria looked at her with raised eyebrows.

Wiping the tears from her eyes, Nora explained; "I was just watching our nurse trying to put a bandage on Spots. He dumped her into the lilac bush."

"She is determined lass, that daughter of yours," said Victoria. "A lot like her mother, at her age."

"Maybe," Nora spoke pensively. "It just seems that they all are growing up awfully fast. This one is three now."
She stroked Caro's blond hair as the toddler sat playing on the floor with some pans. "It was just the other day she was born, at least that's the way it feels. But so many things have happened since we came here."

Victoria nodded. "You've a lot to be thankful for, lassie; three healthy bairns, a good husband and a comfortable home.

Oh, I know you've had some bad times, too, and it's proud I am the way you've handled them."

This was high praise from her mother, who rarely spoke of her inner feelings and Nora felt a lump in her throat. Before tears could form, she jumped up and started to clear the breakfast dishes.

"It would have been a lot harder if you hadn't been here Mama, especially when we lost our baby and when Angus was attacked by the bear." Nora shuddered. "Those were the bad times."

"I'm glad I was here, too, lass. I just wish I could have done more for Hannah when she lost her Danny. The poor soul, she is still in mourning."

"I'm sure one never gets over something like that, no more than we will ever forget our baby. But you did all you could at the time." Nora sympathized.

Hannah and Tom Murphy's second oldest son, Danny, had gone to Panama to work on the canal that was being built. While there, he had contracted malaria and died. It had been terrible blow to the Murphys to whom their sons were their most precious possessions.

At the time, Victoria had gone to her cousin and spent a week with her. Hannah had scarcely responded to her solicitude. She seemed to have wrapped herself in a cocoon of despondency no one could penetrate. She had never quite returned to her old jovial self.

Victoria kept on writing lively letters to Hannah, though she seldom received an answer. At the moment, Victoria's thoughts turned to her other two daughters.

"I've been longing to see Molly and Mairi of late. I'm thinking that if they can't come here I will go over this fall for a visit. Their bairns are getting all grown and I would like to see them."

Nora felt a twinge of guilt for keeping her mother to herself all this time.

"Oh, Mama, of course you should. I'd dearly love to see them, too. But I can't leave here for some time yet. Maybe they will come. Why don't you write today and ask them."

Before Victoria could mail her letter to her daughters, she received one from Molly. She and Mairi had decided to make a visit to the States. They would all come expect for Molly's two oldest boys. They would plan to be in Vermont in mid-July and return the second week in August.

Nora and Victoria were filled with excitement. They started immediately to make plans. It was time to do the spring-cleaning, anyway, so that would come first. Then deciding where everyone would sleep and preparing the rooms would take some time. Perhaps some of them could stay at Harrison and Clara's.

There would be seven people all together. Mairi had two young ones, a girl and a boy. Molly had only one boy that would be coming. There was so much to plan. Nora's head was swimming. Finally, she got her mother to sit down and make out a list of what needed doing and in what sequence. After that she felt a little calmer, as did her mother.

Angus, too, was delighted at the prospect of seeing family from Scotland again. He was genuinely fond of Nora's sisters and had been good friends with his brothers-in-law. It pleased him to see how happy Nora and Victoria were. He knew that Victoria had been very lonesome at times.

The McDonald's still did not have a telephone, so Victoria went over to the Renfrew's to tell them the good news. Sadie Thorne came to the door. Sadie and Victoria had become good friends and the two greeted each other with pleasure. Sadie took her into the study where Clara was knitting by the fireplace and Harrison was going over some papers. Clara asked Sadie to bring them all some tea. But before she even sat down, Victoria blurted out her news.

The faces of her brother and sister-in-law reflected her own pleasure.

"It will be wonderful to have them all here and hear all about our friends in Lochwinnoch." said Clara. Her eyes twinkled in anticipation. "Oh, Harrison, we must plan a barbecue while they are here."

Just then Sadie came in with the tea tray.

Harrison wheeled his chair up to the table to be with the rest of them. He didn't have to stay in the wheelchair all the time now; he was able to pull himself around leaning on a special walker that Claude had designed for him. It was slower than the chair but he felt better being in a standing position. The doctor was amazed that Harrison had improved to this degree.

If the truth were known, his determination to walk again could be attributed to his love for his grandson. Harrison felt a strong sense of duty to the child to make up to him the loss of his mother and his father's indifference. This void in the little boy's life was more or less filled by Harrison, who made himself always available to the boy.

Claude, too, helped. He had been instructed by Harrison to take the boy under his wing and teach him all he needed to know about the farm life. The Renfrew's knew Claude to be honest and trustworthy man. Consequently, the little boy could often be found close by Claude as the foreman went about his duties.

Supleen, who disliked Claude, did not interfere; perhaps because he knew that as a father, he was sadly remiss. He also knew that Claude was Harrison's trusted friend as well as employee. Supleen didn't dare to anger his father any further.

Supleen spent his time in town once his chores on the farm were finished. His evenings were spent in Ginny's private apartment.

Because of her lifestyle, there was no question of his ever marrying her but their relationship was more like a marriage than he'd had with Zoë.

Over the years, he had overheard a few rumors about Zoë's whereabouts but he didn't feel consumed by his anger as he had before. Supleen had never bothered to get a divorce and had never been notified that Zoë had either.

Only when he thought of Zoë did the black anger surface. He rarely did think of her now but his small son reminded him of his wife, which made him feel uncomfortable. He had a certain feeling for the boy which Supleen hardly recognized as affection but he didn't know how to act with him so didn't seek him out.

He was interested in what the boy was doing and sometimes talked to Clara about little Harry. At her suggestion, Supleen occasionally spent time with his son, but little Harry sensed that Supleen was uncomfortable so it wasn't successful. They both felt strained with one another.

While the adults were planning the barbecue one day, the three young cousins were in the Renfrew's barn brushing down the horses. Now that they were getting older, they were allowed to walk back and forth between the two farms. Tad was ten and could ride his filly over, but the two seven year olds could only ride around their own homes. The three spent a lot of time together and had fun making up games together. Once in a while, the two boys would try to exclude Abby from certain activity on the grounds that she was a girl, but she usually ignored them and tagged along anyway.

This day Abby's horse was home so she was helping the two boys groom their horses. Abby lamented the fact that the coming visitors were not her age.

"I wish someone would come to visit that could play with me. Everybody is older than I am except Caro and she's no fun.

She only wants to play dress up or house. I want to play nurse; I think I'll ask mama if I can go over to Aunt Mattie's and play with Katie."

Tad, feeling magnanimous, reassured his sister. "Don't feel bad, Abby, you can still stick around with me and Harry. We don't mind, right, Harry?"

"Sure," Harry responded, but his mind was on something else. His stomach was telling him it was teatime.

"Let's go in the house and see what kind of cookies grandmama has for tea. I'm hungry."

In the library, the children found the grownups talking about the barbecue. This was something they could be a part of. A barbecue was an excuse for inviting every one, friends and neighbors as well as relatives. There would be a great many children coming with their parents. It was going to be a fine summer.

For the next couple of months, there was plenty for everyone to do. Besides the regular planting chores and care of the animals, the house had to be spruced up and readied for the guests.

Nora put Abby to work giving the wicker porch furniture a fresh coat of white paint. She did a good job, with only a little help from her mother.

Tad was needed to help his father in the fields.

Angus had also hired one of Cecile's younger brothers, a short, muscular lad named Nate. The workload had increased considerably since Angus had bought the farm. He was now tapping forty more trees for the maple syrup and every spring had expanded the vegetable garden as well as the wheat planting. He usually had extra grain to sell to other farmers or the feed to store in town. The wood lot was growing nicely but it would be several more years before any cutting could be done.

Both Clara and Jack offered their homes to put up some of Angus and Nora's coming guests. It was decided that one of the visiting couples could stay at the Renfrew's and the others would stay at Belltrees.

None of the visitors had ever met Jack and Annie. Nora thought her sisters might be uncomfortable staying with strangers. Besides, Nora knew that her sisters would want to be near their mother for the little time they were going to be in Vermont.

CHAPTER EIGHTEEN

The arrival day dawned clear and warm, a beautiful July day in Vermont. Wild roses bloomed everywhere. In the fields the pink and white of clover mingled with the orange-tipped devil's paintbrushes and yellow buttercups.

The McDonald and Renfrew households had been awake before dawn. There was much hustle and bustle as last minute preparations were finished.

It had been decided that they would need two carriages, since nearly everyone wanted to go to the train station. Only Clara and Harrison would wait at home. So Claude was to drive a double-seated wagon to have room for the luggage. Angus would drive the family in their own carriage. They could all split up coming home.

The train was due to arrive at twelve but the family was at the station at eleven in case the train should be early. Angus, Nora, and Claude paced the platform. The children explored the station and pretended they were going on a long trip. Victoria sat quietly on a bench, clasping and unclasping her hands.

When they finally heard the far-off rumble of the train and then the whistle there was a great scrambling among the children to see who would be first in line. Angus collared the boys and made them all stand back so that the passengers could have room to leave the train. Nora guided her mother to the front so she could be the first to greet her daughters.

Victoria gave a little cry when Mairi and then Molly appeared first, surrounded by their children and followed closely by their husbands. There was a flurry of hugs and kisses mingled with happy tears. Everyone spoke at once, expect for the children, who didn't remember any of these relatives. They watched with interest, until they were finally brought forward and introduced with pride by their parents.

Tad and Abby shook hands solemnly, but Caro clung to her mother's hand. Little Harry was also introduced, as Harrison's grandson. He got his share of hugs, too.

They finally divided up for the ride home. All the boys chose to pile into the back of the wagon that Claude was driving, with the luggage. The two girls sat up front with Claude. Angus and his two brothers-in-law took the second seat. The four women squeezed together in the McDonald's carriage, with Nora driving. Caro sat on Angus' lap.

The boys were soon chatting together noisily, but the two girls, Abby and Katrine, were quiet. They cast shy glances at each other. Katrine was three years older than Abby but being on her cousin's home ground took away some of her confidence. As for Abby, she thought Katrine was beautiful with her long black hair halfway down her back, her pink cheeks and bright blue eyes.

But soon her natural friendliness won over her shyness. She asked Katrine about her school in Scotland and Katrine responded by questioning Abby about Vermont schools and they were soon at ease with each other.

Claude, who had been observing the inter-action between the girls, chuckled to himself and snapped the reins to cover his amusement.

Among the adults, questions flew back and forth. The McDonald's asked their guests about their trip from Scotland. Mairi's husband Colum wanted to know what kind of crops Angus was growing. James, the quieter one, listened with interest. Mairi and Molly wanted to hear how their mother had been and what she had been doing since they last saw her.

At the Renfrew's, Clara met them at the door with her husband right behind her, leaning on his walker. No guests could have felt more welcome. Clara's cheeks were flushed with excitement. She herded them all inside.

"Come in and rest yourselves. We'll bring in the luggage later. We'll have an early tea. I'm sure the young ones are famished. Nora will show you women where Molly and James' room is so you can freshen up. Come down when you're ready."

Then Harrison led the way into the parlor with the rest of the party. Tad, Alex, and Albert would share Harry's room, as it was very large. Katrine would stay at the McDonald's with her parents. She and Abby would share the room Abby and Caro used. Tad's room was prepared for Mairi and Colum

The adults, replete with the sumptuous meal the housekeeper had prepared, were relaxing in the parlor. There was so much news to catch up on. Although letters had gone back and forth to Scotland, there was so much that hadn't been in the letters. The small details about the fire and the accident that had crippled Uncle Harrison, for instance.

"'Twas a fair miracle that you got out of it alive, Uncle," said Colum.

Harrison put his hand on Angus' shoulder. "If not for this lad." he said. "I wouldn't be here, for a fact. He came along and saved me, he did."

"And you don't know how the fire started?" James asked.

Before his uncle could answer, Angus spoke up. "No! It's a puzzle, but we're mighty glad no one was killed."

To himself, James thought, there's more here than meets the eye. He decided to find out more for himself. A thought occurred to him. He turned to his Aunt Clara.

"And where is Supleen? I've never met him. Nor has Colum" James inquired.

An uneasy look crossed Clara's face, but she answered brightly.

"Oh, he'll be here anytime. He has a lot of business in town."

At this point, Angus stood up, holding out his hand to Nora. "Com' n, love, its time these weary travelers went to bed."

In truth, they were all pretty tired. After promising to see each other early in the morning, the McDonald's took their leave, taking Mairi, Colum and Katrine with them.

Arriving at Belltrees, Colum and Angus went to the barn to put up the horses and do the evening chores. The others went into the house to get the three girls ready for bed.

Nora, pleased to have her sister with her at last, proudly took Mairi from room to room, telling her how it looked when they first moved in. The number of rooms impressed Mairi.

"Oh, my, Nora, this is so grand. No wonder you are so happy here!" Mairi said.

Nora beamed with pleasure. She squeezed her sister's arm. "It would be perfect if only you and Molly lived here, too."

"I would like to, Nora, but there are so many things tying us to Scotland. You know Colum's mother is not well, and he would hate to leave his Da to care for her alone."

"Oh, I didn't know. But we can talk more about it later. Right now, we better see what those little lassies are doing."

Gales of laughter were coming from Abby's bedroom. As the two mothers came in, they saw Abby and Katrine throwing pillows at each other while Caro, in her crib, clapped her hands and laughed.

Nora and Mairi just stood and watched for a while, enjoying the sight of their daughters having fun together. Victoria came in, wondering what all the noise was.

After a few moments, Nora called a halt, seeing her youngest daughter rubbing her eyes.

"All right now, lassies, its time for Caro to get to sleep. Mairi, would you take these two to the kitchen for a bite to eat while I get Caro settled?"

When the little girls were finally in bed, the two men returned from the barn and they all had coffee and apple dumplings Victoria had made. They all had so much to tell each other.

Victoria was content to bask in the presence of her daughters and their husbands. She had been more lonesome than she had ever told Nora. Mairi sat close to her mother.

"It's been too long since I tasted your apple dumplings, Mama. They are as good as I remembered. Now, you're looking a bit tired, love. And it's time we all went to bed. I'm sure the little ones will be up with the birds."

The women went up and the two men soon followed.

"I'll be up to help with the chores, Angus." Declared Colum.

"I'll sure be pleased to have you, if you're not too tired." Angus replied. "Then I can show you around the farm."

Angus took the lamp from the table and led the way upstairs.

The first few days passed quickly. There were the usual chores to do and so much talking to catch up on. The four families went back and forth between the two farms, just enjoying each other's company.

The children were constantly busy. The four boys, Albert, Alex, Tad and Harry, all helped to muck out the stables at the Renfrew's barn. Tad took them to his favorite fishing place. Harry and Alex were allowed to go only if the older boys promised to look after them. They actually brought back five catfish, which the housekeeper cooked for their lunch.

Abby and Katrine, with Caro trailing, were doing all the things little girls do. They played dress-up with some old clothes Nora had saved for that purpose. When the two older girls decided to go outside, they moved too fast for Caro's chubby legs to keep up. She sat herself down and screamed in frustration until they came back and waited for her.

Each day Molly would come to Nora's house or Mairi, Nora and Victoria would go to Clara's so that no time would be wasted.

They all spent one day looking over the McDonald's farm. Angus showed them where he made the maple syrup. They were each given some to take back to Scotland with them. James and Colum listened attentively as Angus explained the process of making the syrup from tapping the trees to the finished product.

Then they went to view the site of the fire in the wood lot. Blackened stumps and fallen trees were still visible through the new growth.

Colum, his curiosity aroused, turned to Angus and asked, "Does no one know what started the fire? I had a feeling last night that Uncle Harrison at least suspected that someone started it."

"Well, we don't know really. If uncle suspects it was started by someone we know, he never spoke to me about it."

The subject was dropped. But a short while later, as they were still walking around the wood lot, James spoke up.

"What's wrong with Cousin Supleen? We met him the other night and he's downright lacking in manners. He was barely civil to us."

Angus was slow to reply. "I'm not sure what is wrong with him. He treats us the same way. Nora thinks he is jealous of the attention his parents pay to us and the fact that Harrison loaned me the money to buy the farm."

Nora added, "He is very upset, too, about Zoë leaving. I wrote you what happened."

"That was upsetting, truly, but it was no fault of ours. He makes us feel like intruders instead of relatives." James replied.

"I know," said Angus. "But for the sake of Clara and Harrison, we try to ignore his attitude. That's all we can do."

Molly spoke up. "I know Aunt Clara and Harrison want us here. They enjoy the children so. I wouldn't want to hurt them for the world. Supleen doesn't seem to be around very much, anyway."

James said, "Well, we don't intend to let him spoil our visit. I for one will be pleasant to him. He can do what he likes."

The subject of Supleen was dropped by common consent, but Colum vowed to himself, to find out more about his strange cousin.

A picnic was planned for Thursday, to be held near the brook. It was the perfect spot. The children could go swimming in the pool that had been made by damming up a small area with large rocks. The women cooked or made cold salads to bring. The picnic was planned for the noon meal so the men could be between chores and could take off for an hour or two.

It was a perfect July afternoon. Everyone got wet, even Victoria, who took off her shoes and dangled her feet in the cold water.

Tad was quite taken with his cousin, Katrine. He had never seen such a pretty girl and she liked to play ball and swim, too. He asked her if she wanted to go fishing with him and the other boys the next day.

But Nora had planned to take her sisters and the younger children to visit with Mattie and Annie. She was anxious to have her sisters meet her two best friends.

Her friends were just as eager to meet Nora's sisters but had not wanted to intrude during the first few days of the visit. So they had invited the McDonald's and their guests for a special lunch. The women and children could come, but because it was the middle of the haying season, the men would stay behind to help Angus. They would all meet at the barbecue on Sunday.

The lunch was at Mattie's house. She and Annie had arranged things so that the children would eat at a table on the porch, to make it seem like a picnic. The women would have their lunch in the dining room, from where they could also keep an eye on the porch.

Mairi and Molly both liked Nora's Vermont friends and they were soon chatting as though they'd known each other for years. Nora was pleased and proud of her family.

It was pretty quiet, at first, at the children's table. Tad and the other boys were not pleased at giving up a day of fishing to have to go visiting. Albert felt that he was too old to be here with the little kids.

Then Andy told them about the big turtles in their pond and offered to show them to the visitors, so the boys became more interested. Also, the lunch was delicious. They all had a good laugh when Harry reached for his lemonade and knocked over his plate of salad. Some of it landed on Alec's dish. He picked it up and threw it back to Harry, who tossed it in Tad's direction. The girls screamed and before it became a full-fledged food fight, Annie came out and restored order.

After the lunch, Andy took the boy's to see the turtles. Mattie's husband, Andrew, was working in the field near the pond, so she felt comfortable leaving them. Albert was told he was responsible for the younger ones, as well.

While the boy's were gone, Annie took the women and girls to see her shop. They were all interested in the latest fashions and Annie was proud to bring out her best.

Mairi and Molly exclaimed over the tastefully decorated shop. Katrine and the other girls were allowed to look at some finished girls dresses and tried on a few. There were many cries of, "Oh, Mama, I love this. Could I have one like it, please?"

When Annie offered to let Katrine have a dress for just the price of the materials, Mairi bought it for her. When the other girls begged to be given one as well, they were told they would have to wait until later. Katrine would soon be going back to Scotland; she could take her dress with her.

When they got back to Mattie's house, they found five mud-covered boys sprawled on the grass. They had gone to see the turtles and somehow got into a mud slinging game.

Sunday, the day of the barbecue, started out cloudy. Everyone was afraid it was going to rain but Claude declared it would be a beautiful day. He was right.

Pits had been dug in which a pig was being roasted on a spit. Potatoes were buried in coals and covered with leaves and hay to slow bake. On long, covered tables scores of dishes were mounded high with fresh vegetables and fruits and breads, all covered with cloths.

By noontime delicious, mouthwatering odors were wafting about the Renfrew's farm. All the men had been working since dawn to have everything ready.

Soon people began to arrive. The family was the first to come but soon friends from all over drove in, all dressed in their best. The ladies wore calicos or sprigged muslin.

They had each brought their favorite dessert so all sweet-tooth's would be satisfied. They would be stored in the cool pantry until later, when they would be served with tea or coffee.

The children were bursting with excitement. Anticipating this, Claude had designated a certain area, well away from the food, where the youngsters could play.

At one o'clock, Uncle Harrison called for everyone to be seated. Then he asked the guests from Scotland to stand. He spoke solemnly.

"I want you all to know my nieces and nephews from Scotland. This barbecue is in their honor."

He introduced them each by name, making Mairi and Molly blush and shy James turn a beet red. But Harrison went on.

"I think you'll all have a good time. Eat hearty. There will be fiddlin' later with dessert."

There was a loud clapping. The Scottish guests were glad to be out of the spotlight.

For the next couple of hours, everyone stuffed themselves with the huge feast. Soon some were stretched upon the ground to rest. Blankets had been spread for the ladies and smaller children.

By four o'clock, some were ready to participate in the planned games. There were the usual; the three-legged race, the bag race (a person puts both feet into a burlap bag and attempts to run to the finish line), as well as a horseshoe contest.

Harrison had also planned some Scottish games, new to the Vermonters. The caber throw, to see how far a heavy log could be thrown; and one for the ladies in which each was asked to see how far she could throw a rolling pin. Only the bravest ladies would try it, amid much laughter from the onlookers. There were contests for the children, too, and Harrison had a prize for each winner.

At five o'clock, two men took up their violins and played, at first sweet, slow tunes, then later, faster songs for dancing. Many couples joined in and soon most of them were dancing.

When the fiddlers took a rest, Uncle Harrison surprised them all by having Claude bring out his bagpipes for him. He played some haunting, Scottish melodies for them. Most of the company had never heard bagpipes before. Many liked the sound, though a few of the children covered their ears at the unusual sounds. Those of the Scottish heritage had tears in their eyes.

By eight o'clock, friends started taking their leave, with their sleepy offspring. The McDonalds stayed to help with cleaning up.

James, extremely moved by the whole occasion, sat down beside his Uncle and Aunt.

"I just want to tell you what a wonderful day this has been for me and for all of my family. We will have an unforgettable memory."

This, from quiet James, brought a lump to Harrison's throat. He could only put out his hand and shake James' hand vigorously. But Aunt Clara gave her nephew a big hug.

"Twas our pleasure, for sure, to have all you young people here. A rare blessing!" she said.

At that moment, Colum joined the group and started to express his gratitude for their hospitality.

Aunt Clara patted his hand, saying, "Dear boy, I was just telling James, here, that we enjoyed the day more than any of you."

Uncle Harrison agreed, adding, "Now, it seems to be getting a bit damp out. Would one of you lads give us a hand to the house?"

With James pushing the wheelchair and Colum escorting his Aunt, they made their way inside. It was a slow progress as the relatives and friends, who were still there, came up in two's or three's to thank the host and hostess for the festivities and take their leave.

Then Nora and Angus with Mairi and Colum left to put their young ones to bed.

Back at the farm, Katrine and Abby were dispatched to the bedroom while Mairi fixed some warm milk for the children. Nora prepared Caro for bed. When the mothers went up to the bedroom, Abby and Katrine were having another pillow fight. As it was getting late, the girls were admonished to be quiet as Caro needed to go to sleep.

Nora and Mairi went downstairs to enjoy a last cup of coffee and conversation with Angus and Colum.

The next few days seemed to fly by. Katrine and Abby were allowed to go fishing with the boys on Wednesday. Albert would supervise and see that no one fell into the pond.

Tad was pleased that Katrine would be going. He spent most of his time helping her bait her hook and giving her advice on how to catch a fish. But the fish were not cooperating. Only Albert had caught anything and it was too small to keep. So they headed for home in time for the noonday meal.

They had a grand time on the way back playing follow the leader, with Albert in the lead. He balanced on fallen logs, crawled through underbrush and turned somersaults. By the time they reached the house they all needed a change of clothes.

The day when the visitors had to leave came all too soon. The family was all gathered at the train station. Dr. Belden, Jack and Annie were there, too. Even the children were subdued.

Tad shyly offered Katrine his favorite slingshot. "Here," he said. "You can keep this if you want to." Blushing, Katrine took it saying only murmured thanks.

As the train whistle sounded, they all started talking at once, giving last minute instructions. Then, in a flurry of hugs and kisses, the travelers boarded the train and were gone. Hands waved out of the train windows as long as they could be seen.

Then the ones left behind, some of them with damp eyes, silently turned toward home. Annie and Jack were invited to the farm for dinner, as well as Dr. Belden. They waited while the doctor checked with his housekeeper, in case anyone was in need of his services. There were no messages, so they all continued back to the farm.

It was an overcast day, matching the mood of the family. On the way home, it started to drizzle.

Nora tried to lighten everyone's spirits by making a special dinner she knew her mother liked. Victoria, though a tear occasionally found its way down her cheek, bustled about helping.

The men wandered out to the barn, as usual, while Abby, Tad and Harry sat on the back steps, not knowing what to do with themselves. That is, until Victoria came to the door and interrupted their moping.

"C'mon, now, you three get busy and feed the chickens and Spot, too. There's plenty to be done around here for everybody. Get along, now." Then she added, "When you're finished with that, tell the men and you all come in to eat."

Victoria was a great believer in keeping busy to take your mind off your troubles.

Jack, Annie and the doctor kept the conversational ball rolling during the meal and soon the others joined in.

It would be several days before the lonely feelings would wear off and everyone was absorbed in the old routine.

CHAPTER NINETEEN

Charles Belden had been a lonely man since the death of his wife, ten years ago. His only child, a girl, was married and living in New York State, where her husband had been brought up. She had two children who Charles doted on, but seldom saw. They would usually come to visit him for a week about once a year and he went to their home for one of the holidays.

Since his wife died, several of the townswomen had set her cap for the good doctor. But, for whatever reason, none of them had appealed to him.

When he met Victoria, however, it wasn't long before Charles decided here was a woman he could live with. At that time, though, Victoria's husband hadn't been gone very long and he could see that she was not ready to let another man in to her life.

So for a year or so he hadn't let her know how he felt. Then, when he finally proposed, Victoria insisted that Nora needed her too much, especially after Angus' encounter with the bear, so she couldn't leave her.

The truth was, Victoria wasn't sure how she felt about the doctor.

The evening that the visitors from Scotland left, Charles decided to have another talk with Victoria. She had always seen him to the door whenever he came to the house. Now, after saying goodbye to the rest of the family, Charles turned to Victoria.

"Will you come outside with me for a bit, Victoria? I need to talk to you for a moment."

At the look on his face, she wasn't surprised when he brought up the subject of marriage again. They sat on the porch swing.

"I've been asking you to marry me for two years now, Victoria." As she held up a protesting hand, he caught it in his own. "I know you think Nora can't get along with out you. I do think you underestimate her, but, I have a plan I'd like you to listen to." He paused for a moment, and then, as she said nothing, he went on. "I've already spoken to Angus about leasing me a small piece of land where we could build a house. That way you wouldn't be far away in case Nora needs you and yet we could have our own place. What do you say, my dear?"

Victoria drew a deep breath. "I think I'm ready to get married now, Charles, not just because of your plan. Because Angus has recovered pretty well from his accident and I think they can get along for now. Most importantly, I do love you, Charles, and think we have both been alone long enough."

For a moment Dr. Belden was speechless; he really hadn't expected such an easy victory.

"Do you mean it? I can't believe it!" He jumped to his feet, grabbing her hand and pulling her up. Then he spoke gently, "We'll be happy together, my love." He held her closely for a few minutes. Then he said. "C'mon, let's go and tell everyone, now."

The family and Jack and Annie were still chatting around the kitchen table when the doctor and Victoria returned to the room. When Charles made the announcement, everyone jumped up to come over and congratulate the pair. There was even a toast made, with a bottle of Scotch Whiskey that Angus and Nora had brought from Scotland with them, kept for just such a special occasion.

Nora had mixed feelings about her mother's plans. It had been so pleasant having her around when she needed to talk to her. At least she won't be far away, Nora mused, and after all she needs to have a life of her own. And the whole family liked Doctor Belden.

Victoria was already writing to Molly and Mairi to tell them of her plans. She was a little nervous about their reaction, although they had all seemed to like Dr. Belden. She didn't think her children realized how close she and the doctor had become.

Victoria needn't have worried because both of her daughter's wrote their congratulations and good wishes for their mother's happiness. Victoria's eyes filled with tears as she read the loving notes.

She decided to ask Charles if they could go to Scotland for their honeymoon. When she told him about it he was as excited as she was about it.

After much discussion, they decided to wait until spring to make the trip as it would be well into the fall when the house would be finished. Winter travel would not be pleasant so they settled on early May for the trip. The weather in Scotland would be perfect then.

Nora was amazed at the change in her mother; she had a glow about her as she went about her work.

"Why," Nora said to Aunt Clara one day. "I assumed that Mother was perfectly contented with us but now she seems to be really happy. I guess I was only looking at it from my point of view."

Her aunt laughed. "Don't blame yourself, lass, we all are guilty of the same thing. And the closer we are to a person the harder it is to be truly aware of the other's feelings, it seems."

This new development served to take the family's minds off the departure of their relatives. Building on the new house began in the second week of August. Doctor Belden planned to keep his office in town because it was well equipped for minor surgery and more convenient for most of his patients.

Tad, Harry and Abby spent hours watching the men work on the house. It was fascinating to watch it grow from bare ground and develop into a home. The house would have only four rooms finished, with a second floor, which would be finished off later if Victoria and Charles wanted more room. They would install a telephone, of course, so that patients could reach the doctor, if necessary.

Nora and Clara began to plan a party for the engaged couple. They would invite all the neighbors and friends that knew Victoria. Of course, the whole country knew Charles, but the party would be just for those who were good friends.

As for Victoria, she went about doing all the same things she had done for Nora's family since she moved to Vermont.

Although she enjoyed doing for them, she started looking forward to having her own little place again. Her thoughts were busy with plans to make the house a comfortable haven for them both.

This is strange, she thought to herself, I had never even thought of marrying again, and now it seems so natural. I still miss my William but I don't think he would want me to be alone forever.

The house was scheduled to be completed about the last of October. So the wedding was planned for the first weekend in November. It was to be a small one at their church in town, with a reception held at Belltrees afterward.

When Victoria told Clara about their plans, however, Clara had a different idea.

"Why don't we have the reception at our house, Victoria? We have plenty of room. And Nora has her hands full with the children. I would love to do it!" Clara exclaimed.

Victoria exchanged glances with Nora. "What do you think, Nora? She asked. Is that alright with you?"

"I think it would be just fine, mother. It's awfully nice of you, Aunt Clara."

"Nonsense! I'll love it. Now, tell me how many you want and we'll start with the invitations."

In fact, Nora was a little relieved, as it had seemed like a lot to do as well as planning the wedding. Christmas was coming soon, too. Now she could leave the plans for the reception to her Aunt and Mother. There was still plenty to do.

At least, now, Abby was old enough to help entertain Caro sometimes, leaving Nora more time to do other things. She would really miss Victoria when she moved; she was so good with the little ones.

Victoria's only attendant would be Nora, with the two little girls acting as flower girls. Annie volunteered to have her dressmaker make them matching dresses of red velvet. Tad vehemently rejected the idea of a blue velvet suit.

Nora was thoughtful; she had always thought of ways to change something on one of her dresses to make it look different for a special occasion. Anyway, there was seldom any money left for clothing for the grownups only for the necessities for the children.

Then she had remembered some things she had packed away which had been given her for her own wedding. She hurried to find them.

Here, in the bottom of her trunk, were some lengths of material. As she recalled, someone had given her a length of royal blue velvet and several yards of royal taffeta. This is perfect, Nora thought. I can make the top in the velvet and the skirt in the taffeta. It will take a while, though. Maybe Sadie would help.

Victoria and Charles were stunned at how their simple wedding ceremony had grown.

One evening Charles had stopped by to visit after attending a patient. They sat in the kitchen drinking a cup of tea, while Nora was getting the children to bed. Angus was doing the milking. Nora had finished telling Charles about the plans that Clara and Nora had worked out. He shook his head in wonder.

"Whatever happened to our idea for a small wedding?" He asked.

Victoria laughed. "That's what happens when we women start thinking about weddings. But don't worry, dear, it'll be all right. Let them have their fun. They're doing it because they care for us."

She hugged him. Charles relaxed.

"It's fine with me." He said. "I'd like the whole world to see us get married."

Angus came in from the barn, pulling his gloves off and blowing on his hands.

"I think it's going to be a cold winter. Feels like snow in the air." he said.

Dr. Belden chuckled. "That's the only kind we have here, son. You aren't used to it yet?"

Angus grinned sheepishly. "Well, I keep hoping for something different. But you are right; I haven't seen a warm one yet. Where's Nora?"

"She's up with the bairns," said his mother-in-law. She should be right down."

She rose and poured two cups of tea and handed one to Angus. She covered the other one with a saucer to keep it warm for Nora.

"Warm yourself with this and I'll give you some fresh scones".

At that moment, Nora appeared in the door. She felt of Angus' cold cheek.

"Winter's starting early, as usual." She commented.

The four spent a companionable hour chatting about the coming winter and the wedding.

Going up to their room later, Nora snuggled close to her husband.

"It's going to be lonesome without Mama when she goes." She said.

Angus folded her in his arms tightly, saying, "I'll be here, love."

The house was finished almost on schedule. The wedding was held in the local church on a blustery, snowy day. Still, the church was almost filled with family and friends.

Afterward, they all went to the Renfrew's for the reception. There was a lot of good food and Uncle Harrison even played his bagpipes for the occasion.

Because of the weather, the party broke up about seven o'clock and the newly married couple went to their new home.

Later, when Nora was getting the children ready for bed Caro asked her mother in a plaintive voice, "Isn't Grandmamma ever coming back, mama?"

Her small lip was trembling. Nora hugged her close.

"Of course, baby, she is only a little ways away. She will be here often to see us and you can walk over to her house with Abby to visit her, too." Nora reassured Caro as she pulled her nightgown over her tousled head.

Then Abby chimed in. "Don't worry, Caro, I'll take you over to see Grandmama every day if you want to."

Caro smiled and jumped up and down on the bed. "Oh, boy, Oh, boy! Oh boy!" She chanted until her mother captured her and tucked her into bed.

But as Nora went downstairs the house felt a little empty. She put some more wood on the fire as she waited for Angus to come in from the barn.

When he came in she was working on some mittens for Abby. She poured him some tea. As she came near him, he caught her hand.

"Lonesome?" he asked.

Nora laid her cheek on his hand. Suddenly she didn't feel so lonely.

"Not now, love. I have you and the wee ones, and soon maybe one more," she said.

Startled, Angus put his cup down quickly and looked at his wife.

"Are you sure, Nora? He asked.

Nora laughed at his surprised expression. "Pretty sure, do you mind, love?" She answered.

Angus pulled her down onto his lap. "Not likely, we need some more men to help on the farm."

"There are no guarantees, you know. It might be another wee lassie." Nora said.

"Just as long as she is healthy and you take care of yourself. Abby and Tad are old enough to help you a little more now."

"I'll be just fine." she replied.

Angus pulled her to her feet. "I'll see to that," he said. "Right now, it's off to bed with you, lass."

Nora went upstairs, while Angus banked the fires for the night and turned out the lamps. He stopped a couple of times to rub his bad arm. It had been bothering him a lot of late, since the cold weather had begun. He just hoped it wouldn't get any worse.

It was a long, cold winter that year, with the snowstorms coming one after the other. Angus had strung a rope between the house and barn to be a guide in case of heavy snow. It came in handy more than once. Tad was a great help to his father this year, taking a lot of pride in his chores.

The children didn't go to their grandmother's house as often as they would have liked because some one needed to accompany them in the deep snow and often their mother and father were too busy. A few times Tad went with them.

Victoria did come over two or three times a week. Nora and she were sewing for the expected baby in their free time.

Abby and Tad were excited about the coming addition, but Caro was less enthusiastic. She wasn't sure she wanted to share her mother with another baby.

Nora and Victoria tried to make her feel better by including her in helping prepare for the new one. There was plenty of time for her to get used to the idea, anyway. The baby would be born about the first of August or the last of July.

It was April before sugaring could begin that year. Nora was getting a bit awkward by this time, but she hated to miss the fun of collecting the sap and watching it turn into syrup in the big vats. So she bundled up the girls and accompanied Angus and Tad a few times, but more often Tad and his father went alone.

It was a good year for maple syrup and they had a rewarding harvest. Angus was grateful and was optimistic that this year he would be able, finally, to pay off his mortgage. Each year, it seemed, some expense had come up that prevented him from making extra payments. Sometimes it had been a strain just to make one.

It would still be a couple of years before he could start selling wood again.

Things had been slow at Jack's mill this winter, but he still found some work for Angus in the store when things slowed down at the farm.

Nora and Tad would milk the cow and feed the animals when Angus worked at the lumber mill.

Abby was a great help at watching Caro at play in the house while her mother was busy. She liked it better, though, when she was allowed to help tend the animals. A born nurturer, she lavished attention on them all, petting and brushing, watering and feeding them. Goat, dog, horse, or cow it was all the same to her, if they needed something.

Caro, used to most of the attention, wasn't too pleased when her mother and sister spent a lot of their time on other pursuits.

A few times during the winter, Tad and Abby would pull Caro on a sled to which a box had been nailed and lined with an old blanket; they would then trudge through the snow to their grandmother's house. And Victoria would give them hot chocolate and scones.

Sometimes, Victoria would feel housebound and hitch the sleigh up and visit her daughter's family.

Spring was a welcome visitor after the harsh winter. When Abby came rushing in one day shouting that she had seen a robin, Nora had to take Caro out to see it, too. The robin had disappeared, but they examined the new green shoots of the daffodils and admired the colorful crocus' that were pushing their way up through the snow by the house.

Caro ran from one thing to another calling, "Mama, mama, look, here is another one. Come quick."

Nora, laughing at her enthusiasm, followed the girls around the yard. It felt wonderful to be outside without several layers of heavy clothing.

There was an unusual amount of rain all spring. That, coupled with all the melting snow, made the fields so wet that plowing had to be delayed. It was June before it was dry enough, so they missed the planting of the early crops. A couple of calves, born in the field had to be rescued from the mud.

Victoria and Charles Belden left on their delayed honeymoon the first week in May. They planned to stay the entire month. Dr. Costain, from the next town would handle the doctor's patients while they were gone.

Victoria had been full of excitement as she made her preparations.

Abby and Caro were in tears on the day of the departure. Their grandmother hugged them both and reassured them.

"Don't waste those tears, lassies. I'll be back before you know it. And then we'll have a wee bairn to look forward to. You must help Mama while I'm gone. Promise me, now."

They both nodded solemnly and Victoria wiped away their tears.

Nora and Angus wished them bon voyage and then they were gone.

On the way home Nora was quiet.

Finally, Angus asked. "What is it, love? Are you missing them already?"

"I don't know exactly. I just have a bad feeling about them leaving." she answered.

Then, seeing the concerned look in Angus' face, she added, "Maybe it's just feeling lonely."

She smiled and changed the subject. "Let's stop to see Uncle Harrison on the way home. I hope he's feeling better."

Clara and her husband had not gone with the family to see the Beldens off because Harrison hadn't been feeling well. Clara was pleased to see the McDonald's when they arrived. She met them at the door.

"Oh, I'm so glad you stopped! It will be good for Harrison to talk to you."

She looked tired and Nora put an arm around her.

"Come now, Aunt Clara, why don't you and I sit here and talk while Angus goes up to see Uncle. You look like you need a rest."

Clara sank into the nearest chair with a sigh.

"I am tired, but I've been so worried about Harrison."

She was close to tears, Nora could see.

Harry had come into the room and the children were laughing and talking. Nora asked them to go outside to play so Clara and she could have some quiet time. Then she found the housekeeper and helped her fix a tea tray for them. While the tea was being readied, Nora went back into the parlor with Clara.

"Now," she said. "You and I will just relax for a while. Did Dr. Belden see Uncle Harrison before he left?"

"Oh, yes, he said it's just a cold, but Harrison is so listless and he isn't sleeping well. I'm so worried about him."

Nora could see that her Aunt was exhausted. She tried to think of something to do to help her.

At that moment, Sadie Thorne came into the room. She had brought in the tea tray. Clara seemed too tired to talk much and after they had eaten, Nora made a suggestion.

"Aunt Clara, you must get some rest, before you get sick, too. Why don't you sleep in the room across the hall from Uncle? Angus can stay with him as long as he wants. I'll take the children to our house."

Clara was too tired to resist, so Nora went upstairs with her and tucked her into bed, making sure there was a fire in the fireplace before she left. Her aunt was asleep before she left the room.

She went down to the parlor to talk to Sadie. The lady looked relieved.

"I'm so glad you came, Nora, she wouldn't listen to me and she insisted on staying in Mr. Renfrew's room all the time." Sadie said.

Nora asked her what she thought about Harrison's illness.

"I just don't know." Sadie answered. "The doctor said it's just a cold but Mr. Renfrew isn't shaking it." She shook her head worriedly.

Nora tried to reassure her. "I'm sure he'll be alright. It's easy to get depressed in his condition and having had a long winter. I'm sure Angus will cheer him up. Would you tell Angus for me that I went home and explain why? I don't want to go in and interrupt their talk. Angus is so good for Uncle."

"Of course, Nora, I'll keep you posted on what's happening. I feel much better about it myself, now."

"Good! I'm glad you're here. I'll ask Angus if he thinks they should have Dr. Costain come over too just to make Aunt Clara feel better."

When Angus came home, Nora questioned him about his Uncle.

"What do you think, Angus? Aunt Clara seemed so worried."

Angus gave her a big hug before he answered. "Well, love, he does have a bad cold, but I think he also feels pretty useless sometimes. We've had a hard winter and he couldn't get out much. That's enough to make a person depressed, and then he got sick, which made it all worse."

"Will he be alright? Should we get Dr. Costain?" Nora asked, anxiously.

"I don't think so, yet, anyway. We've got to pick up his spirits. I'll go over often and get him out of the room as much as I can. I think that's what he needs. I'll have a talk with Claude, too."

True to his word, Angus made the time each day to go and see his Uncle. He encouraged Harrison to play checkers with him and make plans for the summer planting.

One sunny day, Angus wheeled him out to the barn, where he talked to Claude about the farm work. Angus enlisted Claude's help to keep Harrison deeply involved with everything that went on at the farm.

Seeing her husband in better spirits did wonders for Clara, too.

CHAPTER TWENTY

The first week in June, Nora began to look for a letter from her mother about their return. It was not until the tenth that they received a letter. Dr. Belden had become ill the second week of their visit and they had to delay their return until he felt well enough to travel. Victoria hoped they would be home in time for the birth of the baby.

Victoria said in her letter that they weren't to worry. That it was not serious.

Nora was upset because she wanted her mother at home to be with the children when the baby was born. And she knew that Victoria would be devastated if anything was to happen to Dr. Belden.

Dr. Belden and his wife did not get back to Vermont until three days after Master Robert Terrance McDonald first saw the light of day. He was born on June thirtieth with Sadie and Dr. Costain in attendance. He was a cute little fellow who enchanted his sisters.

Tad privately thought he looked kind of funny, with his wrinkled, pink face and dark, fuzzy hair. But he, too, fell under his brother's spell when the baby curled his hand tightly around Tad's finger.

Angus was pleased as could be and brought Clara and Harrison over to view the new addition.

Nora was a bit more tired than she had been with the others, but contented, especially when Angus came in to sit with her. She could see he was pleased with his baby son.

Mrs. Thorne stayed with Nora for two weeks; to help with the children and Nora was very grateful. It gave her a chance to get strong enough to cope with everything.

Angus, Abby and Tad met Victoria and Charles on their return. They were glad to be home. The return voyage had been hard on them.

Angus brought them directly to Belltrees, so they could have a good meal before going to their own place.

Clara and Harrison were there to greet them, too. Sadie and Clara had made a wonderful welcome home supper. Angus even carried Nora downstairs to celebrate the occasion.

The children were all excited when they sat down to eat. Baby Robert had been brought down in his cradle and set close to the others.

Victoria was anxious to hold him and exclaimed over how much he looked like Angus.

Dr. Belden insisted on examining the baby to make sure he was in perfect health. The doctor himself still showed the effects of his sickness while away.

In fact, Nora and Angus were quite shocked to see how much weight he had lost.

So, soon after they finished supper, Angus took the two travelers to their home to rest. He and Tad had been there the day before to see that every thing was in order for the travelers return.

The two little girls had missed their grandmother, especially Abby. Now that she was home, Abby began to spend a part of each day at the little house.

She was interested in everything that Dr. Belden was doing. She loved to hear him talk about his patients, what their ailment was and how he had treated them. Of course, he was usually talking to his wife, but Abby would sit as quiet as a mouse so she could take in every word.

She loved it when Victoria let her help with the cooking, especially if it was making her favorite, scones with lots of raisins and cinnamon.

Caro always wanted to go with Abby but Abby tried to get out of the house without her. Like most older sisters she didn't like her little sister always tagging along. Nora understood Abby's feelings and would find other things for Caro to do.

Tad, too, had missed his grandmother but being older he had developed other interests of his own. He spent many hours with Harry, grooming their horses, mucking out the stables and riding. He was very interested in anything to do with horses and read everything on the subject he could find. Claude was very informative about it, too, because his own father had been a horse breeder in Canada.

Harry had hardly ever mentioned his mother, so Tad was surprised one day when Harry brought the subject up. They were pulling down forkfuls of hay for the cows, when Harry suddenly sat down and leaned back against a stall.

After a few moments, Tad called to him. "Com' on, Harry, let's get this finished so we can take a ride before supper."

Then as Harry didn't respond, Tad stood in front of his cousin and demanded. "What's the matter, Harry, you alright?"

Harry snapped out of his reverie and spoke hesitantly. "Tad, do you remember my mother?"

"No, not really, I was only a small fellow when she went away, I guess. At least I don't remember ever seeing her. Why?"

Harry shook his head, saying. "Oh, nothing." Then after a moment, "Well, I heard grandfather talking to my father last night. I went downstairs for a drink. They were talking about her."

Tad cocked his head with interest. "Well, what did they say?"

"I'm not sure what they meant, but grandfather told papa that he should do something so that my mother couldn't come back and take me. It made me kind of scared."

Tad asked, "What did your father say?"

"He just shouted something and stamped his feet when he went out and slammed the door."

"Well, why don't you ask Uncle Harrison about it? He always talks to you a lot." Tad sensed that his cousin was concerned.

But Harry seemed willing to drop the subject as quickly as he had brought it up.

He jumped to his feet. "Maybe I will. Com' on, lets jump in the hay."

Both boys forgot about Harry's mother for the moment.

But that night, as Harry was getting ready for bed, he remembered and went to find his grandfather. He found him in his study working on his books when he came in. As usual he was happy to see his grandson.

"Hello, lad, on your way to bed?"

Harry came closer to his grandfather and leaned against his arm. "Well, grandpapa, I was thinking about my mother. I heard you and papa talking the other night. Is my mother a bad person? What did she do?" Harry's small face looked anxious.

Harrison felt a twinge of pity for his young boy who had never known a real mother. He wondered how much the lad had overheard. He answered him gently.

"Your mother is not a bad person, lad. No one knows what makes any person act as they do. She loved you but I guess she didn't want to stay here on the farm."

Harrison himself doubted that Zoe could love anyone except herself but he did not want to be the one to spoil any illusions the boy might have of his mother. The boy might learn the truth some day but by then he might be better able to handle the knowledge.

Harrison noted that the anxiety had left his grandson's face. He had complete faith in his grandfather.

"Well, do you think she will come back sometime? I'd kind of like to see her."

"I don't know for sure, lad. Now you'd better be off to bed now. You're supposed to be going into town with me tomorrow, remember?"

Harry's face brightened. "Oh, yes, I'll be ready! Good night grandpapa."

Harry went upstairs, but he didn't entirely forget about the subject. He had sensed that his grandfather did not like to talk about his mother. He decided that when he was grown up he would find his mother and ask her why she had left the farm.

By the next morning, he had put it out of his mind, temporarily.

When Harrison repeated the conversation to his wife, she was disturbed. She didn't like little Harry to be reminded of his unusual family situation. But since Supleen wouldn't listen to reason, Harrison decided to talk to his lawyer. He needed to be sure that his grandson would be provided for in case he and Clara were not around.

Though Vermont was little disturbed by it, conflicts were breaking out all over Europe. In a few years most of the world would be involved in a vicious war. Germany supported Morocco in it's bid for independence from France. Then the Serbs threatened war against Austria. In a short while, these conflicts would deeply affect the family at Belltrees and their new country.

But in Vermont at that time, Europe seemed very far away. Summer on the farm was the busiest time of the year. Hay had to be planted and later cut and stored for the winter. Food crops needed to be planted and tended to provide the family with their food needs during the long winter. Berries were to be picked as each kind became ripe and quickly canned. Anyone able to help was pressed into service. Even Tad and Abby helped to plant the garden and pick berries and feed the animals. Summer was a good time.

One day, Nora took a break from work to visit Victoria. She tucked baby Robert into his pram and, with Caro walking beside her, they started out.

It was a perfect July day. The older children were helping Angus in the hay field. The air was soft and fragrant with honeysuckle and wild roses. So Nora had left behind her chores to enjoy some time with the little ones.

Caro stopped often to chase a butterfly or pick a flower for her grandma. Their progress was leisurely. When they arrived at Victoria's, they found her in the back yard hanging out some sheets. She was glad to see them.

Caro gave her the slightly wilted flowers she had picked. Victoria picked up her little granddaughter, putting her soft cheek against her own.

"The flowers are beautiful! I'll put them in a glass. Would you like me to push you on the swing?"

She set Caro in the swing her husband had made especially for the little ones. It was very low to the ground and had a back on it so they could balance better. Nora and her mother then settled in the wicker chairs.

"It's good to be out of doors again. I've some cleaning to do, but it will keep. Charles is off making his rounds. The man never stops, though I've tried to get him to slow down since his illness." There was a little worried frown on Victoria's face.

Nora tried to reassure her.

"Now, Mama, I'm sure Dr. Belden knows what he is doing. And that is his life, taking care of others."

"I know, but life is so short, we need to enjoy some of it while we're here." said Victoria. "Oh, let me hold the wee lad."

She picked up the baby and cradled him on her lap, cooing over him.

Nora watched contentedly. Her thoughts turned to her friend, Annie, who had been on her mind lately.

"You know, mama, Annie hasn't been to see Robert yet. Jack has been over twice and always has an excuse for why Annie isn't with him. I really miss her, the way she used to be."

"You know it's very hard for her to see you with all the wee ones and her with none of her own yet. It reminds me of my Aunt Willa who never had any bairns of her own. But she spent her time helping out all the other mothers and was always taking care of a bairn or two. That was her way of feeling better about it. She used to say you have to take what the good Lord sends you and make the most of it."

"I don't know how I would be feeling if I didn't have any babies. Angus told me that Jack has tried to get Annie to consider adopting a child, but she won't hear of it. I hate to think of her being so lonely and unhappy."

"Well, daughter," Victoria answered. "We can't take on everyone's burdens. We each have our own. If Annie started thinking of her husband's feelings she would be a bit happier herself." She gently rocked her grandson back and forth on her knees.

Nora had to go home soon to start the evening meal. Caro stayed with Victoria for the rest of the day. Annie was much on Nora's mind as she walked home with Robert.

That same evening Jack came home to find a note from Annie saying that she had a meeting and would be home by eight. There was some cold chicken and potato salad in the icebox.

To Jack, the house looked sadly neglected and lonely. He sank into an armchair in the sitting room, his hand over his eyes. He had no objection to Annie spending time at the store during the day but more and more she was working late, or, the past few months, going to meetings of the suffragette's movement, at night.

He was an unusually open-minded man for the era. He had no objections to women voting; he felt that most of the women he knew were very intelligent. But he still wanted his wife to be home when he was, at least most of the time. He loved her company and didn't enjoy eating alone every evening.

Hunger made Jack get up and go into the kitchen to retrieve the chicken and salad. To ward off the loneliness, he read the newspaper while he ate.

Afterward, he scraped his plate, left it in the sink, and went outside. He walked out behind the barn to the corral.

His sleek riding horse, Flash, came trotting over to him to have his nose rubbed. Jack petted him for a few minutes then saddled him and rode off toward the back of his property.

Annie returned about eight-thirty and was not too surprised to find the house empty. Lately Jack had been going riding when she was late coming home. She puttered about the kitchen for a while, cleaning up the dishes left this morning. Then she went up to put on her housecoat.

In the middle of changing, the familiar feeling of depression enveloped her. She sat down on the bed half doubled over with the pain of it. Tears ran down her cheeks. Her mind was full of thoughts of her marriage. Why can't I accept this, she thought. I love Jack so much but I feel such a failure. I just seem to be frozen inside. I want him to hold me but when he does, I can't respond. All I can think of is I can't have a child. I am ruining things for myself and I can't stop it. Oh, God help me! She lay face down on the bed, sobbing.

When Jack came home, he found her there, sleeping, her face tear-stained. He sat down beside her and brushed the hair back from her face.

"Wake up, sleepyhead, come down and we'll have supper. Are you feeling alright?"

Annie sat up and spoke brightly. "I'm fine, I was a little tired, that's all. Did you eat the chicken I left for you?"

"Oh, yes. But you know me. I'm hungry again. I'll make some coffee and you can scare us up some food. How's that?" Jack coaxed.

Annie combed her hair at the dressing table; she avoided looking into Jack's eyes. "I'll be right down. Go ahead and fix the coffee. It will taste good." She said. Neither mentioned the tears or their cause.

Jack went downstairs with a heavy heart. "What can I do?" he asked himself. "She just won't listen to me. If she would only talk to Nora or Mattie she might feel better. I think Nora could convince her to adopt. But she won't even go out to the farm. Maybe she would ask Angus and Nora out here, for dinner or something."

The coffee had started perking before Annie appeared. She had splashed her eyes with cold water to reduce the redness. She went directly to the icebox and brought out the rest of the chicken and salad and busied herself with fixing their evening meal.

While they ate, Jack asked Annie about how the shop was going and some details about it. Annie answered shortly at first and then she opened up gradually, telling Jack about an especially difficult customer they had. One of the well-to-do matrons in town who wanted the best materials on her dresses but she constantly haggled about the price. Annie could even chuckle a little as she told of the seamstress' reaction.

"Mrs. Crandall taxed poor Agnes's patience to the limit. It's lucky I came in when I did or I think Agnes would have stuck pins in her."

Jack laughed, glad that Annie had shaken her previous mood. She even started talking about the suffragette meeting.

As he watched his wife talking, Jack decided to postpone asking her to invite the McDonald's over. He didn't want to change her mood.

So he waited until they were getting ready for bed that night. Then he nonchalantly brought it up.

"Why don't we have Maggie and Andy and Angus and Nora sometime soon for a picnic? We haven't done that in a while."

Annie frowned for a second before replying. Then she said, "Instead of a picnic, why don't we just have them to supper one evening? They would probably appreciate an evening out without responsibilities."

Jack understood what she meant; that it would be an occasion when the adults would come without the children.

He answered lightly. "You're right. That would be nice."

The matter was dropped for the time.

The next day Jack took a ride out to Belltrees in the early afternoon.

He found Nora outdoors with Caro and the baby. She was watching Caro on the swing while she pushed Robert back and forth in his pram. Jack felt the familiar stirring in his heart as always when he caught sight of Nora.

Just then she raised her eyes and saw him. Her pleasure at seeing him was apparent.

"Jack! What a nice surprise! Come and sit down. Angus is off in the back field but he should be coming soon."

Jack took a seat beside her.

"I'll go out and see what he's up to in a moment. Right now, I'd like to talk to you and ask you a favor."

Nora looked closely at him. She spoke with concern.

"What is it, Jack. Is Annie alright?" she asked.

"Oh, yes, it's not that. Annie is fine, physically, at least. But I am very concerned because she is often depressed lately. She doesn't talk much about it but I think that she is dwelling constantly on having a baby."

Jack looked uncomfortable but he went on doggedly. "I need someone else to talk to her about giving some thought to adoption. I would really like to try it and, well maybe, coming from another woman, it might help. I'm probably grasping at straws, but I don't know what else to do. She feels so miserable."

Nora was thoughtful for a moment. She knew Jack must be extremely concerned to have come to her for help. He was not a man to talk to others about his private life.

"Jack, of course I would be glad to try, only Annie never comes out here anymore. Perhaps I could go into the shop one day soon---" Nora spoke slowly.

Then Jack interrupted her. "You won't have to do that, Nora, Annie said she was going to invite you and Angus over one evening with Maggie and Andrew. Then you could perhaps bring up the subject." Jack rubbed his furrowed brow. "I'll tell her I've invited you both for next Thursday. Would that be alright?"

"That should be fine, Jack. We'd love to come; it's been a while since we went to an adult only occasion. I'll ask mama to watch the bairns, or maybe Sadie. In any case we will be there,"

Jack looked relieved. "Thanks, Nora, I'll see you then. Now I'll ride out and say hello to Angus and make sure it's alright with him."

Caro began to jump up and down with excitement. She pulled on Jack's sleeve. "Take me with you, Uncle Jack, please."

Jack looked down into that earnest little face and laughed. "Sure, little one, if Mama says it's alright."

Nora gave her permission and the two rode off, Caro sitting in front of Jack and looking very small on the big horse. She waved gaily to her mother as they rode off.

If Annie was upset that Jack had gone ahead with the invitation, she didn't show it. She invited her sister and husband for the following Thursday and planned a pleasant evening. She started looking forward to seeing Nora again; she had missed her friendship a lot.

CHAPTER TWENTY-ONE

The following Thursday, Victoria and her husband went up to the farm to stay with the children so Angus and Nora could go to the supper at Jack and Annie's house.

It was the first time in months that Nora and Angus had been anywhere without the children.

Nora was pleased that she could fit into one of her favorite dresses that she hadn't worn since before Robert's birth. It was white voile with a green print scattered over it. It was perfect for the warm summer evening. Her dark hair was smoothed back into a chignon with small curls at the nape and in front of each ear. She took great pains to look nice and was rewarded when Angus came into the room.

"You're looking especially bonny today, love." His eyes repeated the compliment.

Nora kissed him, saying, "And you're looking entirely too good yourself, for the father of four. My, my!"

She straightened his tie. "We'd better be off if we're to be on time. I do feel a bit guilty, leaving Mama with all four."

She'll love it and the bairns will too." said Angus. "Anyway, we won't be late. Com' on, now."

There was a chorus of "'Bye, 'bye, Mama, 'bye Papa." from Tad, Abby and Caro. Robert was indifferent, as long as he was fed and cuddled by someone.

At Jack and Annie's they found Maggie and Andrew had already arrived. It was the first time the adults had been together socially in a long time. They were all genuinely glad to see one another.

Annie had prepared delicious roast pork with new, small potatoes boiled in their jackets. There were side dishes of sliced, juicy tomatoes and sweet cucumbers. For dessert there was homemade ice cream with apple pie. It was a typical American meal and enjoyed as much by the Scottish couple as their friends.

A short time later, when the men went out to inspect a new horse that Jack had acquired, Nora brought up the subject of children.

First, she told of something funny that Abby had done while practicing her nursing skills. Maggie chimed in with a description of some of her children's antics. Then Nora brought up the story of a recently orphaned brother and sister.

"Oh, did you hear about the Nelson family in Hardwick? The mother and father were killed when they had a flat tire going down a steep hill and the car rolled over into a ravine.

"Yes, I heard about that," answered Maggie. "Automobiles are dangerous. I don't think I ever want to own one."

"The worst thing is, " continued Nora. "They don't have any other family. I heard they would be put into a home."

Annie was listening in stony silence. Nora was wishing fervently that she had never brought up the subject. Maggie took the ball out of her hands by speaking directly to Annie.

"Would you consider taking them, temporarily, Annie? You are so good with children." Maggie asked.

Her sister answered tersely. "No, thank you just the same. I would never take a chance on raising someone else's children. Suppose they turned out to be undisciplined brats?"

She poured some more coffee into her cup. Maggie pursued the subject, though she had already read the danger signals on her sister's face.

"But if they are all alone it would be dreadful if they were sent to a home. I heard they are only five and six years old." She looked at Annie hopefully.

Annie ignored her. She stood up and collected the coffee cups and left the room with them. Maggie and Nora looked at each other. Nora shook her head.

"Well, we didn't do very well with that, did we?" Maggie said ruefully.

"I'm afraid we just made things worse. Now she is probably so angry she won't ever come out to the farm again." Nora responded.

She felt depressed to think she had annoyed her friend, whom she had hoped would come back into her life again.

Nora followed Annie into the kitchen. She walked up to where Annie was standing at the sink and put her hand on her shoulder. Annie turned to face her with steel in her eyes. Nora quickly apologized.

"Annie, I'm sorry I was so pushy before. I guess I just thought of how good you would be for those children, that's all."

Annie turned back to rinsing the coffee cups. She answered coolly. "Don't give it another thought. It's forgotten."

But the voice was merely polite. The rest of the evening was uncomfortable, at least for Nora, who felt less welcome than she had before the episode.

It was different for Maggie. She was Annie's sister and knew that she would always be accepted.

When the men returned from the barn, it became obvious to them that the atmosphere was strained. Nora and Angus left soon after, blaming it on not wanting to leave the children too long with Victoria.

On the way home Nora explained to Angus what had happened. He wasn't too sympathetic.

"You know it is never a wise thing to interfere in a marriage, lassie. Now you may be regretting it for a long time."

"I know, Angus. I only did it because Jack asked me to and he seemed so concerned. Anyway, I meant to go about it in a different way but then Maggie started talking about the Nelson children needing a home, so I went along with it. Maybe if Annie could take care of a child for a while she would like the idea of having one permanently. But it all turned out wrong."

Nora sounded so sad that Angus relented. He patted her hand.

"Now, don't get yourself all fashed about it. Annie will probably forget it," he said.

But Nora shook her head. "No, I don't think so, Angus, I don't feel that I know Annie anymore, she is so different."

"Well, love, there's not a thing you can do about it. I sure feel mighty sorry for Jack, though."

Nora was right. Annie was very upset and vowed it would be a long time before she would have another dinner party.

She was distant and unsmiling as she and Jack straightened up a little after their guests had left. Jack was anxious to find out what had happened. Finally he caught Annie's arm and gently pulled her down into a big chair beside him.

"Now, miss, tell me what is bothering you. You don't act like a lady who has just had her closest friends for a visit."

Annie jumped up, her face angry. She exploded with anger.

"They can't stay out of our business! They always have to talk about adopting children, as if it was the only way of life! I'm sick of it!"

She picked up some glasses and flounced out of the room.

Jack slumped in the chair for a few minutes before following his wife into the kitchen. He tried to pacify her by telling her that her sister and Nora had only spoken about these things because they wanted her happiness and because they loved her.

But Annie was not to be mollified. She remained cool and distant to Jack, though in her heart she knew it wasn't his fault. She couldn't seem to stop her own reaction.

Jack sat a long time by the fire that evening, trying to sort things out in his mind. He knew if he went upstairs Annie would be pretending to be asleep as usual.

Although Nora sadly missed her friend, Annie, she had so many things that filled her life she had very little time to dwell on it.

The children were growing fast. Each one had his or her own particular need of her.

Tad was always busy, usually with Harry trailing him, doing things about the farm for his father or on projects of his own. His chores were done with care and sometimes even he found a better or easier method of doing them.

He became very interested in the invention of the automobile. Although there were very few cars in Vermont at that time, his Uncle Jack had bought a Ford that he used when the weather was good. Every chance he had, Tad would beg for a ride. He bombarded Jack with questions about what made it run.

Tad was torn between his love of horses and his fascination with motorcars. He had many long conversations with Jack about that. Jack told him that someday the cars would replace horses almost entirely.

Tad had a dream, since his Uncle Harrison had given him Peggy, that someday he would raise riding horses. Now, his interests had broadened to include automobiles and a desire to do as his father did, farming. He felt confused about what he would do when he grew up.

Angus could see this in his son. He remembered how he had felt when he was his son's age. He brought up the subject one morning as they worked in the barn. Angus was milking the cow while Tad pulled down forks full of hay for the animals.

"You know, lad, when I was about your age I had to go to live with my grandfather. He was a blacksmith and he wanted me to learn the trade. But I really didn't like it at all, though I did help him in the smithy to help pay for my keep."

Tad stopped and leaned on the hay fork to hear what his father was saying.

"What did you do then, Papa?" he asked.

"Well, I really didn't know what I wanted. I just wanted to learn about a lot of different things. I don't think many lads decide what they want until they are a bit older. I guess you are feeling a lot like that yourself right now. It's natural at your age, so don't let it worry you."

Tad wondered how his father seemed to always read his mind. Angus chuckled at the puzzled look on his son's face.

"Don't forget, I was your age once myself. You've plenty of time."

Angus drained the last drop of milk from Betsy. He handed the pail to Tad.

"Here, lad, take this to your mother."

As Tad was leaving, Angus added. "You're a good lad, the best helper I'll ever have."

Angus cleared his throat as he finished pulling down the hay and filling the bins. He was very moved by the sight of his earnest young son.

Tad's heart swelled with pride at the unusual compliment. He gave the milk to his mother, who was making scones for breakfast.

Robert was in his cradle by the table. Tad paused to look at his baby brother. He put his finger in the baby's hand; it closed tightly around it. Tad laughed, tickled at how strong the tiny hand seemed.

Abby had started shooting up the last year. She was getting tall and slender as a young colt. Much of the time she had to watch Caro for her mother, especially since Robert was born. She didn't have much patience with her sister, perhaps because they were so different.

Abby, still the tomboy, loved to climb trees, play ball or practice her nursing skills.

None of these appealed to Caro. She didn't like to get her hands or clothes dirty. Her favorite toys were her dolls and she loved dressing up in her mother's old clothes. She refused to let Abby bandage her leg or arm or anything else. She did allow her to doctor her doll when it was needed.

In return, Abby would cut paper dolls out of the Sears Roebuck catalog as well as several sets of clothing. She mounted the paper dolls on cardboard so that they could be stood up. It was a game Caro never tired of but soon bored her sister.

As often as possible, Abby would get Caro settled with her dolls and then ask her mother permission to visit her grandmother. She loved the little house and followed Victoria around as she tended the garden or did other chores. She liked most of all to listen to Charles talk to his wife about the cases he'd dealt with that day.

Often the doctor would let Abby watch as he cleaned his instruments and prepared his bag for the next day. Though it was the same thing over and over, she never tired of watching.

Because she was so interested, Dr. Belden would explain the use of each instrument and pill he put up and told her about some of his simplest cases, especially if it had been a child he had treated.

Abby's best friend was Mrs. Dufrense' youngest. Marie didn't seem to take after her mother much, as she was rather quiet, at least in the presence of grown-ups. But with Abby, she opened up and as they enjoyed the same things, they got along famously.

She spent many hours on the weekends at Belltrees. Sometimes, if Nora didn't need Abby to watch Caro, she was allowed to go to Marie's house. Abby especially liked to eat there, not so much because of the food; it fascinated her to see the eleven Dufrense' and their mother and father all eating in unison.

She watched in awe as Mrs. Dufrense, covered neck to toe in an immaculate white apron, held a loaf of homemade bread against her stomach as she cut off thick slices.

Mr. Dufrense, seated at the head of the table, said not much of anything. But if any of the children became boisterous, he only had to look at the offender to squelch him.

Abby wondered why they seemed so in awe of him, to her he looked harmless.

Anyway, she wasn't allowed to go there very often. Nora thought Mrs. Dufrense had too many children to be able to watch each one and Nora liked to know what her own children were doing at any given time.

Caro was still too young to go very far, in fact, she still liked to be in her mother's vicinity. As for Robert, Caro didn't think he was of much use. Mostly he lay there and ate and slept. He also took up a lot of her mother's time. Nora had told her that it wouldn't be long before he would be able to play, but to the five year old it seemed impossible that would ever happen.

She would take her dolls and play as close as she could to wherever Nora was working. Sometimes Nora would put a dishpan of water on a chair and let Caro play at washing her doll clothes.

Nora was having a difficult time recuperating from Robert's birth. It seemed to be taking a lot longer than after the first three. She had developed a nagging backache, perhaps from leaning over the wash so much. A small baby created so many diapers and other dirty clothes. Of course, she had Tansy or Victoria with her when the others were born which had helped a lot.

One Wednesday her mother had walked over for a visit and found Nora sitting in a chair outside, with Robert in his pram beside her and Caro playing nearby. Nora looked so white and drawn that Victoria was disturbed. She settled in a chair near her daughter.

"Well, lass, you're looking a mite peaked. What seems to be the problem? Too many bairns to look after, I suppose."

She looked closely at Nora's tense face.

As Nora started to answer, tears of exhaustion rolled down her cheeks.

"No, no, it's not the babies. It's just--I can't ever get caught up and it is so hard to get out of the bed every day."

She wiped furiously at her eyes to stop the flow. She hated to appear so helpless, but it seemed beyond her control. She didn't want her mother to worry about her and she didn't want to ask her for help. Victoria rose briskly to her feet. She put a hand on Nora's shoulder.

"Now, lass, you just relax here a while. Tell me where to find that small lassie of yours. She is old enough now to help out a bit."

Nora protested. "She's still so young; I don't want to burden her with work already. I'll manage," she said.

Victoria snorted. "You'll manage yourself right into a sick bed, that's what you'll do! Don't worry about Abby. I'll not ask too much of her. Now tell me where to find the lass and stop this nonsense."

Nora explained that Abby was playing with Marie in the back yard and Tad was helping his father in the fields.

Victoria found the girls romping with Spots. She enlisted their help by giving them some grown-up chores to do. Soon they were taking the clothes off the line and folding them as they had seen Nora do before.

Nora was marched off for a much-needed nap while Victoria made lunch for them all. Then she tied big aprons around Abby and Marie so they could do the washing up and tidying of the kitchen, while she tended to Robert's needs.

Even Caro was allowed to help. When Nora came downstairs about four, she found everything in order; the older girls playing with Caro outside while Victoria mixed up some bread and Robert slept peacefully.

Nora felt guilty about her mother doing all the work but Victoria refused to listen to her apologies for sleeping too long.

"You're long overdue for a rest, love. I've enjoyed myself and the two young lassies were a big help and proud of themselves, too."

She told Nora about how the girls had worked. She admonished Nora not to let Abby spend her entire time just playing.

"She's a bright one and can handle a little responsibility. She'll be better for it. Now, I'll be over every afternoon for a while and you will take a little rest each day. I've nothing much to do while Charles is making his rounds, anyway." declared Victoria.

Nora knew her mother could always find pleasant things to keep herself busy but she accepted Victoria's offer of help with gratitude and no more protests.

By the end of the third week, Nora was feeling more like herself. Her backache had lessened and she insisted that Victoria not spend all of her afternoons helping her.

Her mother gave in but insisted that she would send the farm girl that Charles had hired to do his office cleaning, to help with Nora's washing for a while.

Martha was a large, rather stoic young woman with the strength of a man, it seemed. She made short work of the washing and, without being prodded, cleaned anything else she thought was in need of it.

That, plus having Abby helping as well, soon had Nora feeling more relaxed and able to enjoy her children and any spare time she could spend with Angus.

Once again they could sit on the porch in the evening and admire the Belltrees, which had grown considerably. Or they would walk down the lane, enjoying the sweet summer smells from the honeysuckle. With Angus' arm around her waist, Nora felt all was well with her world.

CHAPTER TWENTY-TWO

1914

On a particularly warm August evening, about dusk, Nora, Angus and Jack were sitting on the front porch of Belltrees idly watching the children playing hide and seek.

Abby, Harry, Caro and Robert were running widely about, screaming when caught and racing back to the tag tree.

Tad sat on the steps of the porch, feeling very grown up. He had graduated from school and was making plans to go to the University in the fall. He was thinking about that now. He felt guilty to be leaving the farm work all to his father.

He had been at the top of his class in all his subjects and his Uncle Harrison had insisted that he have the pleasure of putting his grandnephew through the University.

Tad would be studying agriculture and he was very excited at the prospect.

It had taken some doing for Harrison to convince Angus to allow him to finance Tad's studies. But Harrison had won, declaring that it would be worth it if Tad could come home and show them all how to increase production on the farms.

Now, Tad became aware that the grown-ups were talking about the war going on in Europe. Jack had brought a newspaper out with him and it was filled with reports about what was happening.

On August fourth, Great Britain had declared war on Germany after that country had declared its' intention of marching through Belgium, a neutral, to attack France. Just two days ago, on August twenty third, Japan had declared war on Germany.

"Half of the world has gone mad, it seems." said Nora. "What will it mean to us here, Angus?"

She turned, anxiety on her face, to her husband.

Angus' response showed his concern. "I'm not sure, but with most of the countries in this thing it will be pretty hard for the U.S to stay out of it. Though President Wilson seems to be the kind of a man who would keep us out of it, if at all possible." Jack's face showed his worry. "I wish Great Britain had stayed out of it, but of course, it couldn't. Think what it will mean to all the young men there and all the other countries. Your sister's sons, Nora, are the age to join the army, aren't they?" he said.

Then as he saw Nora's face turn white, "I'm sorry, Nora! What a fool I am?"

Nora put out a protesting hand. "No, no! It's true! I just hadn't thought of it yet. They must all be so upset! How I wish I could talk to them!" She declared.

Tad, like all young men who see war as a great adventure, was excited at the prospect.

Without thinking of its' effect on his mother, he spoke hastily. "Alex is the same age as I am, Papa. Do you think I should be going off to college if this country is going to war?"

Angus, who saw what this was doing to Nora, hastened to stop Tad from making any more such comments. "We aren't at war yet, lad, so don't worry your mother over that right now." Angus spoke lightly but sent Tad a severe warning look. "Why don't you bring us all out some lemonade now, lad?" Tad, understanding the message, went into the house.

Nora, however, was not distracted from the subject of the war.

Her heart went out to her sisters and their families. "If only they had moved here with us." She mused.

Angus answered her sympathetically. "Don't fash yourself so, love, you know it wouldn't matter where they were. All our heart's are with our homeland at a time like this."

Nora looked alarmed. "You aren't thinking of going, are you?" She asked.

Angus patted her hand. "Of course, I'm thinking of it, but how could I leave all of you to fend for yourself?"

However, he avoided her eyes and she felt a chill of fear. Just then Tad came out with the lemonade and at the same time Robert fell while running to hide and skinned his knee. It was the younger children's bedtime and for the time being the subject of war was dropped.

When Nora and the young ones went in the house, Jack, Angus and Tad wandered out to the barn. Once there, they sat down on the bales of hay.

After a moment of silence, Jack spoke to Angus. "I've about made up my mind, old friend, to go back to England and see what I can do to help."

Angus protested. "But what about your business; and Annie?"

Jack shook his head. "I don't know how I can work it out right now, but I know I have to go."

He was silent a moment than continued. "I have no children and Annie has her shop. I just have to figure out what to do about the lumberyard."

He stood up. "I think I'll be on my way. I've got a lot of thinking to do."

He put an arm around Tad's shoulder and spoke very earnestly to the boy. "You tend to your studies, son. Your turn will come, if it's to be. In the meantime, your family needs you right here."

As Tad and his father left the barn, each was deep in his own thoughts.

Tad was wishing that he were older so he could go to Scotland and get involved in the war with his cousins. He was also thinking of Katrine. If he went, he would get to see her again.

As for Angus, he also wished that he could return with Jack to fight but to leave Nora with four children and a farm to take care of would be impossible. It would also mean that Tad would have to stay home to care for the farm and forget about going to college. His family must come first.

When Angus and Tad went into the kitchen, Nora was at the table writing a letter to her sister, Molly. Tad said goodnight and went upstairs.

Angus poured some tea for him and Nora and sat down opposite her. She seemed scarcely to notice him, so absorbed she was in her writing. Concern for her sisters was reflected on her face.

When Angus finished his tea, he went to stand behind his wife's chair for a moment. She stopped writing and leaned her head against him. He bent his head to kiss her.

"I'll be going up now, love, don't worry too long."

Although the normal household routine went on as usual the grown-ups thoughts were on what was happening in Europe.

As Nora cared for her family's needs, she was wondering about Molly and Mairi. What was in store for them all? She was grateful that Tad was yet too young to make his own decisions.

As soon as the breakfast things were tidied up, Nora sent Abby and Caro out to feed the chickens and pigs. When these essential chores were finished, she took the three young ones and walked over to the Renfrew's.

She felt she had to talk to someone who would understand, about what was happening. She found Sadie and Aunt Clara still discussing the day's schedule over a cup of tea.

She sat down with them while the children found Harry and went out to the barn. She went over the conversation of the previous evening with Angus and Jack about the war.

Clara was also very concerned about her niece's families. But she tried to allay some of Nora's fears.

"Now, lass, don't fret so, it may be that it will all be over soon and the lad's won't have to be called to serve. We'll all pray that it's so. Have a nice cup of tea, now."

She poured a cupful and set it down in front of Nora. "Now, how is your mother taking it?" She asked.

"I didn't want to upset her by bringing it up right now." Nora answered. "At least until I feel a little calmer about it myself."

Nora took several swallows of her tea. The warm liquid somehow was comforting.

Aunt Clara shook her head. "Don't worry about Victoria. She has a cool head. And as we get older we learn to accept things better."

Sadie nodded in agreement. She offered her opinion. "That's true, and worry never got a person anything expect a headache. Besides, we don't even know if your nephews are in this thing yet. Time to worry when we hear."

The two older women's practical statements helped Nora to relax more than sympathy would have. By the time she left for home, she felt much better.

She stopped by her Uncle's study to say hello. Harrison seemed to Nora to be looking more drawn and tired than usual. She thought "he certainly has a lot to worry him, with a son like Supleen and trying to bring up his grandson. Poor man!" To cheer him up Nora told him Angus would be over to see him later.

The children had found Claude and Harry cleaning the stalls and putting in fresh hay. Their offer to help was accepted and they all worked together for a while. Then the young ones went out to lean on the corral fence and watch the horses.

Harry was quieter than the other children today. His mood was almost sullen. Only Claude knew how the boy suffered by not having a normal father and mother.

Only this morning Harry tried to get his father's attention by asking him to come down to the barn and look at the new colt that had been born the day before. But Supleen had hurried past with barely a word to his son.

Claude and Harrison tried to fill the void of an indifferent father but often failed. This was one of those times.

The boy also missed the constant companionship of Tad, who was now pursuing more mature tasks; helping his father and preparing for college. Though Harry often went over to be where Angus and Tad were working, it wasn't the same.

The chasm between thirteen and sixteen was a wide one.

When Nora came out to the barn to collect the children, Claude called to her from the barn door. He motioned her inside. Nora wondered why he was acting so secretive. He addressed her in his usual polite fashion.

"Ma'am, I hope you don't mind, there was something I wanted to speak with you about. I don't like to worry the Renfrew's about it."

Nora was alarmed by his serious tone. "Of course, what is it, Claude?"

"Well, ma'am, I know it's not exactly your problem, but I've been worried about the boy there. With no mother and hardly any father, it's pretty rough on the boy. And now your Tad has outgrown him, he feels he has no one. Lately he's been bringing home a friend from school who is a tough acting fellow. The other day I caught him teaching Harry how to smoke. Of course, I sent him packing, but it's not going to be that easy."

Claude looked so concerned and worried that Nora felt sorry for him. She tried to reassure him.

"It's good of you to be concerned, Claude. I'll talk it over with Angus and see what we can do to help. Meanwhile he can come over to the farm today and help Abby to shore up the chicken coop. It's about ready to fall down. It will keep his mind off things."

Claude looked relieved.

As they left the barn, Nora said, "Time to go home now. Harry, why don't you ask Aunt Clara if you can come to our house for a bit? Abby needs help to fix the chicken coop and I know Tad would like to see you when they come in for supper. What do you say lad?"

Harry hurried to get permission to go and came out smiling. Both Nora and Claude knew it was only a temporary solution to a deeply rooted problem.

After supper that evening, Nora had a chance to talk to Angus about Harry. She told him of Claude's concerns.

"I just can't talk to Aunt Clara about this. They have both been through so much. You know they are both getting frailer. I can't bear to give them one more thing to worry about."

Concern put a frown on Nora's pretty face.

Angus gently lifted a stray tendril of hair from his wife's face and put it back where it belonged.

"Don't fash yourself, love, there isn't much you can do about the poor lad. He knows we all care about him. But the fact is, no one can take the place of a mother and father that aren't interested in their bairns. It makes for a hard life for the lad." Angus stated.

Nora pursued the subject. "But we have to do something! He's still a little boy and always looks so lost, sort of."

Nora looked pleadingly at her husband until he felt compelled to answer. He took his pipe out of his mouth and knocked the ashes out before he answered.

"Well, I know he misses Tad a lot now that Tad has outgrown him a bit. And Harry is at a difficult age. I could have him help me in the fields more; he's good with the horses, too. Maybe if he's here with our bairns more, he may feel more like he belongs."

Nora's face lit up and she planted a quick kiss on Angus' cheek. "That's a good idea! It's worth a try, at least! You're a good man, Angus McDonald!"

From that day on, Harry was a very busy boy. Between his chores with Claude and working on the McDonald's farm he didn't have much time to feel sorry for himself.

He worked and sweat hard with the others. At night, he slept better, too. His grandparents noticed that his appetite had improved considerably and they were pleased.

Claude, after a talk with Angus, found plenty for Harry to do when he was home, as well. As Angus said "A busy lad is a happy one."

CHAPTER TWENTY-THREE

The end of the summer was announced, as usual, with an explosion of colors. Scarlet, orange and yellow leaves made the woods seem like a giant's flower garden.

Nora stood on the front porch but for once she didn't notice the brilliant foliage. She was waiting for Tad and his father to bring out Tad's luggage. Today they were driving Tad and his friend, Billy Todd, to Burlington to college.

While Nora was proud of her son, she had a funny little lump in her chest knowing he was leaving home and he was a grown up person.

She thought back to the day they had arrived here at Bell trees; how excited they all had been and how the goat had attacked Tad. She smiled then gave a sigh.

The screen door banged shut and she turned to see Angus and Tad coming out loaded with suitcases and clothes. They carried the luggage to the car and stored everything in every available space.

Jack had loaned the 1910 Cadillac Roadster to them for the purpose of transporting the boys and all the necessary equipment to Burlington. The boys were more impressed with the automobile than the prospect of college. It was a splendid vehicle; adorned with wood veneer and gold accents on the hood. There were running boards and even a rumble seat.

Besides their clothes, they had to bring sheets, blankets and towels to last until the Christmas vacation. Nora had made sure Tad had more than enough warm winter clothing. Before they finished packing the car there was barely enough room for the four of them to sit.

It had been difficult for the McDonald's to manage the extra money needed to outfit their son for school. For the social occasions when Tad would need to dress up, Nora had paid Annie's seamstress to alter one of Angus' suits to better fit Tad.

Victoria and Charles had made him a gift of two pair of pants, two shirts and a sport jacket. To supplement these, Nora had added two more new shirts, a sweater and shoes. Some of his old things were in good condition and could be taken, as well. In fact, young Sean felt quite like the well-dressed college man.

It didn't matter that when they arrived at the school it became apparent that many of the young men were from pretty well to do families, judging from their extensive wardrobes; some of them even owned automobiles. But Tad had never worried about nice clothes and it didn't bother him now. He had plenty for his needs and that was all that mattered.

Just the day before, Tad had announced that in the future he would be called by his given name, Sean Edward; he was too old to be called Tad anymore. His brother and sisters had just hooted and ran around calling out "Sean Edward" in haughty voices until Angus had made them stop. Nora and Angus had respectfully agreed with their tall son that it was time to drop childish nicknames.

On this day, when he was leaving home, Sean wasn't thinking about how homesick he might become. He was just excited about this new adventure. It would be the first time he'd even been away from home for more than a night or two except at his grandmother's or Harry's house. Now, he looked at the faces of his family and suddenly felt very grown up.

Abby was excited for him and wished it was her going away to school. Caro was tearful and Robert was trying to give Sean his pet turtle to keep him company. Sean hugged and patted them all and explained to Robert why he couldn't bring the turtle with him.

"A turtle wouldn't like being cooped up in a dorm room, Robbie." He said. "Why don't you take care of it here for me, all right?"

Robert readily agreed, he hadn't really wanted to part with his pet.

Only Harry seemed to accept Sean's leaving stoically, although he was the one who was the most affected by it. He realized that the world of a college man would change his best friend and idol. Harry felt that Sean was lost to him forever.

While everyone was shouting their goodbyes as the roadster left the driveway, Harry left quietly to go home and seek solace in his favorite spot, the tack room in the barn. There he curled up on a horse blanket and cried until he fell asleep.

Claude found him there when he went in to get the currycomb and hang up the bridle he had used. Claude noted the fetal position and the tear stained face. He guessed the cause, as he knew about Tad's leaving for school.

He thought, "This boy is headed for trouble unless I can turn him around now."

Claude spent some time thinking before he woke Harry.

"Harry boy, wake up. It's supper time. C'mon, son."

Harry opened his eyes. As memory returned, his eyes reflected the despair in his heart. He stood up to follow Claude into the house. Claude pretended not to notice Harry's mood. At they walked along, Claude spoke in a hearty voice.

"Oh, I forgot to tell you, I have a message from Tad for you. He wants you to take care of Peggy while he's gone and exercise her for him."

Harry looked up at Claude in disbelief. He stopped walking and exclaimed. "Really, Claude? Tad asked himself?"

"That's what he said. I guess he knew he could trust his best friend to take care of his horse." Claude lied convincingly.

Harry's face took on a glow and he walked briskly toward the house. "Hurry up, Claude, I'm starving!" First thing in the morning, I'll bring Peggy over here so I can take care of her."

Claude made a mental note to tell Nora and Angus about his plan after supper.

When he explained the whole thing to them they agreed it was a great idea. Angus wrote a note to Sean so he could write to Harry about it.

Nora sorely missed her oldest son. Several times a day she wondered what he would be doing and found her eyes misting over. She knew Angus missed him too, especially as they had been working together every day. Angus would have to hire one of Cecile's brothers to help him, since harvest time was coming and there was just too much for one man to do in time so the crops wouldn't spoil.

One day, soon after Sean had left, Jack drove out to Belltrees to say goodbye. He had finally gotten his affairs in order so he could leave to go to England.

He explained that Annie had too much to do that day to come with him. Of course, by now Nora was used to the idea that Annie didn't want to visit them and had got over her first sadness over it.

Jack, Angus and Nora sat at the kitchen table to talk. Nora was fixing some string beans for supper as she listened. Jack was explaining his plans.

"As you know, Angus, I've left Bill Johnson in charge of the mill part of the business. Annie will take charge of the store but with George Olsen to work there full time. We talked before about you helping out, Angus, are you still willing?"

"Aye, I talked it over with Nora and it should work out fine. In the winter I have plenty of time to help out. What is it you will need help with?"

Jack spoke slowly. "Well, you know Bill and George are both good men, but I feel that Annie needs some one to help take charge and kind of take my place. She has a lot to do with her shop already. Here's my plan; you tell me what you think and if you can do it, I will really appreciate it."

Jack went on to explain that he would like Angus to meet with Annie and Bill on a bi-monthly basis to go over what was happening in the business. Besides that, in case of any problems, Annie would call on Angus and in the winter, Angus would work with Bill as co-manger at the lumberyard. Jack looked at Angus quizzically.

"Will you be able to handle all that, my good friend? I know it is a lot to ask of you."

Angus responded without hesitation. "Ooh, mon, think no more about it. I'm happy to do it. And you'll be helping us as well. The extra money will be welcome."

Jack turned to Nora for her reaction. "And, you, Nora? Is it all right with you? I know it will take Angus away from the farm some and I hated to ask it but he is really the only one that I know I can trust. Tell me how you feel about it."

Nora could see on Jack's face the strain of the past few weeks. The decision to leave home and business to help his mother country had not been an easy one. She reached out and touched his hand.

"I agree with Angus, Jack. It's a time to help each other. That's what friends are all about. Now, will you stay for supper with us?"

Jack's frown left his face and he gave a sigh of relief.

"I will, and thank you. Annie is having supper in town with a friend. I will be leaving on Saturday, so I may not have another chance to see you before that. This will be our farewell supper," Jack said rather sadly.

For a moment all three friends were silent, reflecting on what it might mean to have Jack involved in a war.

But Nora was determined not to let this be a gloomy occasion. She jumped up and went to the stove with the beans. She put a happy note in her voice as she urged the men to spend some time just to enjoy the evening.

"C'mon, you two. I'm for letting the supper cook while we take a walk outside."

"Have you noticed the Belltrees lately, Jack? They've grown so much."

She removed her apron and the three went outside for a last look around together. Jack exclaimed over the height of the Belltrees and they reminisced about when they first came to Vermont and how small the trees had been. They walked to the pond where they had enjoyed many picnics together.

Abby, Caro and Robbie joined them from their various pastimes around the yard. The children seemed to sense that this was a special occasion. They were unusually quiet.

Later, at the supper table, Angus told them about Jack going away and the reason for it.

Abby was full of questions about what he would do in England. Robbie wanted to hear about the war part of it. Caro started to cry, as she did so easily. Nora had trouble with a lump in her throat, too, knowing there was a possibility that Jack might never come back.

She quickly changed the subject by asking Abby to help her serve the dessert and the evening ended on a light note.

When it was time to leave, Jack did so quickly, giving Angus a hug and a kiss for Nora. But driving home he had some trouble seeing the road at times because of the tears, which formed in spite of himself.

The past weeks had been extremely stressful for Jack. The repercussion of the decision to go involved many people and would be long-range. Not only leaving his home, friends and business was difficult but also to leave Annie for who-knew-how-long was proving to be harder than he had ever anticipated.

When Jack had told her of his plan to return to England, Annie's response had been one of fury. She saw it as rejection of herself and reacted with a cold anger, saying, "If that's what you want to do, Jack, far be it from me to stop you."

After that she feigned indifference and in private shed bitter tears.

She listened without comment to his plans for the business and only said, at the end, "That's fine with me."

Her attitude hurt Jack immensely though he knew his wife well enough to know she was just erecting another barrier to protect her true feelings.

He tried several times to get her to talk to him in every way he could think of. He brought her flowers and a lovely cameo on a silver chain.

Annie received her husband's offerings with little change in her demeanor.

The day before he was to leave, he went to her shop and insisted she go out to supper with him. She was quiet during the evening and on the way home. As they were walking into the house, Jack put his arm around Annie's waist and turned her to face him.

"Please, Annie, don't let us part with this coldness between us. I love you and I don't want to leave! You must see why I have to!" He pleaded with her.

Annie answered coolly. "Things have not been good for a long time now, Jack. I think this is your way of getting out of it all."

"No! No! It's not that at all. It's my duty to go when England is in trouble. I know you've been unhappy because we haven't had any children but that's no one's fault. Why can't we be happy, just the two of us, as we were at first?"

At the mention of children, Annie stiffened but she only said, "I don't know, Jack, but maybe being apart for a while will help us both to sort things out."

She walked into the house and Jack followed, resigned.

The next morning, as they waited at the train station, they said little. At the last moment, Jack caught Annie to him and kissed her, holding her for a few moments. She was barely responsive but would not allow any crack in the wall she had erected.

Jack left with a heavy heart. Annie went back to the shop and kept herself busy trying to shut out the picture of Jack leaving.

CHAPTER TWENTY-FOUR

Christmas that year was a festive one. Sean was home for school vacation. Harry was elated that his cousin hadn't changed toward him and when Sean declared he had never seen Peggy looking better, Harry's happiness was complete.

The young ones decorated the house with garlands of evergreen they had collected from the woods.

The whole family went, as usual, to find a suitable Christmas tree. Of course, there were a lot of different opinions as to what a perfect tree looked like. But they finally agreed on two trees about six feet tall. One was placed in the parlor at Belltrees. The other was hauled to the Renfrew's.

After decorating their own tree, the whole group went to Clara and Harrison's to help Harry decorate theirs.

Angus and Nora had always made sure that their Aunt and Uncle's home was decorated for the holidays. They knew that the older folks were not up to doing it all themselves and Supleen wouldn't bother. For Harry's sake, especially, Nora thought the holidays should be as festive as possible.

Aunt Clara always rose to the occasion preparing hot chocolate and currant cakes for the crowd. Sadie was an enthusiastic participant at these occasions and contributed her homemade fudge that just "melted in your mouth" as Caro said, and demonstrated. Harrison even brought out his bagpipes and played some tunes while some of the young ones twirled and jigged to the music.

Christmas had always been one of their favorite times of the year. Now, Nora was wondering how many more years they would all be together. Sean was already embarked on his own life path and in a very few more years Abby and Harry would follow.

For the New Year, Nora and Angus had invited some of their closest friends to join their family. Annie, as usual, had refused, saying that she had made other plans. However, Mattie, Andrew and their children, Katie and Andy, came to the party. The von Stubins came with their pretty daughter, Hilda. Of course, Harrison, Clara, Sadie Thorne and Claude were there. Even big, blustery Mrs. Dufrense and her small, quiet husband came with four of their offspring in tow.

The house was full, it seemed, of young people. They were put to work making popcorn balls in the kitchen. Of course, as soon as they were made, they were also eaten.

Sean suddenly noticed how blue Hilda von Stubins' eyes were when she was helping him dip the popcorn balls in the caramel glaze. For the rest of the evening he couldn't take his eyes off her.

Later in the evening, the old Victrola was brought out and some of the guests enjoyed a waltz or a foxtrot. Andy and Sean both claimed Hilda for a dance. Andy won out so Sean asked Katie to dance. She was tempted to refuse because she was second choice but decided she didn't want to miss the rare opportunity to dance with her idol. The younger children danced around the others alone, or with whomever they could grab hold of.

Nora and Angus were delighted with their New Year's party. It wasn't often that they had their good friends gathered around them. They observed the young people's actions with amusement and pride.

Nora whispered to her husband. "We've done a good job with our bairns, haven't we, love?"

In answer, Angus squeezed her hand and took her out on the floor for a waltz.

The von Stubins had to leave early because they had a long drive and the winter weather was threatening snow.

Before they left, Sean managed to ask Hilda to write to him at college and said he might be able to visit her before his vacation was over. Hilda was not given to being coy and was frank about wanting to see him again. She blushed deeply when he held onto her hand too long when saying goodbye.

Mattie and her family stayed to see nineteen fifteen come in and wish everyone a Happy New Year.

Uncle Harrison couldn't admit how tired he was but Clara saw his color fade from his face and insisted on going home.

Everyone left tired but happy, with the exception of Katie, who cried in her pillow that night thinking that she had lost Sean to Hilda.

Nora had observed what was happening between her son and Hilda. She felt sorry for Katie, who, it was obvious, was suffering. It seemed strange for Nora to have her children grow up enough to be romantically involved.

Her thoughts then turned to her sister Molly, whose two eldest sons were probably fighting for their country now. I thank God, she thought, that Sean is yet too young. But if the war dragged on another year he would be old enough and she knew she couldn't stop him from going if that happened. She prayed that the conflict would soon be over.

In March of nineteen fifteen, the British launched a major attack at Neuve Chapelle but only managed to take the advance German Line. Then in May, the British passenger ship the Lusitania was sunk by a German sub with the loss of many lives.

The Americans, as well as the rest of the world, were shocked and angered by the attack on an unarmed civilian ship. People, who at first had wanted no part of the war, now began to feel that the United States should join the allies.

Nora and Angus had heard very little from Jack since he had gone back to England. Only a few short letters had arrived telling them he was all right. Of course, he couldn't tell them much about what was actually happening because of censorship.

He had written some longer letters to Annie telling her of his feelings and trying to encourage her to make plans for their future together.

Annie answered his letters but in the same stiff manner she had displayed when he was at home. She threw herself into her work for the shop and the hardware store.

When Angus had his bi-monthly meetings with Bill and Annie, he reported back to Nora that she was very distant and had lost some weight.

Nora felt a great pity for her friend but any overtures of friendship from her were met with a frosty attitude from Annie.

Nora and Angus still liked to take their evening walks around the farm whenever the weather was good. It was a way of getting away by themselves to relax. Very often, a couple of the young ones followed them, but interested in their own pursuits like catching fireflies or romping with Spots or the dog.

Nowadays, the adults' conversation nearly always turned to the war and the possibility of President Wilson deciding to join the fray.

One evening in late June Nora and Angus started out on their usual walk, Robbie and Caro following. When Angus started talking about the world affairs, Nora put her hand over his mouth.

"No, Angus, I don't want to hear about anything like that tonight. Let's just enjoy this time. The bairns will be grown and gone all too soon."

So they talked of other things and listened to the sounds around them. The crickets and the frogs were playing their usual symphony and mingled with the children's laughter.

When they came to the pond they sat for a while on the bank on the soft grass. Caro and Robbie begged to go in the water so Nora allowed them to take off their clothes and go in swimming. Soon Nora hiked her skirts up around her waist and waded in, too. Angus soon joined them.

The spring fed pond water was cold at first but they got used to it and had a great time splashing and dragging their father around in the water.

It was the first time in a long while that Nora and Angus had such a carefree break in their busy schedule.

The children came out of the water, shivering, pulling on their clothes. They ran home far ahead of their mother and father, who took their time.

Angus grabbed hold of Nora's hand.

"C'mon, wife, see if you can still run! C'mon!" He tugged at her hand.

Nora surprised him by suddenly taking off in a quick sprint. Angus caught up to her and passed her just before they reached the house. They both collapsed on the porch, laughing. Nora held onto her side, panting.

"Oh, I'm getting too old for this kind of thing." She gasped.

Angus pulled her to her feet. "We're not too old, love, just out of practice. Now, I'm hungry again. I'm for some scones and tea."

It was a pleasant respite from a troubled world. After that, Nora made sure that the few hours when she and Angus didn't have to work would not be darkened by war. They needed to enjoy life as long as they could.

When Sean was at home he was admonished by Angus not to dwell on the war too much in front of his mother.

Once a month the local grange would hold a dance and potluck supper. Most of the farmers went, as well as the townspeople. A room off the large hall was designated a nursery for the smaller ones and a couple of the older girls took turns watching them. Most of the babies just slept through the festivities.

The von Stubins brought Hilda and, when Sean was home from school, he attended with his family. Abby, who was getting pretty grown up, was in great demand as a partner by the young boys; but she could most often be found in the nursery tending to the babies.

Caro, on the other hand, would have liked to dance but was still considered a child by the older boys and those of her age didn't like to dance. They would rather play marbles or hand wrestling on the large porch.

Caro still spent a lot of time on her toilette, even when she was going to school. Sometimes Nora worried that her youngest daughter was too vain. She tried to balance this trait by teaching Caro how to cook and sew, since she didn't like outdoor pursuits. She was also required to help with some of the outside chores, though she didn't like it much.

Charles and Victoria would often go to the grange parties because it was a good opportunity to meet with all their friends and, in the winter, it relieved the monotony of being housebound. Charles was beginning to talk about semi-retirement but he was waiting until another doctor could be found who was willing to work in this rural area. He had placed an advertisement in the Burlington paper for an assistant.

Abby had become a real help to the doctor. He had taken her with him on some of his routine calls, with her parents' permission. She also read any of the medical books she had time for and seemed to have an insatiable appetite for any medical information.

Abby had already talked to her mother about going to nursing school after she graduated. Nora was pleased with her daughter's choice, but privately worried about the cost of nurses training. She decided not to broach the subject to Angus until it was time for a decision to be made.

Victoria knew about Abby's plan and brought the subject up to her husband one evening as they sat in front of the fire.

"You know how much Abby wants to be a nurse, Charles. I don't see how Angus and Nora will manage sending her to school with all their other expenses. Of course, it is still a year or more away but...." She looked expectantly at her husband.

Charles puffed on his pipe thoughtfully before he answered. "Well, why don't we start paying her for the work she does in the office. Lord knows she saves me a lot of time by helping with the books and cleaning in there. She deserves it."

Victoria's face lit up at his suggestion. "She certainly does and that's a wonderful way to help Nora without offending her. With the money she saves in the next year or so it will go a long way toward her school expense! You're an old dear to think of it! Just for that, I'll make you some fresh coffee."

She ruffled his thinning hair on her way out to the kitchen. He just smiled.

When Dr. Belden told Abby of his plan she was dubious about taking money for something she loved doing, especially from her step-grandfather. However, he told her that she was close to graduating and would need money to go to school.

He didn't mention that her parents would find it a hardship to pay for the schooling, but Abby was a smart young lady and understood. She agreed to his plan with enthusiasm.

Walking home that day she felt a wondrous happiness. Her childhood dream was going to come true! She felt like skipping and running as she did when she was little.

When she explained Doctor Belden's plan to her parents, they at first protested. It had always been their feeling that you didn't accept pay for helping anyone.

Abby was adamant and insisted it was what Charles and Victoria wanted.

Nora and Angus suddenly realized that their daughter was growing up and deserved to make some of her own choices.

At the end of their conversation, Angus, very moved by his young daughter, said, "We're very proud of you, lass."

Abby blushed, embarrassed by this praise from her quiet father. "Thank you, Papa." She said shyly as she turned to go upstairs to bed.

For Abby's fifteenth birthday in December of that year, Abby asked her mother if she could have a party. She was particularly thinking about one special boy that she wanted to invite. His name was Rob and he was in her class at school. Naturally, they had talked before. There were so few children in the school it would have been hard not to, especially as they sat next to each other. But Rob was a very quiet young fellow and had never asked to walk her home, in spite of her obvious hints.

So Abby issued a verbal invitation to her whole class, which included one girl whose name was Nettie, who very few of the class liked. However, Nettie was part of the class, so she had to be invited, too. Nettie had made herself unpopular by always bragging about how much money her family had and flaunting her expensive clothing in front of the other girls. In fact, she was a rather plain girl and she was jealous of the fact that the boys all liked Abby because she loved to play baseball and was a good sport.

Victoria came over to help with the party preparations. Abby arranged the seating in the dining room and decorated the parlor, which they now called the living room. With Caro and Harry's help she moved the furniture and rolled up the rug so they could play games and dance. They blew up an endless number of balloons in Abby's favorite color of baby blue, suspending a bunch of them in the middle of the living room ceiling. It was Harry's idea to have the balloons descend en masse over the dancers at a specific time. There would be a large bowl of punch on a table in one corner of the room. The birthday feast would be served at the dining room table along with the cake.

Besides Abby's classmates, she invited her friends Andy and Katie, although they were both older. She also invited three of the Dufrenses who were around her age. Of course, Harry, Caro and Robbie would be allowed to attend.

The day of the party dawned clear, with no threat of a snowstorm. Vermont winters were unpredictable and there was already about two feet of the white stuff on the ground.

Everyone would be coming by sleigh, driven by their parents, who would stay for the duration of the party. Nora had planned that the grown-ups would have their own refreshments at the kitchen table so the young people would be more comfortable with their own group.

Abby and Caro, as well, had primped for almost two hours before the guests arrived. Abby, who usually was very casual about her dress, wanted to make an impression on Rob, so she wore her best calico, a lovely shade of blue with a lace collar. She borrowed a hair ribbon from Caro that matched her dress. Caro always had a supply of pretty things she had begged from her mother or grandmother. When Nora saw her oldest daughter all dressed up, she was startled at how grown-up she looked.

"Why, Abby, you look very lovely! And so grown up!" She exclaimed.

Abby glowed with pride and felt pleased with herself.

There was a sudden flurry of several guest's arriving at once. The young people came in all excited, clutching presents for the birthday girl. Parties were not a common occurrence, especially in the winter.

Nearly all of the guests had arrived and Abby was beginning to hope that Nettie was not coming. Rob was one of the last to arrive and Abby's heart jumped when she saw how handsome he looked all dressed up. He barely met her eyes as he handed her a gift, then quickly went to join the other boys.

When they were almost ready to sit down to eat, Nettie arrived, much to Abby's disappointment. She was dressed in an elaborate dress of green taffeta and suddenly every other girl in the room felt a little dowdy.

For the rest of the evening Nettie attached herself to Rob, always choosing a seat near him and patting his arm occasionally. In fact, she thought Rob was a bore but she knew that Abby liked him and she was determined to annoy Abby. Rob was indifferent to Nettie, which made Abby feel a little better.

Other than that, the party was a success. Abby felt as if she had joined the ranks of the grown-ups. When Rob asked her to dance, instead of Nettie, she felt her day was complete. Over Rob's shoulder she caught a glimpse of Nettie's face, twisted in jealousy.

To Nora, that winter of Nineteen fifteen and sixteen seemed longer than usual.

With Sean at school most of the time, he was greatly missed by the whole family.

Nora was worried about Angus. The intense winter cold seemed to get right into the marrow of his injured arm, where the bear had mauled him. It often ached fiercely and Nora would rub it with liniment at night.

Cecile's brother was still helping with the chores when Tad was not home.

Abby, Caro and even Robbie did their part. When it was time for sugaring off, Abby went along on the wagon to help her father and the hired man. When the first spring breezes finally promised kinder weather it was especially welcome.

Caro and Robbie eagerly helped plant seeds in shallow pots to be kept in the house until the little green shoots were a few inches high and the earth was warm enough outside to nurture them. In this manner they would be sure of having their vegetables mature earlier. The growing season in Vermont was a short one and had to be planned for carefully.

By July of that year, Nora's kitchen was constantly filled with activity. Victoria was there almost every day to help with the preserving of the vegetables for the next winter. Later on, when berries and apples and peaches became ripe, the children were sent out to pick the fruits while Nora and Victoria, often with Sadie helping, did the canning.

Nora loved the aroma that filled the house, especially during the peach season. The sweet, succulent peaches were peeled and covered with sugar syrup in the glass jars. Just looking at them made her mouth water. Everyone ate their share while they worked, of course.

The children came back from berry picking with mouth and hands strained with berry juice.

Nearly everyone helped when it came time to start haying. It was always, it seemed, the hottest day's of the summer. If rain threatened, the hay must be brought in quickly for fear of it getting damp, which would cause it to become moldy.

Even Caro and Robbie helped by lugging gallon cans of ginger ale out to the workers. This was made with cold water, ginger, sugar and a little vinegar, combined to make a deliciously refreshing drink. It was really appreciated after working several hours in the hot sun.

The younger ones thought it was all great fun, especially riding atop a huge load of hay on its way to the barn.

During that summer, Nora tried to ignore the news coming from the rest of the world. To think about it caused her sleepless nights of worry for her sister's families. And she was aware of Sean's interest in the war news.

The seemingly senseless fighting raged on in Europe and Asia. Both sides had victories and then defeats. In an attempt to weaken the French forces, the Germans had attacked Verdun. They only succeeded in capturing Fort Vaux and some other fortifications, but the city remained in French hands.

Causalities were reported to be over three hundred thousand on each side.

When Nora heard Sean and Angus discussing this news after supper one evening, she felt the cold hand of fear.

"Is there no end in sight to all this killing of young men?" She appealed to her husband. "Will they not stop until they all are dead? I doubt we can stay out of it much longer!"

Her face was white and she sank into the nearest chair.

Angus and Sean looked at her with concern. They had usually avoided talking about the war in front of her. Angus tried to reassure her.

"Our President wants peace, and if he can possibly manage it we won't go to war. I read that he has already sent a Colonel House to talk to the European heads of state to try to put an end to it all." he said.

But Nora was not appeased and could not shake her sense of dread.

President Wilson, in fact, had been in the role of mediator since the beginning of the war, struggling valiantly to keep his country out of the madness. In January of 1917, the Germans announced that they would attack all ships going to and from Great Britain, carrying goods. On April 6th of that year, the United States declared war on Germany.

At school, all the young men cheered and yelled when they heard the news. Most of them, with the folly of youth, thought of it as a lark, an adventure. A good many of them left the college at once to enlist.

Sean watched them go with envy; he wanted to do the same himself. But the memory of his mother's face when they had last talked about the war stopped him. He didn't want to add to her worry about her sister's sons and he knew it would be much harder on her if he enlisted, too.

At the end of the school year, in May, when he went home, he found the whole town in an uproar. A few of his friends had enlisted already and every family with grown sons was praying their own would not be called. Most of the young men were badly needed to help work on the farms.

Nora was happy to have her son home for the summer. Having her whole family together was her greatest pleasure in life. She knew it was a temporary situation and could change at any moment. She was aware of the conflict going on in her son's mind, knowing that some of his friends had already gone. But for the time being she enjoyed knowing Sean was somewhere on the farm, helping his father or helping one of the younger children with some project of theirs.

To herself she thought; I'm just going to enjoy this time, this summer, while we are all together. This was her comfort while she went about her daily chores, cooking, cleaning, and washing.

The second week that Sean was home, he rode out to see Andy after supper one evening.

Nora said, more to herself than to Angus. "There he goes. It will be different when he comes back."

Angus looked at her, sharply. "What do you mean, love? He's only going over to spend some time with his best friend."

"No, it's eating him that he isn't in the war. And Mattie told me the other day that Andy has been talking about joining up." Her voice was sad.

Angus patted her hand. "We knew, we couldn't keep them with us forever. It will be hard, though, to see him leave for a reason such as this."

Fear and frustration were a heavy weight in Nora's chest. She jumped up, tears forming, and pounded on the porch railing.

"Why doesn't God stop this madness? This waste of young men! To be maimed or killed! For what?"

Angus held her closely as the tears ran down her face. He tried to console her with words he didn't believe himself.

"Don't torture yourself so, love. We don't even know if Sean will go. Or, if he does he will come back to us in one piece, I believe that. Sh, sh!"

He held her gently. And trying to change her mood, he shook her a little. "Now, you may be wasting your tears. He may not be leaving at all and you will have wasted all these lovely tears." He wiped at them with his hand.

Nora managed a wry smile. "You don't believe that, but don't worry, I won't break down again. All the worries of the last months just caught up with me at once."

She caught Angus' hand. "C'mon, let's walk a bit before dark." She said. "I want to go down to the barn and check on Flossie, her foal is due any time now."

Angus said, "When she starts to drop it, I want Robbie to be there, since I've promised it to him."

When Sean arrived at Andy's he was invited in for some apple pie with the family. Katie looked very fetching in a yellow checked gingham dress with a yellow ribbon in her red-gold hair. Suddenly Sean saw her as a young woman instead of his childhood playmate. He even found himself stammering when he told her she looked very pretty; he'd never said anything like that to her before.

He felt embarrassed and as soon as he could, he got Andy to go outside where they could talk privately. Katie was surprised and delighted that her old friend had finally noticed her. She smiled to herself and didn't mind when the young men went out. She knew Sean would be back.

Nora and Angus were already in bed when their son returned home that evening. Nora, at least, was still awake and heard Sean come in but she wasn't in a hurry to hear what she knew he was going to tell them.

The next morning at breakfast, after several tries, Sean told them that he and Andy were going to enlist.

Nora stayed calm and continued serving the hot cakes.

Angus only said, "I hope you've thought this over thoroughly, lad, it is a serious decision. And you haven't finished school as yet."

But he knew it was just prolonging the inevitable.

The younger children started protesting. Caro's eyes were misty; Abby just stared at her older brother. Robbie cheered, wishing he was older.

They were all silenced by a look from their father.

To Sean, he only said. "We'll talk more about this later, lad, we've got to get out there and see how Flossie is and finish mending that north fence."

Robbie finished his breakfast in a gulp.

"Oh, I have to see if my colt is here yet!" He exclaimed and dashed outside, followed by Abby.

But the foal wasn't born that day, either.

When Angus and Sean came in for their dinner, Sean announced that he was going to pick up Andy and go into town to the recruiting office.

His parents, conceding defeat, did not protest. Sean gave Nora an especially tight hug. As he went out the door, he looked back at his mother and father. His eyes thanked them for their understanding.

"I'll be back, Papa, and we can finish the fence today."

"All right, lad." was all Angus could say.

When Sean returned, he sought out his mother before going out to join his father. He found her upstairs making her bed. She straightened up when he came in and they just looked at each other for a second. Sean spoke first.

"I won't be leaving for a couple of weeks, Mama, and then I'll be training only a few miles away for now."

Nora was silent for a moment, and then she only said. "Take some ginger ale out to your father when you go, there's a good lad."

Sean answered in the same manner, thankful she did not cry or carry on. "I will, Mama. And after supper I have to go talk with Uncle Harrison about my decision." His Uncle was financing his education.

"That's good, lad. He is very interested in your future. Run along now, your father is waiting for you."

When he had gone, Nora just sat down on the bed, feeling listless. It was so nice when they were small, she thought, I always knew just where they were. From now on, it's out of my hands. Oh, God, please take care of them all.

Harrison was working on his books in the library when Sean came in. The young man was startled at how his Uncle seemed to have become smaller since he saw him at Christmas. He took Harrison's frail hand in his.

"How are you feeling, Uncle Harrison? It's good to see you."

Harrison smiled with pleasure to see his young nephew. "I'm doing just fine, lad. I'm glad to see you. Tell me about school, How is it coming along?"

Sean explained to his Uncle what was happening in his life and that he had enlisted. He watched anxiously for Harrison's reaction. His Uncle was silent for several moments.

Then he only said, "Well, you know what you have to do for your own peace of mind, lad. War is a terrible thing, but a man has to try to protect his country. I am very proud of you. I am sure you haven't made this decision lightly."

He looked intently at his nephew. Sean explained that he had thought about this for a long time. He expressed his appreciation for all that his Uncle had done for him. Harrison nodded.

"You've done a good job of it. The things you've learned will help both of our farms. When you get back, the money will be there if you want to go back to school."

Sean hardly knew what to say in the face of his Uncle's generosity.

Before he left, Sean embraced the elderly man. Harrison blinked back the tears that stung his eyelids.

Before going home, Sean went to find Harry. He found him caring for one of the horses.

As usual, Harry was happy to see his cousin. He was not as dependent on Sean for his companionship as he once had been. He had plenty of work to keep him busy and felt important in his own right. Also there was a special girl in school he liked a lot. When he saw Sean's face, he lay down the currycomb and sat down on a bale of hay.

"I see you've joined up, cousin. So when do you have to leave?"

Sean was always surprised at Harry's intuitiveness where he was concerned. He explained the whole situation to him. He added, "I won't be going for a while."

Harry said, "Well, if this is still going on next year or when I'm eighteen I'll join, too."

He envied his cousin and like all young people, wished he was older.

Neither one said anything for a while. Then Harry said, "I'm going to try to find my mother when I graduate next summer. I haven't told the family this yet but no matter what they say, I have to do it anyway."

Sean was shocked because it had been a long time since Harry had even mentioned his mother.

"But, why? I thought you hated her for leaving you."

"That was when I was a lot younger. And I would never leave grandmother and grandfather, but I just want to see her and talk to her. I'm not sure why." Harry went back to grooming the horse. "I just wanted to tell you about it."

There was nothing more to say on the subject. Sean assured Harry that he would be seeing him before he left for basic training. They spoke of other things before Sean left to go home.

Sean was satisfied, at least, that Harry would not feel so badly about his leaving as he had when Sean left for school three years ago.

CHAPTER TWENTY-FIVE

When Sean left for training camp two weeks later, his family took it very well. Only Nora's eyes were misty and Caro, as usual, was in tears. There were several young men leaving at the same time.

Abby, whose feelings had always been private, felt a sense of loss as she watched her big brother leaving.

The new recruits were to be transported to their training camp in a huge truck. All the families were present to say goodbye. A small local band was playing "Keep the Home Fires Burning" and other patriotic songs, making the occasion more solemn. They were still playing as the truck went down the road, all the young men waving.

Nora and Angus had seen their oldest daughter turn into a dignified young woman in the last year. She would start her nurse training when she graduated. In the meantime, she was a busy girl. She still had chores to help out at home and worked for Dr. Belden. As well as cleaning and keeping his office in order, she sometimes went on calls with him. She was now greeting his patients and assisting him often, especially with the children. She could usually get them to smile, even when they were about to get a shot.

Dr. Belden's advertisement for an assistant doctor had received three answers. He had eliminated two of them and was about to try out the third one. The young man was due to arrive on June third. He was to stay a few days in order to look everything over before making a decision.

When Abby came to work the first day Doctor Samuels arrived, she had forgotten that the new doctor was due. So she was surprised, upon walking into the office, to see a strange young man examining the contents of the medicine supply cupboard.

Hearing a footstep, Dr. Samuels turned and saw a lovely young lady with long, black hair and wide, questioning eyes standing in the doorway. At her expression, he smiled and held out his hand.

"Sorry if I startled you. I'm Mike Samuels. You must be Abby. I've heard a lot about you already."

Abby managed to thrust out her hand and find her voice. "Oh, of course. I had forgotten for a minute. Where is Dr. Belden?"

She was thinking that Dr. Samuels was a very pleasant looking man. He was nearly as tall as Sean and had sandy hair and dark blue eyes. Of course he was old, she thought, at least twenty-four.

Just as Mike Samuels was answering her question, Dr. Belden came into the room. He spoke briskly.

"Well, I see you two have met. Good! You'll be working together, that is, I hope you'll decide to stay with us, Mike,". He looked quizzically at Dr. Samuels, who before this had not been told that he was accepted. Dr. Belden went on, "We've got a lot of ground to cover, so we'd best get started."

Abby stayed in the office to do her usual work after they left.

When her mother asked her later what she thought of the new doctor, she said, "He seems very nice. He's from New York. Dr. Belden likes him a lot, I guess. He said he hopes that Dr. Samuels stays."

"If Dr. Belden likes him, he must be all right." replied Nora. "He's a good judge of people."

Abby was surprised at how glad she was when young Mike Samuels decided to stay in Morristown and work with Dr. Belden. She had always enjoyed her work with the doctor but now it seemed to be a little more exciting. The new doctor brought with him some new ideas and Dr. Belden was a clever enough man that he accepted them, while educating his new assistant in the tried and true methods. Fortunately, Dr. Samuels was clever enough to accept these; so they got along extremely well.

Harry, true to his word to Sean, left home after his graduation from high school, to search for his mother. He promised his grandfather to return within a year, if not before and go to college. It was Harrison's dearest wish and Harry did not want to let him down.

He found it much easier to locate Zoë than he had anticipated. Clara had told him of his mother's Aunt Charlotte in Charleston, so he headed there first.

That venerable lady was on her deathbed when he found her. Her daughter, son and other relatives surrounded her.

They welcomed Harry and insisted that he stay with them. Of course, they were his relatives, even though he had never seen them. He met a whole new, to him, branch of his family. Some of them he liked a lot, especially some cousins of his own age.

None of theses people wanted to talk about Zoë. He couldn't get any information at all until his Great Aunt Charlotte's daughter called him into the parlor the second morning he was there. Her name was Hattie, a large, buxom woman, with a lot of hair piled high and adorned with a black ostrich feather. But she had a soft, southern voice and kind manner. Now she sat on a sofa and patted the seat beside her.

"Come and sit down, Harry, we need to talk."

He did as she suggested, wondering what she had to tell him.

"I like you, young Harry. I feel sorry that we never knew each other before. Now, I'll you all that I know of your mother, although I have not set eyes on her for years. It was about eighteen years ago, I think. I was a young woman then. You must have been a mere babe. I can't imagine how Zoë could have left you."

She looked thoughtfully at Harry for a moment, and then continued talking. She explained that Zoë had stayed at their home for a short while. Then she had left with a man whose name she could not recall. But, she added that she thought her brother might know his name. She would try to find out for Harry.

It turned out that her brother, Matthew, did remember the man. He said, in fact, that he was working at a speakeasy downtown. He would take Harry there if he wanted.

That evening, Harry and Matthew went out together. Harry was nervous, thinking he would soon meet someone who actually knew his mother.

Larry Deauveau was working as a shill, a person who inveigled patrons to the gambling tables.

Harry disliked the man instantly. Matthew, who was familiar with Larry's type, finally got him to talk by suggesting there might be some money in it for him. Harry seethed inside, listening to this low-life speak with disdain of his mother.

But Matthew put his hand on Harry's arm and shook his head at him.

It took only a few minutes to find out what Larry knew. Matthew gave him a bill, and then Harry and Matthew went outside.

Harry was shaking with suppressed anger. Matthew looked at him sympathetically.

"I know how you feel, son, but that type isn't worth fighting. Anyway, he told me that your mother could be found at a place called "The Pink Lady." It's a river boat that's been permanently docked and used as a nightclub."

Harry's stomach felt as though it was filled with butterflies as he and Matthew approached the riverboat. A shifty eyed man, speaking through a peephole, demanded to know their business. Matthew didn't know the password, but explained that they were relatives of Zoë.

The man knew the name. He closed the peephole and after a few minutes, reappeared and opened the door. He pointed to a curtained alcove in the back of the room and said briefly, "in there".

When Matthew pulled back the curtain, they saw a man and woman seated in plush chairs with a table between them. There were drinks and a bottle on the table. The man was probably in his sixties, judging by his bald pate and wrinkled countenance. But he had a pleasant expression.

Harry didn't notice, for he only had eyes for the woman. She was slouched back in her chair with a drink in one hand and a cigarette in the other. She wore a pink satin dress in the currant flapper style, which did little for her overblown figure. But Harry looked only at her face, which reflected the dissipation of years. She looked at the men with half opened eyes, totally disinterested.

Harry couldn't speak.

The man spoke pleasantly. "I am Sol Kincaid. I understand you are relatives of Miss Zoë, here?"

The woman said nothing.

Matthew replied for them both. "I am Matthew Stewart. This is Harry Renfrew." Then turning to Zoë, he said. "This young man is your son, Miss Zoë, he wanted to see you."

At the mention of Harry's name, the heavy lidded eyes opened wide at last. Zoë set her drink down, noisily. She stared at Harry, who was still speechless.

He finally found his voice. "Are-are you my mother?" he stammered foolishly, feeling about ten years old.

Sol Kincaid stood up and speaking to Matthew, he said, "If you'll come with me, I'll buy you a drink."

They left the alcove together.

Harry and Zoe stared at each other for a moment. Harry then sat down in the other chair. Zoe finally spoke.

"So you're my kid, eh? Well, you look pretty good. What're you doing down here, anyway?" Her voice was slightly slurred.

Harry felt like he was the adult of the two, now.

"I wanted to see you and ask you why you left Vermont. Did someone force you to go?"

Harry was thinking of his father and how difficult it could be to live with him. He was trying to find a good reason why she would leave him without a backward glance.

Zoë laughed. "I was glad to get out of that stinking hole. I wanted a life. You were better off without me. I wasn't made to be a mother."

Harry felt a hollow inside of him. The air in the small alcove became oppressive. He stood up. Zoë waved her glass at him.

"Have a drink, kid. Relax."

Shaking his head, Harry managed to say; "No, thanks, I'd better be going. Bye."

He backed out through the curtain. He looked around frantically for Matt. He found him talking to Sol in a corner.

Seeing the boy's face, Matt said a hurried goodbye and took Harry outside. The boy leaned on the boat's railing and took some deep breaths.

Matthew looked the other way and waited for Harry to regain his composure.

Neither of them spoke on the way back to Matthew's house.

Harry left to go home that same day.

The only one he told the whole story to was his Aunt Nora. To his grandparents and other members of the family he only said that he had found Zoë and talked to her.

Claude knew the boy was upset about it and had a fair idea of what he had seen. He made a point of bringing it up one day while they were working in the barn. He chose his words carefully.

"The worst thing a person can do, son, is to feel sorry for himself. We have each been given a life to do the best we can with it. What other people have done, we can't take responsibility for."

Harry just nodded. He always understood Claude.

The following fall, Harry enrolled in college. His beloved grandfather died two years later.

Harrison was a clever man. He designed his will to protect his wife and grandson. Everything was left to Clara. On Harry's twenty-fifth birthday, the estate was to be divided equally between Supleen and his son, Harry. Clara was to live in and have charge of the house while she lived.

The year that Sean had enlisted, Angus was able to make the last payment on the farm to Uncle Harrison. Nora and Angus had celebrated with a family party.

Sean had a weekend pass from training so he could attend. The Renfrew's were invited as well as Mattie and Andrew and their children and, of course, Sadie Thorne and Claude.

Victoria had prepared her own version of haggis with tatties and neets. (The original recipe for haggis called for stuffing the cleaned sheep's stomach with a combination of mutton and cereal.) Victoria had developed her own recipe, which was simply a lamb loaf with mashed potatoes and turnips.

Nora made a roast chicken and for dessert; shortbread, currant cakes and fruit pudding.

Everybody had dressed up and the Victrola had brought out for music and dancing.

The next day, Sean left for camp. They all knew he wouldn't be back until the war was finished. He would be leaving for overseas soon. The exact time and place was a military secret. Everyone went to the station to see Sean off.

As the truck carrying her oldest son drove out of sight, Nora had a heavy lump in her chest that would stay there until Sean returned home.

CHAPTER TWENTY-SIX

Just six months after young Dr. Samuels had come to work for Charles Belden, he was called to serve in the army. He and Abby corresponded while he was gone. Their letters brought them close and their friendship developed into a deep affection.

When Mike Samuels returned to Morristown, they both worked in the small clinic that had been established there.

A year later, they were married in a lovely ceremony in the garden at Belltrees.

Caro was her sister's only attendant; she wore a sweet, yellow, organdy dress. Robbie was the best man for Mike, who had no brothers of his own. He felt very important.

Robbie had become an automobile enthusiast. After he graduated from school, he had applied for a job on the assembly line, building cars. He moved to Michigan and he eventually became a designer of cars.

When Sean came home from war, he had found it hard to settle down into the old routine. His best friend, Andy, had come home minus his left leg; he was hospitalized a long time, mostly because he could not come to terms with his disability. Sean spent a lot of time with him, not necessarily talking about the war but taking comfort in the knowledge that the other one had been through the same things.

Sean went back to helping Angus on the farm, partly because his father was suffering more and more from the effects of his crippled arm. It ached fiercely in the winter months and seemed to be losing some strength.

Harrison had died in his sleep just a few months before Sean had come back.

Sean missed his Uncle and felt awfully sorry for Clara, who looked like a lost soul. The McDonald's and Sadie Thorne, as well as Claude tried to console her. Her greatest supporter was, of course, young Harry. He stayed around the house a great deal and took his grandmother out often, until she finally began to shake her depression.

Sean had written to Katie and to Hilda while he was overseas. News from home was always welcome. But when he visited Andy, he saw more and more of Katie. He went to see Hilda occasionally as well. They enjoyed each other's company too.

Then, one day, when Sean went to visit Andy, he ran into Katie coming out accompanied by a young man.

He was introduced to Sean as Adam, who Katie had met at the U.S.O. Sean was puzzled by his own strong reaction to seeing Katie with another man. He only knew he didn't like it.

From that day, Sean made it a point to ask Katie to go places with him. He brought her flowers and candy. Then, one day as he sat with Andy on the porch, waiting for Katie to join them, Andy glanced at his friend and chuckled.

"Boy, you have a strange look about you lately, Sean."

"What do you mean?" Sean asked in surprise.

"You sure look like a man in love. You can't take your eyes off Katie lately. And you talk about her all the time. I can't get a decent conversation out of you any more."

Sean colored deeply. He had no answer. He knew it was true. Even when he was working in the fields or in the barn, he kept thinking of Katie.

Now he looked at Andy, an abashed grin on his face.

"Well, I guess I'd better do something about that, don't you think?"

Just then Katie came out on the porch, looking especially lovely in a blue gingham dress with tiny flowers all over it. Her eyes were shining as she looked at Sean and he became suddenly tongue-tied. Katie wondered why her brother was laughing as she and Sean left in the Ford Roadster that Sean bought from Jack.

When they returned, much later that evening, they were an engaged couple, to no one's surprise.

They planned to marry in the spring.

Both families were pleased, though. Caroline, who was visiting a friend in Burlington at the time, heard the news when she arrived home the following weekend. She had always been a little jealous of Katie as an older, more sophisticated girl. And anyway, no one could be good enough for her adored, elder brother.

But when she saw how happy Sean was and particularly when she was asked to be a bride's maid, she felt mollified. As a matter of fact, she had some news of her own.

She had met a man while visiting Nancy in Burlington. He was some older than she and owned a good-sized department store. He was very interested in Caroline and they had decided to write to each other.

She told her mother all about it the first night she was home, while they were preparing supper together. Nora was interested, as she had been in all of Caro's past young men.

There had been a lot of them through the years, since she had been in the first grade. This current one was ten years older than Caro and quite well off. This might well be different, Nora mused, as she listened to Caro's chatter. Caroline always seemed to want a lot of nice things. Perhaps this man would be the one.

This is going to be a mighty big house, Nora thought, when the children are all gone.

At Christmas time, Caro invited her young man from Burlington for a visit. He arrived the day after Christmas and stayed for two days. His name was Harley Munson and he seemed to fit into the family nicely. He endeared himself to Nora and Angus at once with his admiration of Belltrees and his obvious deep regard for Caro. They took him on a tour of the ground and woods. He explained that his father had started the department store when Harley was a small boy. His father had taught Harley all about the business. In the past two years his father's health had been failing, so Harley had become the store manager.

When Harley had gone back to Burlington, Caro told her parents that he had asked her to marry him. She had looked up at this tall, shy man and felt a wave of pure love for him. They sat there, under the Belltrees, and talked for a very long time. Harley asked her to wait to tell anyone until he had brought a proper ring for her.

A week later Caroline got a telephone call from Harley saying that his father was failing fast. Could Caroline consider coming to Burlington so they could be married before his father died. It was the elder Mr. Munson's wish to see his son married while he was still alive.

There were some lengthy discussions about the matter between Caro and her parents. Angus didn't think his daughter should get married in such a hurried fashion. But in the end, Caro won out and she called Harley to say he could go ahead with plans for the wedding and she and her parents would be there in a few days.

So, about a week later, the McDonald family stood quietly in the back of Mr. Munson's sick room while the minister read the wedding service.

The bride was very stylish in a pink silk dress and carried small pink roses. The attendants were Nancy and Sean. Mrs. Monson stood towards the back with the McDonalds, weeping silently into her handkerchief.

There was a lovely wedding dinner served for all the guests, although without the usual gaiety.

When Angus and Nora had returned home to Belltrees, the house seemed terribly empty.

The next morning, while she was getting breakfast, Nora felt curiously empty. When Angus was seated across from her at the table her eyes filled with tears.

"Oh, Angus, this is terrible! This big house! And so empty!"

"So." He joked. "I'm not enough for you any more, love?"

But his wife didn't laugh. She spoke thoughtfully.

"Angus, why don't we move in with mama when Sean gets married? She's all alone now and I know she is lonesome."

"Well, that might be a good idea. I'm not crazy about living with a pair of newlyweds myself, and I still need Sean's help here. You talk it over with mama and the two of you decide. I guess I can put up with the two of you."

He chuckled and swept Nora up in a tight embrace before he went out to the barn.

She felt a good deal better and fled the quiet house to go and talk it over with Victoria.

Nora found her mother working with her roses in the back yard near the house. She was always glad to see her daughter.

She had many a lonely hour since Dr. Charles had died. And she hadn't felt awfully well for a while now. So when Nora told her about her plan for moving in the cottage with her, Victoria was pleased.

The spring of 1924, Sean and Katie were married in a pretty ceremony, attended by his two married sisters and his brother, Robbie, who had come from Detroit for the occasion.

After all the festivities, when everyone had gone home, Robbie was visiting old friends and Nora took Victoria to the cottage.

Angus had chores to do. Victoria invited them to stay for supper that evening.

While Victoria cut some of her favorite roses for the table, Nora relaxed in the gazebo, which had been built in the back under a huge weeping willow tree. She sat there a long time lost in memories.

When Angus returned from his chores and rounded the corner of the house, he paused for a moment to admire the picture she made, still in the blue, voile dress she wore to the wedding.

Then as she noticed him, he waved and went to join her.

"I invited Jack to join us for supper. Victoria said she would be happy to see him. You don't mind, do you?" Angus asked.

"Of course not. We don't see much of him any more. He seems such a lost soul. I'm glad he came to the wedding."

"Well, he blames himself for Annie's breakdown. There seems to be little hope that she will be cured."

Soon after Jack had returned from the war, Annie had gradually withdrawn from society, even her beloved business.

Then one day, when Jack came home, he found Annie lying on the bed, cradling an old doll of Abby's and crooning to herself. She didn't appear to know her husband.

When the doctor came he decided she should be hospitalized for treatment.

Jack had refused to have her taken to the state facility. He had found a private home for her not too far away so he could visit her often.

Now, Nora replied to her husband. "It's terribly sad. We must have him out here more often I'm sure it would make him feel better to work with you around the farm, don't you think?"

Angus pulled Nora to her feet with an arm around her waist. "I'll insist on it; I'd enjoy his company, too."

As they strolled back to the cottage, Nora remarked; "There have been so many changes since we came here, Angus. Now, our wee ones have grown up and gone....." She trailed off sadly.

Angus chuckled. "Don't fash yourself, darlin', there'll be the patter of little feet around Belltrees soon enough, I'm thinking."

Nora's face brightened at the thought. "True. And meanwhile, you and I can enjoy our time together. We'll take a trip to Niagara Falls and have that honeymoon we never had!"

Made in the USA
Lexington, KY
01 November 2010